ANGEL

A NOVEL BY ANTHONY FIELDS

Angel

Cover Design by Black Market Logos
Book Interior Design by Lashonda Johnson & Ghostwriter Inc.

A Novel by Anthony Fields

CHAPTER ONE

ANGEL

As the music drifted throughout the house, I silently sang along.

"Don't want to make a scene, but I really don't care when people stare at us/ sometimes I think I'm dreaming I pinch myself just to see if I'm awake and I…"

That Jagged Edge CD be cranking like shit, I thought to myself as I sang the rest of the song. *Plus, those twins in the group are fine as hell, talk about doubling your pleasure.*

I put a little more seasoning on the steaks and flipped them over. Tony likes his steaks medium well and I make one of the best steaks in the metro area, if I must say. At least, that's what I've been told. I always cook my baby something special when I have good news. And I have very good news for Tony. I can't wait to tell him and I know he's going to be anxious to hear what I have to say.

I tossed the fresh greens of salad and sat them in the fridge to marinate. A good salad always brings out a meal. I cooked the broccoli a little too much, but the cheese sauce I made should set it off very nicely.

I bet none of those hood-rat chicks in Congress Park cook for Tony the way I do. I bet his baby momma don't do half the shit I do for him. If she did, the nigga wouldn't be here with me.

It's been two years since Tony and I met at the HOBO Shop fashion show. I remember that day like it was yesterday….

3

Angel

The HOBO Shop Fashion Show was held at the Ramada Inn on Annapolis Road off of Route 450 in New Carrolton. HOBO stood for Helping Our Brothers Out. I personally knew Moochie, who owned the shop. He made some hitting fly shit the whole family could wear. I was a regular customer, so when the tickets for the fashion show went on sale, I copped me one. The hotel ballroom was packed with people, cameras, local celebrities, and the whole nine. I kicked it with a few of my friends, Sharmba Mitchell, Keith Holmes, Jermaine Fields and Fat Trell, an upcoming local rapper, before I took my seat in the back of the ballroom. *I can't believe Moochie sold me these fucked up seats. Shit, I'm all the way in the back of this motherfucker.* I looked up and saw Paul staring at me. Paul was Moochie's father. He waved at me to come to him. *I hope he got a better seat for me than this,* I prayed to myself.

"How you doing, Paul? Where's Moochie so I can cuss him out for sitting me all the way in the back of this show."

"Don't worry I got a seat for you. Moochie went to California. He's getting ready to open the HOBO Shops in LA, Philly, and Atlanta."

Paul was the one who ran things in Moochie's absence and since he took his whole entourage with him to California, all the seats in the front reserved for the VIP, were empty. That's how I ended up in the VIP section. I took a seat next to Paul, who introduced me to a man sitting next to him. His name was Tony Bills. If he hadn't had on so much ice, I would have thought he was a bamma. At first glance, I didn't like Tony that much. He was fine, don't get me wrong, but something about him screamed out playa, liar, and a cheat.

I still checked him out though, and I liked what I saw. He was pretty fly. Boyfriend was hurting them at the show. He had on brand

4

new Prada loafers, black linen shorts, a Prada contour tee-shirt, and a Prada hat flipped up in the front. His jewels consisted of a large diamond earring in his left ear, an iced out Frank Muller, and a diamond platinum chain. I couldn't see the pendant hid under his shirt. But I knew it was iced out as well.

His Aviator sunglasses complemented the whole outfit. He flashed an award-winning smile at me with the whitest teeth I had ever seen in my life. We exchanged numbers after the show and I really went home anxious to see him again. So anxious that I literally sat by the phone waiting for him to call. But he never did. Two days went by, so I decided to be proactive and called him instead. I believed in going after what I wanted. I called his cell phone. He answered on the third ring.

"Hello, is this Tony?" I asked.

"Yeah, who's this?"

"This is Angel. Do you remember me?"

"How can I forget you? We met at the fashion show a few days ago. I was going to call you. It's just been hectic as hell. What's up?"

"Nothing much, I just wanted to call and say hello." I lied, wishing he was on his way over to see me.

"Okay, well now that you've said hello, would you mind calling me back in ten minutes?"

Is he trying to get rid of me? Maybe he's busy. What if he's with another chick?

"I'm sorry; I forgot to ask you if you were busy. Sure I'll call you back." I felt kind of dumb. *What if he doesn't want to talk to me? Maybe I shouldn't have called him.*

"I'm on the other line with my daughter's teacher at school. So, make sure you call me back and we'll talk alright."

Daughter's teacher, thank God.

I gave him fifteen minutes instead of ten. We talked all day on the phone. He told me everything about himself. That is why I liked him so much. He never lied to me, not even once. He told me all about his baby momma, how they still fucking around, how he got her a house in Kettering, Maryland and how he takes care of his kid.

And I guess because he kept it so real with me, I didn't mind. It wasn't no need in tripping because he was with his baby's momma. Shit, actually it was better, that way, when I got tired of his ass, I could send him right on home. From the beginning, I accepted the fact that I could only have a piece of Tony, but that piece would be the only piece I would need.

Tony was a known street hustler, but he didn't serve shit hand to hand on the street corner. He was a major supplier to all the other dudes in his hood and beyond. Tony had his eyes and ears in tune with the streets and the people roaming around in them so much that he preferred to hang on the curb with everybody else. I really started to dig Tony. He took me everywhere there was to go. From the movies to concerts, we hung out every day, even if it was just going out to eat.

His physical appearance was awesome. He was 6'3 and weighed 235 pounds, all muscles. Tony had a Range Rover, a S600 Mercedes Benz, and a Continental Flying Spur. He told me that he got his baby momma in a BMW X5 and his momma was pushing an E Class Benz. He was always dressed in some fly expensive designer shit like Armani and Versace and the nigga had so much money his shit was like the Federal Reserve. That's why I decided to give him the pussy to hold on to him. He was definitely a keeper. From the first time I saw Tony at the fashion show, I knew we was going to fuck.

I knew that he wanted to do me just as bad as I wanted to do him. I saw the nigga watching my ass all night long and I mean literally watching my ass, staring at my print, and licking his lips. He was sweating me and I loved every minute of watching him lose control. Tony hung out on 14th Place in Congress Park, which was a small section of Congress Heights. I would hang out with him on the curb sometime. All the dudes he fucked with gave me the utmost respect.

They knew I was fucking with Tony, so they had no choice. However, every now and then I would catch them undressing me with their eyes when Tony wasn't around. Honestly, I couldn't blame them if I tried. I was fine as old wine. Truth is, I practically live in the gym trying to keep my figure in blast as my old boyfriend, Buck, use to say.

"Bitch, keep that ass in blast."

I can still hear him to this day. I'm 5'3 and weigh 135 pounds, all hips and ass. So it's a lot to keep in blast. My caramel complexion accents my hazel eyes. I keep my fingernails and toenails done up real proper. My naturally curly hair is cut short. It has often gotten me mistaken for some sort of exotic mixed breed.

I have really nice skin, glowing and blemish free. My ass and thighs are too big for my taste, but my breasts are just right. A real trademark stamped with perfection. When I started seeing Tony, I decided to cut off all my other male friends and other sex partners. After snagging Tony, who needed them?

I would go around to Liberty Park and literally sit on a bench for hours and eye hustle as Tony conducted his business. At first, he didn't like me hanging around so much. But in time I guess I just grew on him. It seems to me that Tony knew half of the people in DC. People would drive up and get out of their cars just to speak to him or shake his hand. I knew that he was ghetto fabulously rich, but I didn't know that he was famous as well. 14th Street was like an office to Tony and every day including Sunday, he ruled the hood like a powerful CEO.

Angel

I would always roll out by midnight. I had to get up early to go to work. Every night though before I would leave; I would sit on Tony's lap. I would straddle him fully clothed and kiss his juicy lips for what seemed like hours. Every day, I'd call Tony to see if he was hanging out on 14th Street and then I'd drive over there as soon as I got off work.

One night when I was sitting in the truck with Tony, listening to a CD he started kissing me and using his hands to hike up my skirt. Like magic, it was up to my waist and he had my thong to the side with the skill of a pick-pocketer. In one fluid motion he had his face between my legs, awakening the inner demons in me until they roared their approval. It was broad daylight and I had only known the nigga for two weeks. It was way too soon for me to be giving him my goodies. But like R. Kelly said, *'My mind is telling me no, but my body is telling me yeah.'* I tried to stop him, but he licked my clit and that was all she wrote. My legs ended up wide open with my knees holding themselves up on the dash board. His tongue was a dangerous weapon that had me open in broad daylight in front of everybody. *What was I supposed to do?*

Tony's tongue danced around my womanhood like an explorer in search of the new world. His head game was the bomb. I tried not to let him know that, but my moans betrayed me. *What was I supposed to do with three inches of tongue hitting my spot?* Like an expert Tony's tongue stayed inside me until I responded by orgasming all over his freshly trimmed mustache. Then we hopped in the back seat like the Rover was a hotel room.

"I want some of him."

"Who, this big guy right here?" Tony said pointing to his dick.

"You got some condoms?"

He played coy for a minute. Then he pulled out a pack of condoms and unzipped his pants. I watched as he pulled out his perfect brown dick that looked to be about nine inches with a curve in it. As he slid on the condom, I became conscious of where we were and what was about to happen. I glanced at the windows of the truck and was relieved to see that the truck was equipped with factory dark tints, so that no one could see us in the back seat. Tony hit every tender spot inside my body as we put in work. Both of us coming as he laid on top of me and shivered violently. From that day on we were inseparable. Tony continued to live at his house in Kettering with his baby momma and their daughter, but he also lives with me in an apartment on Martin Luther King Jr. Highway in Seat Pleasant.

CHAPTER TWO

ANGEL

The rice was a little sticky, but Tony won't mind. Other than that the meal was perfect. I set two places at the table, then went and got Tony from in front of the TV. *All he does is play them damn video games like a big ass kid.* We sat down to our meal.

"Baby, this steak is good as shit and this cheese sauce is the bomb. Boo, you did this. I'm gonna have to hit the gym for a whole week straight to work this off."

"You should have been up Run and Shoot trying to work out. You're getting love handles on your six pack. When you go to the gym I'm going with you. My butt's getting too big." I stood up and showed Tony my butt.

"Your butt looks fine to me, boo." He said as he got up, grabbed my butt and kissed me.

We talked some more during the rest of the meal as I carefully thought out my plan.

Our apartment in Glen Willow was laid out. Tony had me living ghetto fabulously with a sixty-inch big screen plasma TV, high-tech stereo systems with surround sound, theater vision, and the finest Italian leather furniture that money could buy. I always was fly and I always had a little money, but with Tony, I was spending his big money and he didn't mind. I took a trip to New York and shopped in Barney's and Saks on 5ᵗʰ Avenue and complemented my closet with all the latest fashions. From shoes to handbags, I had it going on.

There wasn't a chick in the DMV area who could out do me. Tony even went so far as to cop me a SL55 AMG. So, I'm rolling with my top down screaming out 'money ain't a thang', especially since the money was Tony's. For the past two years that I have been with him, nothing has changed since the first time we met. After dinner, I ran a bath for the two of us. The bathroom was equipped with an oversized Jacuzzi. I lit some candles and played an old Isley Brothers CD in the background.

Of course, our naked bodies in the tub couldn't resist one another. He lathered me with soap and I returned the favor. Rubbing his rock hard body with soap made me want him so bad. I gently lathered his balls and took my time washing his dick as it poked straight up at me. Forget the bath. We rinsed each other off in the shower, before Tony gently forced me on my knees. I dropped down and put half of him in my mouth. I let his head tickle the back of my throat as I tried to engulf his whole dick.

Tony couldn't help but to grab the back of my head as he started to make love to my face. I loved the way he forced his self on me, holding and guiding my head to do as he pleased. Giving Tony head actually turned me on and I felt myself climax as Tony grabbed my curly locks and drove his dick deep into my throat. I couldn't help but to gag as Tony let go in my mouth. His juices went straight down my throat and I swallowed it all, loving every drop. What can I say? Real bitches do real things.

And just when I thought it was over, it was actually just getting ready to begin. Tony must have snuck one of those Viagra's in on me, because his dick never got soft. He went down on me causing me to cum, from his slightest touch. Then he did the unexpected. He turned me around so that I was facing the wall, rubbed some soap into the crack of my ass and stuck his finger in my back-door. Before I could turn around or protest, he replaced his finger with his dick. I rose up on my tip-toes to ease the pain and I tried to close my eyes as I bit down on my lip, but I couldn't relax.

I knew this was what he wanted and I knew that I had to give it to him. I wanted to scream out in pain, but I didn't. I let him have his way, pushing in and out of me. It felt like I was being ripped in two, but once he got it in real good, I relaxed. And to my surprise, the pain turned to pleasure. As Tony began to thrust in and out of me, I actually felt myself about to cum. My legs got weak and I came harder than I ever had in my life. Seconds later, Tony came inside me.

"I love you!" he whispered.

"I love you too."

We made our way into the bedroom and both of us collapsed on the bed. I could tell Tony was still up for a little more bumping and grinding so I started to kiss his neck a little.

"Daddy, I want to try something I saw in one of those nasty videos."

"You ain't stickin' me with nothin' or putting nothin' crazy on my body."

I laughed and tried to lighten the mood.

"No silly, you can do all the stickin'. I want to tie you up and then I want you to tie me up. In the video, the guy was all tied up and the girl was sucking his dick like crazy and all he could do was lay there and enjoy it. And after I do you, then you can tie me up and do things to me. I even want you to fuck me in my ass, again."

His brain started working in overtime and I could see the curiosity building in Tony's eyes mixed with the thought of much pleasure. I went to the closet and got the cord that I had placed there earlier. Tony looked a little nervous at the cord.

"What? Relax, I got you." I said smiling from ear-to-ear as I stretched the cord out in my hands.

I tied both of Tony's feet together and then his wrists.

"Girl, this better be good or I swear I'm going to kick your ass later. Don't be pinching my nipples, be gentle with the nuts, and don't go anywhere near my ass. I'm not playing."

Promises, promises, I thought to myself and licked all over his neck, as I licked him from head to toe, I even sucked on his toes. I turned Tony to the side and laid down to give him a little head.

"Damn, baby, you got the best head this side of the Mason Dixon Line.

"I know, that's what you tell me." I responded with my mouth full of him. I stopped and got behind him and licked his back. I sat up and jerked his dick with one hand and reached under the bed with my other hand. I felt the handle of a .40 Caliber I had placed there earlier. I pulled the gun from under the bed, turned Tony onto his stomach, and whispered sweet nothings in his ear. Then I put the barrel of the gun near his head and quickly pulled the trigger.

The music inside the apartment was on as it always was. All the neighbors heard was a loud pop. Tony's body jerked once as blood splattered on my face. His body went still as the Federal Hydrashock bullet penetrated the back of his skull, turning his brain into a bloody pulp. I knew Tony was dead, but I checked his pulse anyway. I quickly went to the bathroom to wash up. I looked into the mirror and the face that stared back at me was the same face that stared at me in Charlotte, North Carolina so long ago.

Pull yourself together. Stop acting like this is the first time you've killed someone. A little bit of blood won't hurt you.

I went back in the bedroom and retrieved the gun. I carefully wiped it off, leaving no fingerprints on it and put it in the trash can. I slipped on my slippers and took the trash outside to the dumpster. Then, I took a flat head screwdriver out of my robe pocket and jimmied the locking mechanism on the balcony door. That would help support my story of a break-in. *Relax, you've got everything covered.* I kept telling myself.

I put on latex gloves and opened Tony's safe. My pussy caught fire at the sight of all his money. *Damn, this nigga had a rack of money in this motherfucker the whole time. I knew it. Jackpot.* It was way more than I expected. It was so much money, I felt like playing with myself right there as I fondled the cash. I stuffed all the money into two Louis Vuitton carrying bags. I put the two kilos of coke in there too that were in the safe. I took the bags outside to my truck which was parked conveniently by the dumpster. *No one will see me, no one will remember, it's too late.*

I cut the latex gloves up into tiny pieces and flushed them down the toilet. The trash people came promptly at 3:30 a.m. and they would unknowingly dispose the gun. I checked the balcony door. My work looked good. Real good. I left the door ajar and then went back in the bedroom to check on Tony. His naked body was laying silently still on the bed with the bullet hole in the back of his head. I had carefully planned this night for the past thirteen months and so far, everything was going as planned.

Looking at Tony made me think of Andre. He was the first man I ever killed that I had ever truly loved. *Stop crying. What's wrong with you, finish what you started.* I had to stay focused. It was time to call the police and play the grieving girlfriend. The acting class I took in high school had certainly come in handy in my older years.

I picked up the phone and dialed 911.

'Someone just killed my boyfriend." I screamed hysterically.

The police arrived in minutes and were all over the place. Both the plain clothes detectives and the uniformed cops were all over the apartment like roaches. A detective had me in the living room asking me all kinds of questions. How many dudes did I see? What did they look like? Height and weight? What were they wearing? Then what happened? Did you hear the gunshot from the bathroom?

For the twentieth time I told the same story. I had it memorized. In between sobs and plenty of tears I told my story over and over.

"Tony and I ate dinner in the living room. After dinner we got into the tub. We made love in the tub for about an hour. Then we dried off and rubbed lotion on each other. We got in bed and called it a night. I was awakened by two hands snatching me out of bed. Two gloved hands picked me up as if weighed nothing. One of those hands quickly covered my mouth.

"The lights were dim but I could see two other dudes standing over Tony. They carried me into the bathroom and told me not to scream or they would kill me. They said I would be safe as long as I stayed calm and seemed followed their instructions. The big dude held me for what seemed like an eternity. Then I heard a single loud pop. The dude holding me said that he would keep his promise and wouldn't hurt me. He told me to stay in the bathroom, count to one thousand, and then come out.

"He said if I came out of the bathroom before I finished counting, he would kill me. I was so scared I just did what he told me to do. When I walked out of the bathroom, the dudes were gone; that's when I saw Tony. He was lying there on the bed tied up. I saw the hole in his head. I felt for a pulse; there was none. I saw that the safe was open and that's when I called 911."

I watched the coroners carry Tony's body out in a black bag and that's when I really performed. I cried and screamed and even convinced myself that intruders had really been there. The detectives had to hold me down and even offered me tissue and a glass of water.

"Calm down, ma'am. It's going to be okay. We're here now."

Angel

They let me get dressed and pack my things that I had in his apartment, then the area was officially sealed off as a crime scene.

I drove straight to Fatima's house, my best friend who lived in Silver Springs. Fatima woke up and let me. I showed her the bags and their contents.

"What have you done?" she asked a little nervous.

"Sit down and let me tell you."

A Novel by Anthony Fields

1978
TO
1999

CHAPTER THREE

ANGEL

Everybody close to me calls me Angel, but my real name is Kareemah El-Amin. I was born on June 7, 1978 at D.C. General Hospital. I was raised in the Benning Heights area. My family lived on 46th Street and Hillside Road in Southeast D.C. My father was the assistant Imam of the Masjid that my family attended. Everybody in the neighborhood knew my father because of all the things he did to try and improve conditions of Benning Heights and the community. My father, Abdul-Khalif El-Amin was strict on me and my little sister, but my mother, Sister Naimah El-Amin, let us get away with murder for the most part.

Mom was a housewife. She also taught Islam 101 at the Masjid on Fridays after Jumah. My little sister, Adirah and I were raised in a strict Muslim household. Growing up, we spent a lot of time at the Masjid. I was the oldest child and therefore had a lot of responsibilities. I had to wear the traditional Islamic clothing. The hijab drove me nuts as I got older. I hated wearing the head covering. I honestly did.

"We must guard our modesty. It's a sin for men to lust. We mustn't provoke them." My mother would say.

"So, why do I have to wear this stupid head covering and wear garb so men don't lust. If it's their sin, it should be on their head, not mine!"

All the yelling and screaming in the world wouldn't change anything. I was garbed down, covered up, and miserable. The boys and girls were always separated at school and in the Masjid. I never understood why. And the boys were always treated as if they were above the girls. I hated that too. Besides the discrimination of being a girl and having to cover myself, my childhood wasn't that bad.

I attended an Islamic Elementary School called Sister Clara Muhammad School. Then I attended my neighborhood public junior high school, Fletcher Johnson; since there were no Islamic Junior high schools nearby. *Al-hum-dil-li-lah!* And H.D. Woodson High was filled with all the dunya one could imagine to poison the righteous Muslim mind. That's what I wanted, that's what I needed and luckily I got a dose full of regular kids who wore designer clothes and had drugs, sex, alcohol, and cigarettes. They had all the material possessions Islam stood against.

Unfortunately, my father refused to let me outside without being properly covered. So, I was ridiculed because of my clothes, my religion, and my refusal to participate in the school's holiday events. Still, I was glad I was there. *Sticks and stones can break my bones, but words can't hurt me.* Plus, I had my best friend in the whole world, Fatima. She was also raised by the Islamic faith. We stuck together throughout junior and high school years like crazy glue.

I can remember back to the day this boy named Kyle Dunley asked me to the school dance. He was nice, well-mannered, well-groomed, and a good student. I told him yes. I figured being as though I was about to turn twelve-years old, my parents had to let me go. I was so excited, I rushed home from school to tell my mom, but she wasn't home when I got there. No one was home yet. I went in my room and started rummaging through my closet. *There has to be something here to wear. I have to have something.*

I took off my garb and hijab and began trying on various gifts. *Ain't no way they gonna let me out the house with this on.* As I started to undress, I felt a silent presence. It was my father. He was standing in my doorway.

19

Angel

"What are you doing, Kareemah?"

"Oh, daddy, nothing." I said quickly trying to cover up my nakedness. "I was asked to the dance and I was just looking for something to wear."

My father didn't hear a word I said. His eyes focused dead on me and before I knew it, he was standing behind me with his hands feeling my bare shoulders, his fingers moving down my back.

"Daddy, what are you do..."

"Sshh, you're daddy's good little girl, Kareemah. Be a good girl."

I was so scared I didn't say a word. I just stood there, still as a board as my father's hands felt between my legs.

"Why aren't you grooming yourself, Kareemah? We have to groom you. Lay down."

He walked out my room and came back within seconds, holding a pair of clippers in his hands.

"Lay down and open your legs, Kareemah."

Meticulously, he trimmed the hair around the lips and vaginal opening of my pussy. This is how he always began sex with me. First, he'd make me lie down while he shaved and cleaned me, then he'd use his hands to finger me, then he'd eat my pussy, then he'd fuck me. That was the routine, but he would always shave and clean me first.

I was so scared, I never told anybody, not my mother, not Fatima, not a soul. I carried my dirty little secret with me for years until one day I came home from school earlier and I was scared my father might have been waiting for me, so I tried to be as quiet as I could. I tiptoed down the hall but before I got to my bedroom door, I heard strange noises coming from my little sister, Adirah's bedroom door. Gently, I peeked in her room and saw my father on top of my little sister.

"Daddy, please stop! Daddy, stop. You're hurting me. Please!" Adirah cried out.

Tears began to well up in my eyes for her. I knew I had to do something to stop him. But what? I knew couldn't tell anyone. No one would believe me.

Quickly, I went back to the front door, I opened it, yelling, "I'm home. Anybody here." I walked down to Adirah's door way and opened her door.

"Adirah, you home?"

I saw Adirah run into the bathroom and my father as he was buckling his pants. I looked at him and at that moment I no longer saw the strong minded, righteous man everyone knew at the Masjid. I saw a hermit, and a look of fear that my father didn't want me to know about him and my sister. I pretended I didn't have a clue as to what was going on. But I did, and I knew I had to do something to save my little sister. She was all I could think about. She was only nine. For days, I couldn't eat or sleep.

I had to devise a plan to protect Adirah. So I always made sure she was never in the house alone with our father. I skipped school leaving a half hour early just to get home at the same time Ahdeerah did so she wouldn't be alone. I couldn't eat or sleep and all I could remember hearing was her sad plea for our father to stop. I went to school in tears, and it was then that I told Fatima what was going on. Fatima couldn't believe it, she felt so bad for me and Adirah that she started crying too.

"What are you going to do?" Fatima asked.

"I don't know. I just don't know."

******

Three days later my Aunt Doreen fell down three stairs. She twisted her ankle and was in a soft cast. She had been given crutches, but fell down again trying to walk with them and had to go back to the hospital. My mother went over to her house to help take care of her. It was the perfect opportunity to fix a never ending problem. I knew exactly what to do. I bought some ecstacy pills at school. I crushed them up and put them in my father's iced tea.

"Let me take it to him. Stay here." I told Ahdeerah, taking the ice tea in my hand.

I walked out to the living room and handed my father the glass. He looked at me, focusing his eyes on my fourteen-year-old breasts. I wasn't wearing a bra, just a t-shirt and I had conveniently taken off my panties as I walked down the hall.

"Here you go." I said real nice and slow conveniently standing in front of him. "Do you want anything else?" I asked slightly lifting my tee-shirt so he could see the lips of my shaven pussy. It was really quick and I let the tee-shirt go once he saw what I wanted him to see. I looked at his crotch and his bulge was poking through his pants.

"Let me see." He said as he fondled me and looked at my nakedness.

Both of us could hear Adirah coming down the hall and he quickly withdrew his finger out my pussy and let my shirt fall back down.

"I'll be back." I whispered and followed Adirah down the hall to her bedroom. After she fell asleep, I went back out to the living room. It seemed as if my father had been patiently waiting. He turned into an octopus that had twelve arms. The E-pills had definitely worked.

"Stop, we can't do this here. Adirah's in the next room and could walk out and find us. We need to go somewhere." I lied knowing that my sister was sleep.

His perverted mind went into over-drive as he appeared to be in deep thought.

"Okay, I know a place. It's dark and private. Go get dressed and meet me outside."

We ended up at Anacostia Park, in a secluded area. We both got out of the car and walked to a little patch of grass by the water. *Boy oh boy, is he in for a surprise. Sick bastard.*

The E-pills had him nodding in and out as if in a heroin-induced daze. I kissed him on his thigh and on his stomach. I even kissed his penis and that was something that I never did. He rolled his head back and closed his eyes as I pulled a razor sharp knife out of my pocket and then stabbed him three times in the neck.

He fell back, stumbled, and looked at me as he gasped for air. Little did I know, but I had severed his jugular and the oxygen supply that went to his brain. His eyes widened in shock and horror as he realized that he was about to die. He lunged towards me, but I stepped back and he fell to the ground, his hands wrapped around his own neck as he tried to stop the blood from gushing out between his fingers. His mouth opened and he tried to scream, but no sound came out. I heard him gurgling and choking on his own blood.

I threw the knife into the Anacostia River and stared out at the open body of water. It was so peaceful and serene. I looked over at my father's dead body lying on the ground as the realization of what I had just done set in. *I killed my father. But, I had to.* It didn't even upset me. I felt secure in the fact that Ahdeerah and I didn't have to worry about him violating us anymore and I didn't have to worry about anymore dirty secrets.

We both sat side by side at the funeral and watched our mother cry her eyes out. We just looked at each other, with no remorse. We watched them lower the casket into the ground. *Good riddance,* I thought to myself. After that day, I never thought about my father again or what had happened. Adirah and I never spoke another word about it. I guess for us, some things were better left unsaid.

Angel

After graduating high school, Fatima and I separated. Since I had a 4.0 grade average, I received an academic scholarship to Johnson C. Smith University in Charlotte North Carolina. Fatima got a Pell Grant and went away to Clark University in Atlanta Georgia. As I attended college and grew more aware of myself, I still held fast to my belief in Allah and his Prophet, but I moved further and further away from the Islam faith. It's hard to explain, I still felt and believed like a Muslim, but I wasn't on my deen. I stopped practicing and I stopped wearing my hijab and the other Islamic clothes. I dressed more fashionably wearing regular jeans and tee-shirts.

I got a part-time job at Sonic's Fast Food Restaurant so I'd have extra money in my pocket. The restaurant wasn't far from school so I could walk there and walk back to campus. I lived in a dorm with three hundred other raving lunatic females whose main concern only seemed to be men, men, and more men!

But me, I kept my mind on my studies. I majored in communications and minored in child development. I had plans on becoming a radio or TV personality and then on to bigger and better things. The drama class I took in high school gave me the acting bug. From day one, it wasn't hard to tell that I was different from everybody else, so I stayed to myself.

Between school and work, a whole year passed by in no time. In the beginning of my sophomore year I met Andre. The campus grapevine had it that Andre was a major catch. He was invited to all the hot spots and all the parties and his circle of friends were the in-crowd and the most popular on campus. I met Andre at the Sonic. He came in one day and ordered a number five special. I couldn't stop staring at him. He was gorgeous in a rugged sort of way, standing over six feet tall with a lanky frame. His eyes were mesmerizing, changing colors at different angles. His hair was cut short and his skin was the color of pure honey.

I was attracted to his style. He wore a multicolored Coogi sweater and a matching hat with Coogi blue jeans and butter Timberland boots. He looked at me as I placed his order and I swear it felt as if he stared straight through me to my soul. He made small talk as I rang him up.

"What's your name?"

"Uhh, the tag." I said pointing to my name tag that read Angel.

I gave him my number at the dorm and he said he would call me. After Andre left the store I recognized him. He played point guard for the school's basketball team. Everybody that knew him or knew of his basketball skills said he was destined to be in the NBA. It was even rumored that he'd forgo his senior year to make himself available to the draft.

I didn't think that Andre was really that interested in me; but to my surprise he called me the next day and then every day after that for about three months. Basically, all we did was talk on the phone. He seemed to really like talking to me. We talked about everything from DC, Islam, and myself. He was a big fan of go-go music although he was from Detroit and used to partying to house music and rap. He told me all about his life too.

"I grew up on the basketball courts in Detroit. I used to go all over Detroit playing the best basketball players on the court. I always knew that basketball would be my ticket out of the hood. My parents both worked like slaves in the GM auto factory. We were poor and my mom and dad really struggled to make ends meet. I played ball at Cleveland Elementary, post middle school and then at Cooley High School. I was approached three years in a row by college scouts. It was my mother's prayers to see her son get a college education and ball has done that for me. Now, it's my dream to get in the NBA. All I ever wanted to do was to play ball, that's my dream, it always has been."

Angel

He told me about his life growing up on Finkle and Hurbert on the Westside of Detroit. He told me about the movie *Cooley High* being based on his high school. He expressed anger over racism. He vented about Malice Green, the black man who was killed by white police officers during a traffic stop, a couple years after the Rodney King beating. We talked about world events, music, cars, clothes, and school, but eventually the conversation always ended up back at basketball.

Basketball was his life; although I couldn't talk basketball talk, I listened a lot. On our first date Andre took me to a cabaret being held at the campus auditorium. The cabaret featured a go-go band from DC called Rare Essence. I had no idea why it took so long for Andre to ask me out. But it took him a while. I was actually starting to think he was never going to.

Growing up in DC all my life, I knew about go-go music and I even sang along with the catchy 'call and response' hooks. But until that day I never saw a go-go band live. It was better than I anticipated. The band was cranking like hell and everybody was feeling them. The whole auditorium was out of control; it was off the chain.

The band had a song called *'Work the Walls and Take it Off'*. All the chicks were dancing, shaking their asses and gyrating seductively all over the guys. Some couples were so risqué they actually simulated sex acts out in the open. Andre moved through the crowd as if he owned it; he grabbed my hand and guided me through throngs of people. I wasn't a very good dancer, but I faked it. Thank God for a crowded dance floor. Tired, sweaty, and tingling, I went to get a soda at the bar.

When I came back, Andre was dancing with another girl, she had her back to him with her ass pressed into his crotch. If they didn't have clothes on, they would've been fuckin' on the dance floor. I was livid! I never thought I had any jealous bones in my body, but apparently I did. I didn't know what to do or how to respond. Was I supposed to go over to him and shake my ass harder?

Fuck him! I thought to myself and left the campus auditorium and walked across the campus to my dorm. A little while later, Andre called me begging me to come downstairs. I was mad and I didn't really want to see him on one hand and on the other hand I was glad he called me and wanted to see me.

"Why did you leave me?" Andre asked with a hurt look on his face.

"I left because you were all up on that big booty girl when I came back from the bar. I felt stupid so I left."

"Angel, you can't get mad at stuff like that. I know plenty of females. I'm the star point guard. You can't sweat the small stuff."

He went on about me having to be able to deal with his celebrity status on campus and after a little coaxing, we ended up in my dorm. My roommate Shelia was at home in Boston for the weekend, so that meant that Andre and I would be alone, without interruption. I was a little nervous about being in the dorm with him, but he had a strange way of making me feel comfortable. I turned on the radio and sat down next to him.

"I've been in love with you ever since the first day I met you." He said before kissing me.

I was young and believed every word that came out of his mouth. When he reached over to kiss me, I readily kissed him back and when his hands started to caress my nipple through my blouse, I willingly let him. Inside me, my body was yearning to experience life's simplest and greatest pleasure. An orgasm. I wanted him to want me, so I didn't dare stop him. Andre reached under my blouse and expertly unsnapped my bra from my back. Before I could blink my blouse and my bra were on the floor. My nakedness embarrassed me somewhat and I couldn't help but to hear my mother in the background messing up the mood.

Never let any man see or touch your body, his intentions must be to marry you and if he's not your husband, he has no rights to you.

But, just as quickly as that thought entered my head was as quickly as it left. I felt Andre's finger between my thighs and I opened my legs for him like the whores I had seen in the nasty videos. I threw my head back and gave into the wonderful exotic feelings that electrified my body. His hand found its way to the center of me. My womanhood expanded and I opened my legs a little wider for him to do as he pleased. He stuck his finger in me probing my warm wetness as his lips locked on my nipple and sucked it.

I didn't know if I should cry or scream out in pleasure. I couldn't believe I was nineteen-years-old and about to become a woman in every sense of the word. Andre laid me on my back and began stroking my inner thighs with his tongue. He licked all around my pussy and I would have never thought anything in this world could feel so good. Then he began to go down on me, licking at my clit as if it were a lollipop. When his lips kissed me down there I screamed out in ecstasy. When his tongue slipped up to the top of my lips, I could feel his fingers pushing me apart as he opened me and began sucking my clit.

I rode the wave of ecstasy for what seemed like hours but were actually only minutes. Andre was slow and methodical in his quest to turn me on. I felt my soul grow hot and then an intense burning sensation emanated from deep within my inner self. The vibrations started at my toes and then rose throughout my whole body. I came so hard, I cried. Tears were running down my face, but I quickly wiped them away.

"Are you a virgin?"

"Yes." I lied. "So, please be gentle with me."

Andre must've sensed my trepidation because he snuggled against me and talked about how beautiful and special I was. Then he climbed back on top of me and slowly entered me. I was so caught up in a sea of emotion. I clung to Andre in an attempt to hold him hostage. He was like water that quenched my thirst; he was food to curb my hunger. I was in love. I cried softly to myself as R. Kelly sang on the radio, *I believe I can fly.*

Andre got up and showered, kissed me all over my face, promised to call me in the morning, and left. I toasted my newfound love with a cup of herbal tea, then I fell asleep. The next morning, I couldn't wait to see Andre. I had so many plans for us. I rang his dorm, but he wasn't there. I was in a daze and I started to wonder if the night before had really taken place or if it was all just a dream.

I looked at the crumpled bed sheets in the corner of the room so I knew that last night was real. *Where's Andre? He said he'd call me.* I rang his dorm again, but no answer. I couldn't help myself. I felt like a stalker. I called several more times.

"Naw, he not here. I'm not sure where he at. I'll tell him to call you when he gets back."

Okay, don't worry. He'll call when he gets the message. Maybe he had some things to do this morning. Maybe he's just busy.

I tried to tell myself that he'd call, but my gut instinct said bullshit! I tried to be calm, but I couldn't. All I remembered about last night was that Andre told me he loved me, and that I was special. But at that moment, I didn't feel special. I felt violated and lied to. I felt used. I showered again and cleaned up my room and did the laundry. I needed to wash away the evidence of Andre's betrayal. I was clean on the outside but I felt dirty on the inside. To take my mind off Andre I studied. By the time the clock read midnight, I was thoroughly agitated.

Angel

He's not going to call. He just said the things he did so he could fuck me. How could I be so dumb?

The next morning when my roommate came back to school I told her about the situation with Andre. Then she dropped the bomb on me.

"Damn, girl I should have told you about him. I am so sorry."

I was puzzled by her apology. "Sheila, why are you apologizing?"

"Because, I forgot to warn you about Andre Ford. That nigga is the lowest of the low. All he does is go around using his popularity to sleep with everybody, especially the freshmen and sophomores. He's a whore and a heartbreaker, girl. He ain't shit. I was supposed to warn you about him, but I forgot. Last year a girl tried to commit suicide over Andre. Angel, I'm so sorry I didn't tell you and I'm sorry he did this to you."

Sheila ended up telling me all the stories about Mr. Andre Ford as I sat there on my bed mortified. The part that really hurt the most was that Shelia felt sorry for me. As tears welled up in my eyes, I went into the bathroom to cry. I didn't need anyone's pity. As my tears dried, my resolve strengthened. I decided right then and there in that bathroom, that Andre Ford might have tricked me out my panties, but I had a trick or two up my sleeve for him.

Thirty minutes later I came out of the bathroom with evil thoughts cemented in my mind. Sheila and I didn't exchange any words. She must've figured that I had had a good cry and was okay. But I wasn't, I was heated and I wanted revenge. That was my destiny and I accepted it. I wasn't sure when I'd get Andre but I wouldn't rest until I did.

About a week later, I went to the gym and watched the basketball team practice. There was Andre, my Andre, everybody's Andre and he was there playing his part to the fullest. The star point guard running the floor, doing what he did best. *Basketball might be what he did second best,* I thought as my insides shivered a little at the thought of him eating my pussy. I sat in the second row of the bleachers and applauded every assist, steal, and basket that he made. I pretended to be his greatest fan, his biggest groupie, and the most gullible girl he could have whenever he wanted.

When Andre looked into the stands and saw me he looked a little uncomfortable.

I guess I'm not supposed to be following you around, cheering you on since you dumped me huh?

He played the rest of the game like his concentration was off. After practice was over, I walked out onto the court and approached Andre. He braced himself for a nasty fall-out.

"How are you doing?" I smiled seductively.

"Hi yourself, Angel. I've been meaning to call you but I've been really busy with my classes and basketball. I've been cramming all night for exams the last couple of nights. I apologize." He smiled a Twizzler commercial smile.

"I understand baby. I know how it gets sometimes. I didn't expect you to be around me 24-7. I just need you to do me a favor."

"What?"

"I'll be leaving school soon, going back home, but before I go I just want to see you one more time. My scholarship wasn't renewed and I don't have the money to continue. I'm leaving, but before I leave, I want to be with you. One last time.

I can't help it, but I'll do anything you want."

His shocked reaction was genuine, but it quickly turned to conceit. "Sure I think I can find some time to make love to you real good one last time before you go."

"Okay, meet me on the roof tonight, 9:00." I turned and walked away and pretended to drop my dorm keys. Carefully, I bent down giving him and everybody in eye sight a quick glance of my goodies. I heard the guys around him, they saw my thong panties. But more importantly he saw them and I knew he'd meet me later.

"Bye." I said waving at him as if nothing happened.

******

"**W**hy do you wanna do it up here?" He asked as he laid a blanket on the roof.

"I don't know, I just thought it was a great place being outside on the roof and all." I said and walked over to the roof's end.

Andre walked over and stood behind me and we both looked at the view of the campus. I turned around and began kissing him.

"Andre I love you. I will always love you." Then I dropped to my knees and unzipped his pants.

"Angel, I love you too!"

Fucking liar, you love no one but yourself.

As I licked his penis it got hard. I wanted to relax him, so I did something that I thought I'd never do in a million years. I put his penis in my mouth and started to suck on it. Andre's eyes were closed as he moaned with pleasure. I didn't know what the hell I was doing. I just went with the flow and sucked him off like the girls did in the nasty videos. He grabbed the back of my head and guided his penis in and out of my mouth. Sometimes he'd push it a little too far and cause me to choke, but like the trooper I was, I kept sucking.

Before I knew what was happening, he was humping my face, thrusting in and out as the warm thick liquid rushed into my mouth. He held my head so hard, I was forced to swallow his cum and I thought I would vomit. He pulled me up off my knees and zipped up his pants.

No this nigga isn't done?

"I love you Andre."

Before he could respond, I gave him a hard shove that sent him over the ledge and out into the open sky. I looked over the edge and watched his free-fall to the waiting earth down below. Andre's twisted body hit the ground with a loud thud.

See, that's just what you get, liar.

I picked up all evidence that I was there and I walked back to the door that we came through and descended the stairs to the gym. I left out of the side door that Andre had jimmied to get us in, so no one paid me any mind as I walked slowly across the campus. People quickly gathered around Andre. I heard them crying, shouting, and screaming as I walked back to my dorm. I showered, then got in my bed, and went to sleep as if nothing had happened.

The next day the news of Andre's death was all over the local news and all over campus. No one understood why he would commit suicide when his life was so promising. I finished the school year at Johnson C. Smith, then I decided that college wasn't for me. I wanted to go back home, back to D.C. I had plans, really big plans and it was just a matter of time before they manifested themselves. I rode the Greyhound back home. I knew that my life had changed, I just didn't realize how much.

CHAPTER FOUR

ANGEL

The one thing I left behind, I ended up needing most of all. The money-counting machine. Tony had a digital IBM money counter. In my haste, I forgot that I would need it. So, Fatima and I had to count the money manually. I emptied out all the money from the carrying bags. It was so much money, it was like hitting the lotto.

A bitch can eat good now, for real.

Fatima and I sat on the floor and started to count the money. Shit, we was counting money for so long, my got-damn fingers started to get sore. *Now how's that for ching-ching?* After an hour we had counted out $250,000. *Damn, I didn't know counting money could be so hard.* By the time we finished, it was daybreak. The clock on Fatima's wall read 6:45 a.m. and I was $1,373,000 richer. I gave Fatima $20,000 for helping me count the money and another $10,000 just because she was my best friend. Fatima held onto that $30,000 and smiled like a Somalian child with a bag of food.

"Girl, I got plans for this little $30,000, honey. But, I don't know, Angel. You think I should take it?"

"Why the hell not?" I stopped and looked at her as if she was crazy.

"Girl, this here is real blood money." Fatima said as if the money were diseased. "From a real dope dealer."

"Blood money? Bitch is your crazy? Let me find out, money is money. If you don't want it, give it back to me. I need all the dope money I can get. I'm trying to get to LA."

"You have over $1,000,000 right there; you can go to LA right now."

"Naw. Not yet. I need more than $1,000,000. See I gotta plan. Give me two years and I'm outta here." I said and got up off the floor to stretch. My bones cracked and my butt was still sore from the pounding Tony gave it the night before. I walked into the bathroom and showered. I was tired as hell and looked it.

As I looked into the mirror, I thought about a book I once read; *The Art of War*, by Niccolo Machiavelli. One of the main principles of war was to get enough rest. The book says that the body doesn't function well when it's weary. Sleep is a weapon when used properly. So, I laid in Fatima's bed which was so comfortable and I fell asleep.

******

The hallway was long, it seemed like it stretched a mile every few steps I took made my legs heavier and heavier and heavier. I tried to open the first door I came to, but it was locked, the next door I tried was locked. Door after door after door, they were all locked, until one opened. And the light brightened the hallway. I peeked in and saw a man, a naked man. He called my name as he was waiting for me. The sight of his nakedness frightened me and I dropped my book bag and ran down the hall. He ran after me, chasing me. Chasing me down the hall as it narrowed until he reached out his long arm and wrapped it around my waist, pulling at my clothes, ripping them off of me.

"Noooo!" I screamed and kicked and yelled. "No, Daddy, no!"

I rolled over seeing my father's face and wiped the sweat off of my forehead. I jumped up and ran into the bathroom. I looked in the mirror. *It was just a dream, just a dream.* I told myself as I patted my face with cold water and went back to bed.

Angel

When I opened my eyes later that afternoon, it was almost 4:00. I called out for Fatima, but she was gone. She left a note on the kitchen table saying that she'd be back soon. I laughed to myself, *I bet she done went shopping.* Fatima was a clothes and shoes fanatic. Her closet was filled with Chanel, Gucci, and Prada. I couldn't talk, I was the same way. Sure enough, she called me a few minutes later from Tyson's Corner Mall bragging about her shopping spree.

"Girl, you need to get down here. They got some shit up in here, for real. I got these Versace sandals on sale for $199.00." She continued to tempt me with shop talk, but I couldn't oblige her. I had a few personal things I had to do.

"You not wearing that stuff to Jumah are you?" I joked with her.

"I know you not talking, you don't even go."

Fatima was a practicing Muslim, but she was what they called a radical. Like, for instance, she rarely covered her hair anymore, but she always went to Jumah.

And she still offered all her prayers. I'm sometimes tempted to go to the Masjid with Fatima, but my evil nafs always get in the way. I know that I'm not on the straight path. I don't read my Qu'ran anymore. I haven't offered the Salat in years. But every now and then, I'll say *Insha Allah or Allah-akbar.* When I'm feeling really terrible, I'll say *Dua* or *Dhirk* to *Allah,* in hopes that he forgives me of my sins. Then I feel hypocritical because in my heart I know I'm not through sinning. *It's hard to be righteous.*

I got the card from my pocket and called the detective investigating Tony's case, Sean Jones. He told me that some people call him Mason because he solves cases like the infamous Perry Mason. *Whatever,* I thought to myself. *See if you can solve this.* He was nice enough, but I had to be careful with him. Because after all he was the enemy. He asked me a rack of the same questions that he asked me the night before. I told him the exact same story that I told him last night. All I added was a few new tears to my act.

I was starting to get good at playing the grieving girlfriend role. Actually, I should have won an Oscar. Next, I called my answering machine and checked my messages. One of the messages was from Tony's baby mother, Tina. She left a phone number and asked me to call her. *I wonder why?* The news about Tony's death wasn't on the news yet, but it was in the afternoon edition of the Washington Post. Fatima conveniently left it on the table for me to see. The Prince George Police Department (DPGD) was asking for the public's help or any information that would lead to the arrest of the three black males who participated in a home invasion that led to the death of Anthony J. Phillips.

They put what I had told them, in the paper. I told the police that three dudes were involved. I told them that the dudes were wearing masks. But, I knew they were black because I saw the skin on the wrist of the dude who held me. I described the other two dudes as being medium height, 5'10 to 6'0, both kinda stocky. I had only seen them for a few seconds and that was the best I could do. When the detective asked me how they got in which way did they leave, I told him I didn't know because I was in the bathroom when they left.

Then he started asking all kinds of questions about Tony's lifestyle. What did he do? How was he able to afford all the expensive stuff he owned? I played dumb especially when he asked me if I knew what Tony had in the safe? Drugs? Money? Guns? Or all three?

"I don't know." that was all I said over and over and over.

He asked me about Tony's truck and I cursed under my breath for forgetting all about the Escalade parked out in front of the apartment. I told the detective that the keys had to be in the apartment unless the robbers took them. Then he asked me about Tony's connection to Drug Kingpin Carlos Trinidad. I really feigned ignorance. Then he asked me if I knew why the robbers opted to rob my apartment instead of Tony's house in Kettering, Maryland? I told the man I had no clue.

The detective told me that Tony had been shot once through the occipital bone. In layman's terms, he explained that these bones were in the back of the head. He told me that they dusted the whole house for prints, but found none. He said he wasn't surprised since the gunmen were wearing gloves. He then talked police talk about how the first twenty-four hours are always critical in solving homicides. He then promised to stay in touch. And for some reason, I knew he wasn't buying my story.

I checked my mind and then double-checked to make sure that I hadn't forgotten anything else. I still couldn't decide what to do with the two kilos of cocaine I took from the safe. I know all of Tony's friends, even Carlos. Well, I knew of Carlos. I never actually spoke to him, but I did see him on several occasions. I knew that Tony dealt with Carlos on a regular basis. I definitely didn't want the word to get out that I sold two kilos after his death. Carlos would surely want them back if Tony still owed him.

Then I decided to just sit on them. There was no immediate need for me to move them. I just came off with a million and three, in cold hard cash, so I'm straight financially. I flipped the paper to the classified section in search of a new condominium. I know I can afford a house, but it's just not me; I don't need that much space. I knew Tony's family would handle all the funeral arrangements, so I didn't have to stress about that.

I decided to call my mother back later. My next call of duty was to confront the grieving baby's momma who probably wanted my head on a stick. I knew all about Tina, where she and Tony lived, and what kind of car she drove and where she worked. You'd be surprised at all the shit niggas tell broads when the pussy is good. I knew that their daughter's name was Honesty and where she went to school.

But that's were my jeopardy game show skills ran out. Tina and I had never actually met face-to-face, but we did talk on the phone once. I know what she looks like; I saw pictures of her in Tony's wallet, but she doesn't know what I look like. At least I don't think she does. And I don't think she knows about us, but then again Tony might have told her. But, I don't think so.

When we met; Tony told me how to deal with Tina. I remember him saying, "Tina is going to find out about you eventually. She checks my pager, she goes through my pockets, and she scrolls through my cell phone. She'll cross reference them with the numbers that call my pager. If she goes over the bill and sees several calls from the same number, she'll call it."

And he was right. About two months into our little fling, she called me. I remember the phone call. I was at home on 46th Street then. My phone rang and I answered it.

"Hello, who am I speaking to?" she asked me.

"Who do you want to speak to?" I replied.

"I would like to speak to whoever keeps calling and paging my man from this number."

I knew exactly who it was. "Who's your man?"

"Tony!" she said angrily.

I had to do everything in my power to keep from laughing.

Then I shot my spiel. "Look boo, I know Tony. Tony is my connect. We do business together, that's it. I call Tony to see when he'll be ready to see me. I need raffle tickets. His tickets are so hot that I can never keep enough of them. Tony and my man Craig are buddies. Craig got locked up so I had to step in and pay Tony his money. Tony told me about his family, and boo, I would never dream of disrespecting what y'all have. I'm not after your man. Can you deliver my message?" I laid the bullshit on extra thick.

She apologized and then hung up, but I could tell that she wasn't convinced. I talked to Tony later that day and relayed the conversation to him. He told me that I had done the right thing.

That was almost two years ago and I'm not too thrilled that we have to talk again. I dialed the number that she left on my answering machine. After about two rings she picked up the phone.

"Hello?"

I decided maybe that I shouldn't have called. "Hello?" Then I said, "Is this Tina?"

"Yes, this is she; who is this?" I could hear a voice in the background that sounded like a young girl.

"This is Angel. You left a message on my machine asking me to call you. Well, here I am; what's up?"

"Can you hold a moment please?" I waited. "Baby, hang up that phone please." We both listened as the girl hung up the other phone. "Hello, Angel."

"Yeah, I'm here; what's up?"

"You were the last person to see Tony alive, right?"

I knew I couldn't lie because the detective would have already told her everything. So, I decided to tell the truth or at least, my version of it. "Yeah, that would be correct. I was with him when he was killed."

"Listen ho, I've known about you and Tony since day one. Even when your lying ass wasn't woman enough to tell me that we were fucking and sucking the same dick. You could've kept it real. I knew Tony wasn't shit. Tony admitted to me that you and he were more than friends a long time ago. So, you can drop the *'I don't know anything, we're just friends'* shit. I sat back and allowed y'alls little thing to continue because I knew that Tony would be Tony, no matter what. So as long as he brought his ass home at night on most nights and took care of us; which he did, I figured fuck it, we could share the dick. All I want is the keys to his truck and whatever personal effects that he had at y'all little crib in Seat Pleasant. Ho, I can give you your address."

I was starting to get upset at Tina for her lack of respect. She was going a little too far with the cursing and name-calling, but I let her continue. "I would appreciate it if you would gather all his things and put them in the truck. And I'll meet you and get the keys. Do we understand each other?"

I swear I was about to let her funny-looking ass have it, but I knew that she was grieving over Tony's death. I told her that I'd call her when she could pick up the keys.

"And by the way, I talked to the detective on the case. He told me about the absence of footprints and all the other things that make your story some bullshit. Please don't let me find out that you were part of this tragedy and that you set Tony up or something, because bitch…"

Before she could finish her sentence, I hung up on her. She could tell the rest of that shit she was talking to the dial tone. Besides; I was busy thinking about how I wanted to spend some of that million three. I'm not going to spend a lot of it though because I'll need more than that to go to California and live. When I finally leave, I don't want to come back for any reasons.

I hid the two keys in Fatima's bedroom closet. As I got dressed I couldn't take my eyes off the Louis Vuitton bags knowing what they held. I was intoxicated, totally inebriated with excitement. Then I decided to stash the money at my mother's house in Southeast. My mother still lived in the same house that we grew up in on the same block.

Forty Sixth Street looked exactly the same, nothing had changed. My mother still taught Islam 101 at the Masjid and my little sister was in her last year at HD Woodson High. As soon as I walked in the door, I knew I was in for it.

My mother gave me the Muslim greeting. "As-Salaamu Alaikum."

" Wa-alaikum As-Salaam." I replied.

Then she said, "I saw the news today; its mighty strange how much that dead boy looks like that boy you been living with. And they even have the same name. Then I could've sworn that that apartment complex where he was killed looks just like the one you live in. Tell me what's going on, Angel."

I explained the scenario to my mother just like I did with the cops. She gave me the same condescending and contemptuous look that she's been giving me ever since I left home. I told her that I was staying at Fatima's until I found another apartment.

"Girl, Allah is going to punish you. You've turned your back on Allah, he who created you. And now Allah is turning his back on you. I raised you to be a Muslimah. I raised you to accept your true nature and self. All things are in submission to Allah, except for you. You've strayed far from the straight path. No one can guide those who Allah has led astray. I love you because you're my daughter, but I hate you for the sake of Allah. Look at what you've become. The streets that you love so much will bow down to Allah on the day of reckoning and so will you. But the streets will testify against you and say that they never made you forget Allah. You are grown now, and you can make your own decisions, but Angel, you need to come back into the folds of Al-Islam. The only true deen of Allah.

Yada, yada, yada.

I knew that my mother was going to run that *'come back to Islam speech'* on me; I was prepared for it. So I just made a whole lot of empty promises and stepped off. I went to my old bedroom and hid the two bags of money. I hid them in my old clothes stacked in the closet. I knew that nobody ever really came in my old room but my mother, and she wouldn't rummage through my things. I stopped and looked at a lot of my old things. My holy Qu'ran was still on top of my dresser. The pictures of myself as a young girl stared back at me. I remember what I used to be then; and what I am now.

The little Muslim girl with the sheet on my head was now a grown-up sinful Muslim lady with a million three in cash. *One day,* I told myself, *one day I'm going to get back on my deen, but not right now.* I kinda like the woman I've become and I still have things to do, people to see, and places to be. Places where good Muslim women shouldn't be. I looked around one last time and then got up out of there before nostalgia overwhelmed me.

CHAPTER FIVE

ANGEL

On the morning of Tony's funeral, I prayed silently that the next phase of my plan fell into place. If I miscalculated the feelings between two men, then I'd be left with a million and change in cash, two keys of coke, and a lot of blood on my hands. It's either all or nothing for me. A couple of days ago I was allowed to go inside the apartment. The cops still had the premises under investigation, but I was allowed to grab a few more things. I put all of Tony's things in a box. I found the keys to the Escalade in the living room on the floor by the chair where Tony always sat playing video games.

I picked up the keys real fast and shoved them in my pocket before the cops noticed. I grabbed some of my things, the box of Tony's stuff, and rolled out. Tony's Cadillac Escalade was still parked outside in the same space where he left it. Fortunately, the cops didn't see it. I put the box in the truck, locked it up, and walked back to my Benz. I thought that seeing Tony's things and smelling his cologne in the truck might have made me feel bad for killing him, but it didn't. I felt nothing. No remorse. No regrets. No sadness.

Tony's wake was held at Robert G. Mason Funeral Home. I had been to Mason's on a few occasions. I waited behind a long line of cars that vied for a limited amount of parking spaces. The wake and funeral was packed to the hilt. It looked as if a famous foreign dignitary had died. The whole Good Hope Road was blocked off. It seemed like the whole DC was trying to see the great Tony Bills before he was laid to rest. Tony's home-going service resembled a car show.

Every make and model of car and truck that denoted luxury was there. Cadillacs, Lexuses, Benzes, BMW's, Hummers, Navigators, Excursions, Jags, Porches, and Bentleys. The ghetto's fabulous had most definitely come out to see Tony Bills. I wondered if Carlos would show up. I crossed my fingers and stood there in line. When I finally got inside the funeral home, after standing in the street for about forty-five minutes, I took a seat in the back.

The service hadn't started yet and people were still viewing the body. I flipped through the obituary that I got from the lady at the door where I signed the book. The obituary was more like a story of his life. Tony as a baby, Tony as a little boy, Tony in his cap and gown, Tony in jail as a juvenile, Tony locked up in Lorton, Tony on the streets. The obituary showed several pictures of Tony with Tina and Honesty, Tony with just his daughter, and Tony with the rest of his family. I didn't feel a thing.

I decided to view the body so I got in line. The line progressed slowly past a brown mahogany casket that held Tony's body. People were doing the black people thing; crying, screaming, and falling out. The woman who I recognized as Tony's mother wailed at the top of her lung capacity. I recognized Tina off the break and saw how distraught she was. People were screaming questions at God and falling out every couple seconds.

I got up to the coffin and stared at the man who I had spent two years with, the man who I had put in that box and noticed how peaceful he looked. I thought about the pain and poverty that he probably had caused so many and decided that everything was fair in love and war. Since Tony had been shot in the back of the head, he had no visible marks to explain his death. He looked as if he were sleep. He looked handsome in a white Gucci dress shirt and black slacks that were probably Gucci as well.

He had on a black gator belt that had a platinum buckle with his name emblazed on it in diamonds. That joint was mean. He had his customary diamond stud earring that was the size of a dime and an iced out Rolex watch. His hair and face was neatly trimmed. I couldn't make myself cry though. I stood there for a little while before I moved on. I looked into Tina's face and saw a hint of recognition cross her eyes. At 11:00 a.m., the casket was closed and the service began. Tony's daughter made a scene at that point. She went out of control when they locked Tony's casket.

"Daddddddy! Noooooo!" she cried out. "I want my daddy! Mommy, NOOOOOO! I want my daddy! Daddy don't leave me!"

Everybody went crazy then. There wasn't a dry eye in sight. Anthony J. Phillips was eulogized as a loving, caring man who was dedicated to his family and friends. One of his cousins sang that Men at Large song; *'I'm So Alone'* and rocked it. I finally started crying. Through my tears I spotted two men standing by the wall in the back; one resembled Carlos. *Bingo! Let me stop crying.* That was the one person who I was there to see. I had accompanied Tony on a couple of occasions to meet Carlos and I was hoping that he remembered me.

I recognized his companion as the same dude who was always with him. I believe Tony said his name was Benito or something like that. Benito's powerfully built body hid the fact that he was definitely packing heat, but I know that he had to be. At the conclusion of the service, as everyone filed out, I maneuvered my way over to the two Spanish men. I got close enough to whisper in his ear.

"I'm Tony's ex-girlfriend, Angel. Do you remember me?" he nodded. "We need to talk." I said as we walked outside. I asked him to wait one minute as I walked back to the entrance to Mason's. I caught Tina coming out, hugging her daughter.

Without saying a word, I handed her the keys to Tony's truck. She looked at me with malice in her eyes, took the keys, wiped at her tears, and walked right by me. She knew who I was. There was no denying that. Carlos and Benito were standing beside a pearl white Mercedes Benz S600 with dark tinted windows. Carlos asked me how I was holding up and I played the role of the grieving girlfriend. Then I got down to business.

"Carlos, hear me out. I have something that I believe belongs to you. I want to return it, but I also have a business proposition for you. I know this may be out of the ordinary; I know that you really don't know me, but trust me, we need to talk soon."

I gave Carlos all my numbers and he promised to call me in a few days. I decided not to go to Harmony Cemetery because that would be too much. So, I went back to Fatima's house and just chilled. Just when I was starting to give up hope, Carlos called me. He told me to meet him at Denny's on Benning Road. I pulled into the parking lot about fifteen minutes later and spotted a beautiful pearl blue Jaguar XU8. I figured that it had to belong to Carlos.

I walked into the restaurant and saw Carlos. He was alone. He looked kind of different every time I saw him. He sat in the back of the restaurant by the window. I noticed that he had a perfect view of the parking lot, me, and everyone else around him. I greeted him and sat down.

"What do you have that belongs to me?"

I cleared my throat and went for broke. "Carlos, I know that you don't know me. But I was with Tony when he met you at the Showplace Arena in Upper Marlboro the night that Bernard Hopkins fought Andrew Council. I was with him when he met you at Phillips and when y' all met in Vegas about four months ago. Tony trusted me enough to include me in a lot of the major decisions that he made and I'm hoping to establish the same trust with you. I'm not a groupie or a gold-digger. I'm a business woman and I would like to be treated as an equal. I learned everything I could from Tony and from other male associates of mine. I have two whole keys in my house that Tony left there.

"I figure the two keys belong to you, so that's why I have to return them to you. If they're yours. But, if it's okay with you, I'd like to move them. I'll pay you the money for them, in the hope that you might do business with me on a large scale. I know that a man in your position is skeptical, but I'm the real deal." I handed Carlos my licenses and birth certificate.

"These are my credentials. Do a background check and you'll see that I'm as real as they come. I'm straight hood, born and raised up in the street in Benning Heights. Do your homework. If I come back clean, get in touch with me. You can give me the answer then. Agreed?"

Carlos laughed one of those deep throat laughs and said. "I respect your style so far. You're a feisty broad. I'll check things out. Then I'll holler back. I do remember you now that I think about it. I remember thinking Tony had great taste in women. I'm really sorry about what happened to Tony. He was like a son to me. I have an APB out on anyone connected to his murder. I put a quarter million dollars on the head of whoever's responsible. So, I'm hoping that something will turn up. If you're half as smart as Tony was, we should become good friends. Are you hungry? There's no sense in wasting this trip. I'm going to order something."

I declined the meal, but talked for a few minutes more. Then I sashayed my ass right up out of there. In my heart I knew that Carlos would holler. At that moment, I knew that I was about to conquer the world. But DC had to come first.

A Novel by Anthony Fields

******

The next day, Carlos called me and told about a Bally's Fitness Center off of East West Highway in Hyattsville. He asked me to join him there. He told me that he would be in the sauna and that I should come directly there. I was a little apprehensive at first but then I eased up. I packed my trusted friend just in case a nigga wanted to act up. My Ruger has seventeen shots and I won't hesitate to let every last one go, if I have to.

I changed into some sweats and headed for Bally's. I found the spot with no problem. I paid the entrance fee and went to the women's shower. After a quick shower, I wrapped myself in a big towel. I stepped into the sauna. It was coed. Carlos was the only person there. I never thought about Carlos in a sexual way before, but I couldn't help but notice how sexy he was in an attractive way.

His towel was wrapped tightly around his waist, but I could see that he was hairy and muscular. The man looked like he just stepped out of a GQ magazine in only a towel. His hair was wet with perspiration and it was super-curly. My heart was racing. I wanted to ask him if I could see the rest of him. Then, I remembered that I was the grieving girlfriend and that I was there strictly for business. Carlos explained to me that he tried to work out at least three times a week and that the sauna's a good place to conduct business.

"People like to wear wires to try and entrap honest business people such as myself, that's why sauna's are safe. There's no place to hide wires."

"Very smart, Carlos." I said stroking him.

"Angel, I checked you out and you came back alright. I have some pretty good sources and they vouched for you. But, are you sure you wanna take Tony's load? Tony had been in the game for a while. How will you protect yourself? You saw first hand what happened to him. That could be your fate as well. Plus, a lot of dudes probably won't deal with a woman. How do you plan on doing what no other woman in DC has ever accomplished?"

I pondered his question for a minute, then gave him my logic full blast. "First of all, me being a woman doesn't mean jack. Niggas will buy coke from a homosexual as long as the coke is good. So that's neither here nor there. I tote steel and I can bust guns with the best of them. I stay heated at all times and won't hesitate to let my gun clap. In the situation with Tony, we were caught off guard. I kept my Ruger fully loaded under the bed. And for an all-purpose war, Tony had a Mac-11 with a 50-shot clip in the living room.

"Tony and I went to the gun range on a regular. So don't worry about me. I can take care of myself. I've been around the game for a long time. I learned all the tricks of the trade first hand. I can cook 500 grams and bring back 750 easy. And you could still put the yack on an 8 to a 9. Trust me, I know what I know. And what I know is that Tony moved roughly around 50 keys a week, give or take a few. I know that you charged him 15 gees a key. I know that Tony sold those bricks for 25 a key just to make a quick flip.

"I know everybody who Tony hit with bricks. Now pay attention; I know that he hit Wack and J-Rock in Barry Farms; Boobie, Scrubber, and Skeeter in Park Chester. Squirt and Dip in Congress Park; Ves, Demo, and Moosy on Valley Avenue. And there's a broad that he hits named Pretty Lady, she moves major weight in South View. He hits Mike and Sammy on Minnesota, Romeo on 48th Street. Anthony and Jay-Jay were regulars on Elvans Road, and JV from Wellington Park was consistent. The dude Faceman controls a lot of the Uptown strips. He was also hitting Gambino and Ron down on Delaware Avenue, Antwan and Poo from Oak Park, and some other dudes, but for the most part I know where I'm at with everything. I know Nome and Black from Condon Terrace personally, so I know they'll roll with me.

"Doodie on Martin Luther King Avenue went to school with me. He runs everything on Orange Street and beyond. I know Russell and his mob that run shit in Trinidad and Ivy City. I believe everybody will still respect the game enough to roll with me. In the last week, I've done my homework, and I know that I can make it rain. Tony was moving 25 keys a week at 20 a key. That's five hundred thousand. Per week. You made three hundred and seventy-five thousand dollars and he pocketed a hundred and twenty-five grand.

"I don't know about your last transaction or what was in the safe, but I still have 2 keys that I'm willing to sell and I'll give you the money. I'll give you whatever you want just to show you that I come in peace. Then I hope you can respect me and deal with me like I wear boxers instead of a thong. So, what's up Carlos, what are you going to do?"

"I'm glad that you're on top of everything." He said. "I'm impressed. I like you Angel. You have bigger nuts than most men. I accept your offer and will deal with you. I'll give you the same deal that I gave Tony, but only if you can handle it. You start to slack one bit and the deal is off. Since you want to be treated like a man, so be it. You'll receive no special treatment because you're a female. Tony paid me $275,000 on our last deal. He died owing me a $100,000. When you give me the 30 grand, you'll still owe me $70,000. That will kill the hundred thou that Tony owed me. That's my deal. And if you should need any more product, just let me know and I'll make it happen. So as of right now; you owe me a hundred thou. Do you accept my terms?"

I pretended to think the deal over in my head. I knew that $100,000 was a small price to pay to hook up with the big man. I agreed to the deal.

"In a little while, I'll be looking to expand. Since I grew up in Benning Heights, I plan to supply Eastgate, Benning Park, Hillside, Simple City, Alabama Avenue, Central Avenue, 57th and 58th Streets, and Capital Heights. So be ready to roll with the program. I'm trying to do 100 keys a week."

I could tell that Carlos was also impressed with me physically. He let his eyes roam all over my sweaty body. The towel covered my pussy and breasts, but that was it. I knew he was getting turned on by the rest of my exposed body parts.

"Call me when you're ready to proceed and I'll let you know our next move."

I left his gorgeous Spanish ass in that cooker and went to shower again. I had work to do and lots of it.

CHAPTER SIX

ANGEL

Later on that day, as I maneuvered my truck through the streets of DC, I noticed how shabby everything looked. I didn't know if it was just me or if everything was deteriorating right before my eyes. I heard a horn blow behind me. I looked in the rearview mirror and watched the little old lady in a beat-up Volkswagen flip me a bird.

"Fuck you right back." I whispered as I drove through the light extra slow to irk her nerves. I turned off 4th Street onto Condon Terrace and drove down to the circle. I looked around for a minute. I spotted just the man who I needed to see. All eyes were on me as I pulled up and parked. I got out of the truck.

"Girl, kill my mother; I bet you taste as good as you look." Nome said as he walked across the street and met me. "What brings you to this neck of the woods?"

"I came to see you. You heard about Tony?"

"Yeah, I caught that on the news and word hit me on the street. Slim was one of the big boys. I don't do funerals, but I heard it was off the chain. Scooter and Tom went. They told me about it. They say the line to go in was all the way around the corner. What the hell happened out there, Angel?"

"Nome, don't start with me. All I know is these dudes came up in the spot and rough housed shit. They were masked up, so I don't have a clue as to who they were. They took some money and some coke. I'm still messed up about Tony. They didn't even have to do that. Tony was my heart, but look, I'm not here to cry on your shoulder. This visit is about business."

"What business, boo?" Nome asked.

"Tony was hooked up through some people of mine. I knew the whole operation, front to back. I talked to my homies and they want business to continue as usual. I'm here to make sure you and Black are still down with the team, no matter who supplies it. We been knowing each other for a long time, so it's all love from my end. I'ma make sure that you keep fishscales and in time you'll get a better price. So what's up, Nome? Are you still on the team?"

"Of course, I'm with you. You my main apple-scrapple. I been trying to get in your drawers for years, but you keep shooting me down. I guess my money ain't long enough but it's cool though. The buns around here love me. But on the real, I see no problem with us doing business. I'd rather deal with you, if that's what you're asking. That is what you're asking me, right?"

"Exactly. You and Black will cop from me."

"No problem, boo. You look better anyway. I'm still fucked up about Tony, though."

"I knew that I could count on you. Everything will remain the same. I'll call you in a few days. By the way, what was Tony charging you a key?" I asked, already knowing the answer.

"Who me? He was charging me 18 a bird." Nome said.

"Cut the bullshit, Nome." I shot back as I walked toward my truck. "You were paying twenty just like everybody else."

"I had to try you, boo. I see you're on top of your game."

"I just wanted to see where your head was at. I'll call you soon."

I got into my truck and pulled off. I drove to Star Carry Out on Wheeler Road before making my way to my next appointment. I called Doodie's cell phone to let him know I was coming.

"Angel, what do you want now?"

I laughed. I called Doodie three times in the last week and a half and he's acting like I'm bugaboo.

"I need to see you about something, fatboy. Are you close to Portland Street?"

"I'm at the barbershop. I'll be here all day."

I bit into my General Tso chicken and mumbled. "I'm on my way."

Ten minutes later I parked my truck on MLK by the Popeye's. I got out and walked toward K and P's Barbershop. There was a rack of dudes hustling outside on MLK in front of the China Café. When they saw me, several of them decided to get their mack on. After realizing that I wasn't interested and my name wasn't boo; Miss Thang, sweetheart, or aye girl, they relented. I walked into the barbershop. The all-male clientele and barbers all stared at me, but I get that a lot and I'm used to it. I asked Daryl, the dude who runs the shop for Doodie and he pointed to the back room.

I knocked once and entered the office. I sat down in a chair facing the desk. Doodie was on the phone, so I waited patiently for him to finish his call. Dontez McClain, whom everybody called Doodie, is Southeast DC's version of Master P. He runs a little record shop, the barbershop, a laundromat, a car wash, and a detail shop. He's also one of the main suppliers of cocaine in the area. After a few minutes, Doodie got off the phone.

"Angel, what's up loved one?" he asked as he pulled the wrapper off of a fitness bar.

"I know you not eatin' no nutri-bar? You know damn right well you want some fried chicken, candied yams, macaroni and cheese..."

"Yeah, yeah, yeah." He said shutting me up.

"What happened to the diet?"

"I'm still on it." Doodie explained holding up the nutra-bar. "It's just not working fast enough for me. I'ma bout to call that Jenny Craig bitch. She got cake and everything on her menu or I might try the lemon diet."

"What the hell is a lemon diet?"

"It's this joint that China pulled off the Internet. All the stars are on it. You take lemon juice and mix it with cayenne pepper, maple syrup, and water. It's a diet drink that you do for three days. That fat broad Star Jones said that's how she lost a lot of weight."

"Well, she damn sure ain't fat no more, whatever she did."

"I'm thinking about it doing it. But I kinda like being big. Fat dudes are in. Look at Anthony Anderson and that fat nigga Rueben Studdard. Broads be sweating them niggas. I might stay a fatboy."

Doodie was a personal friend of mine before the drug shit with Tony, so I knew that I could be real with him. " Life must go on, but I miss the shit outta Tony."

"Who doesn't? Tony was a man of principle. I should've went to the funeral, but I couldn't stand to see him like that. I'm sorry about that shit. You were there. You must be fucked up in the head."

"Somebody killed him for his money. He'll be caught. I know it. But that brings me to why I'm here. God bless the dead and all that, but I got to live, you know? The dude who Tony was dealing with was a good dude. I met him on several occasions. I talked to him after Tony's death and he wants me to take over Tony's spot. You know I ain't never sold no drugs, but how hard could it be? All I have been with is street niggas, so I know my way around the business. I'm here to offer you the same deal you had with Tony. You and I go back like doo rags and New Edition albums, so I know you don't have a problem copping joints from me. What's up? Holler at your girl."

Doodie leaned back in his chair and smiled. "I can't believe this shit. Look at the good Muslim sister, Kareemah tryna hustle and shit. I remember when you used to be on your deen. Now you wanna be Tony Lewis' lil sister, huh? That's cool. I'm with you until the wheels fall off. Just show me some love. Let's talk money."

"Okay, first things first. I'm hip to the fact that you owed Tony $40,000 for two of the last joints he gave you. Tony died with that knowledge. So, it's a dead issue to me, excuse my pun. All I want you to do is cop your usual quota of bricks at 20 a key. I'm trying to pick up a hundred thou or better from you weekly. You and I both know that shit ain't been right since that September 11th shit and bricks are still going for twenty-seven to thirty gees a piece. Hopefully, I'll be able to offer you a better price in the near future and we can all prosper."

Doodie reached across his desk and shook my hand like we had just concluded a business deal. We both laughed.

"Angel I remember you used to wear all them scarves and long dresses and shit. I ain't knocking the Islam religion, but you were made for those jeans you got on. What are they, Parasucos?"

"Do I look like I'd wear some bullshit like that? I'm outta here, but I'll be in touch." I blew Doodie a kiss and left. Walking back down MLK, the same dudes tried to holler at me again and again I ignored them.

******

I decided to knock out the dudes who I knew first. Eventually I'm going to start treading water in uncharted territories. I honestly believe that most of the dudes on my list will see things my way. If not, then fuck them. I drove toward Park Chester. I was on my way to see Scrubber and Skeeter, the dudes who ran things in that area.

Word on the street was that Scrubber was the one with the strength, so I'll talk directly to him. Tony told me about Scrubber and the rest of the dudes he dealt with, but I know a few dudes from Park Chester so I basically heard a lot about Scrubber's operation from them. A few years ago I was dating a dude named June who lived in Park Chester, but hustled in the Ellos.

Angel

The Ellos is an apartment building that's directly across the street from Park Chester. He was at odds with Scrubber and company so he would mouth off about their operation to me. He talked like he sipped on glasses of pure haterade. I learned from him that Scrubber is the brains and force behind the crew. Scrubber's brother Skeeter was the worker bee and Boobie was the go-getter. It was Boobie who hooked Scrubber up with Tony. But Tony didn't know Scrubber personally like June did.

Tony and Boobie were locked up together at Youth Center One. Scrubber's weakness was women. Skeeter's weakness was PCP and Boobie's was the dice. But whatever their Achilles heel may be, they get money and lots of it, which brings me to Park Chester today.

I turned on Birney Place and rode down the horseshoe-shaped street. The street was packed with kids and street dudes hanging out and serving customers. I could see why Scrubber and company made a lot of money. I saw a gold Lincoln Navigator sitting on twenty-four inch rims in the parking lot and I knew that Scrubber was near. All eyes were on me. It was always that way when a stranger came to the hood, especially a broad in a Benz truck.

I picked up Tony's cell phone and hit the memory button for Scrubber's number and waited. Scrubber answered the phone on the fourth ring.

"Hello? Who dis callin' from a dead man's phone?" Scrubber shouted through the phone. I had to calm him down.

"Calm down, boo. This is Angel. Tony's girlfriend. Do you remember me?"

"I think so. What's up boo? I thought the police was calling me or the dudes who killed Tony. What's up though? What can the Scrubber do for you?"

"You can start by coming outside. I'm parked right beside your truck."

"I'll be right out." He said and then hung up.

Ten minutes later Scrubber walked up to my truck; he was killing them in a hitting ass Boo Yang sweat suit. He was bowlegged and black as pure chocolate. But he was very attractive in a thuggish sort of way. I hopped out of the truck and he whistled.

"What did you say your name was, boo?" he asked.

"My name's Angel. We met at the summer league basketball tournament down Barry Farms last year. I was there with Tony."

"Right, right, I remember you. You were a vision of pure loveliness then and you look even better now. So, what's up with you? Why the hood call?"

"I know that you're the big man around here. And I also know that you buy 8 to 10 keys a month. Up until a few weeks ago you were buying them from Tony. I loved Tony a whole lot but he's gone. I have to live, so I hooked up with the people in charge and I'm taking Tony's spot. I can make the same deals that Tony made and perhaps some better ones down-the-line. I'm here to see if you're still down with the winning team or have you shopped somewhere else?"

He looked at me with a look of confusion.

"Damn boo, Tony ain't been dead but a couple of weeks and you're already shacking up with the big man. You're a scandalous bitch! But I like that. I did make a few moves to keep things going around here, but I'm definitely down with getting the same product and price that Tony was giving me. These other niggas out here on some little kid shit. Tony always played fair with me and for that I'm loyal. So if you come correct with the same butter that Tony had, hell yeah we can do business."

"I know that Tony charged you 20 a key, so the price is the same and the product is the same. You'll deal directly with me. I'll be in touch with you in a few days." I jumped into my truck and backed out of the parking space. I stopped in front of Scrubber and put the window down.

"And Scrubber, I'm not shacking up with the big man. I just suck his dick every now and then." I drove off, leaving him standing there with his mouth hanging open. I hate when niggas say stupid sexist shit. Dudes kill me thinking that women have to fuck to get on top. I hadn't fucked to get my spot. I killed for it.

The next stop was Barry Farms. I turned off Sumner Road onto Wade Road on my way to Stevens. I hated going to Barry Farms because it's too damn hot down there. The National Guards be posted at the corners. They have these high-powered lights that they send up in the air to illuminate the whole neighborhood. Helicopters hover in the sky all day watching the streets.

I rode down Stevens Road and looked for Wack's black Ford Excursion on the street. I didn't see it parked by the railroad tracks and called J-Rock.

"Talk to me."

"Hello, J-Rock, what's up? This is Tony's girlfriend, Angel. I'm on Stevens Road looking for Wack. Do you know where he is?"

"You say you're Tony's girlfriend? Who is this, Tina?"

I was caught off guard a little with that. "Naw, this ain't Tina. She was Tony's main bun. I'm just the hooker on the side. Anyway, it's important that I speak to Wack."

"Well, Wack is out of town, love. If it's important you can holler at me and it's like talking directly to Wack."

"Well I need to holler at you then. Can you come around here?"

"Naw, Stevens is way too hot. Come around to Eaton Road and pull up in the middle of the block. You'll see a mint green Cadillac with dips on it. I'm sitting in it."

I did as I was told and was rewarded by being in the company of the fakest nigga I ever met in my life. This dude had on a Hugo Boss sweatsuit with some Timberland boots, two diamond-studded earrings in one ear, a bamma ass platinum chain and a medallion that said, 'OY Boyz' hanging to his navel. He had a platinum iced out Rolex and a platinum Rolex bracelet on. This dude was blinding me. I needed a pair of sunglasses just to talk to his countrified bamma ass. Once I stifled my urge to bust out laughing in his face, I got down to business.

"J-Rock, Tony told me a lot about you and Wack. He and I were together for a couple years and before he died I was preparing to take over some of his load. I know that you and Wack buy 3 keys a week, at 25 a key. I want to continue doing business with both of you. Tony is gone, but not forgotten. You and Wack can deal with me. You'll get the same good product at the same good price. Anybody else is going to charge you twenty-seven to thirty a key. If you respect Tony, you can respect me. We come from the same source. It may be odd at first dealing with a broad, but trust me, I'm not the average chick. So we do business, you don't play with me, and I don't kill you. Are you in or out?"

His facial expression was unreadable, so I hoped I hadn't gone too far.

"I remember you. You and Tony were down here for Barry Farms Day awhile back. You have a lot of courage coming into the good Farms and selling me death. But Tony was good people and I would roll with whoever wants to roll on the suckers that brought slim that move. I don't know, but out of respect for Tony, I'm going to accept what you're saying. I'll run everything down to Wack tonight and I'll hit your cell in the morning. Now get your pretty ass away from me before you come up missing. Talking all that grown man talk. Sexy as you are, you don't need to be talking about murder-death-kill-shit. I'll holler tomorrow. Peace!"

I swear I wanted to shoot his bamma ass.

Angel

"No offense, boo, just get at me." Talking to him made me tired. I called it a day. I went home and ran some hot bath-water. I let Calgon take me away. I relaxed in the tub and contemplated my next move. Getting everybody onboard was important to me, so tomorrow I decided I would go through Congress Park, Elvans Road, and Wellington Park. I'm going dead up in the hood to see these dudes, so they'll know that I'm a woman of the people. I made a few phone calls and then went to sleep.

CHAPTER SEVEN

FATIMA

When I heard the keys turning in my lock that night about two and half weeks ago, I knew that it was Angel letting herself in. I had known for a while what Angel was planning to do. She methodically thought the whole plan up about two years ago. I remember when she first told me about Tony. I was still living with my mother on Ely Place. Angel came over to my house banging on the door....

"Damn, Angel, you got somebody chasin' you? Banging on the door like you're crazy!"

"Naw, I'm just amped, that's all. Guess who I met today?"

"Who?"

"Tony Bills!" she said animated.

I was lost and didn't have a clue.

"Who?"

"Girl, Tony Bills." She said as if I was supposed to know who she was talking about.

"Who's Tony Bills?" I asked.

"Who is Tony Bills? You never heard of Tony Bills?"

"I don't believe that I have."

"Hello, Fatima, Tony Bills is THE biggest drug dealer that ever walked the face of DC. He's all the way caked up. Everybody's talking about that nigga. I was at the HOBO Shop Fashion Show at the Ramada Inn. I met him there. If I can get my hands on the nigga girl, I'ma work the shit out of him. I'm tired of living hand-to-mouth. Since Buck went to jail I been fucked up. I'm tired of

Angel

messing with these fake ass ballers. These niggas out here ain't really holding no dough. Tony Bills's is going to be my ticket outta here. Watch and see."

******

In the beginning, she never told me that she planned to kill Tony. So,I couldn't believe it when she told me that she had.. I met her at the door and listened to all the morbid details about what she had done to Tony. I looked in her eyes and for the life of me, she wasn't Angel. I don't know who the fuck she was, but the bitch scared me and I'm not no scaredy-cat. I grew up in Southeast DC and was runnin' the streets during the 'murder capital era', so dead bodies, rats, and roaches ain't nothing to me. But, Angel that bitch was the devil sitting on my couch. I was raised to fear nothing or no one except Allah, but between me and you, I'm afraid of Angel.

I just sat there helping her count dead Tony's money. I felt so bad for Tony. *Damn, Angel's crazy, this bitch really killed this nigga.* I would never call Angel crazy to her face, but there's no explanation for this thing she has for killing people. I silently said a prayer for her. *She has to know she's going straight to the hellfire with gasoline thongs on.* I try to get her to at least offer salat, but she won't.

First it was her father, and I understood that, because she was trying to protect her little sister and herself. But, then she killed Andre Ford in college. That's when I knew something wasn't right. She just pushed the nigga off the roof and went on with life like it wasn't nothing. I don't know how she does it, she's like an actress playing in a movie called 'life'. But, me, I feel bad. An even better word for me would be guilty. I feel like I'm some silent partner. If you think about it, aren't I the co-conspirator? The one who doesn't actually do anything but knows it all.

I'm going to jail with this bitch. I hope she don't say my name, never.

A Novel by Anthony Fields

I'm sitting here with a bunch of voices in my head telling me how crazy this bitch is and how crazy I am for sitting here with her counting all this money. *I know she gonna hook a sister up, though. She better, my fingers are hurting like shit. I wonder how much she'll give me. I can't take the money. It's blood money. Damn, I need a new sofa.*

By the time we were done counting, Tony's paper totaled one million three hundred and seventy thousand dollars. With a few odd thousands left over. And that's a lot of mullah, scratch, scrilla, ink, cheddar, dough, or whatever you prefer to call it.

I know one thing; I was happy as a pimp with a stable full of hoes when Angel gave me that thirty thousand. I know several dudes with serious cash, but no one ever gave me that much money in my life. Don't get me wrong, I ain't no broke chick. I've got a little sumpin' sumpin' going on for myself. But never had I seen thirty thousand cash. Shit, I barely make $30,000 working all year at my job. So, Angel, was a life saver.

I know just what I'ma do with this. I'll pay off my credit cards and my car, maybe trade it in for something new and get me a new living room set, honey. And shop a little bit. I went to the Mazza Gallerie and to Tyson's 1&2. I had a ball, shit I was ballin'. When I got back home Angel was gone. *Girlfriend's a nut.* All she talks about is leaving DC and moving to California. She wants to be in movies. The truth is she thinks she's Halle Berry. I told you the bitch is crazy. Believe me not, honey, you'll see though. Angel isn't working with a full deck. Now she's running around DC, in all those spooky ol' projects, tryna locate all the dudes she wants to sell coke to. Brokering deals like she's some high-powered Wall Street exec.

She hollered at some big drug dealer dude named Carlos and he agreed to give her the drugs that he used to give Tony. He doesn't know she's the one who killed Tony.

Angel

I wonder what he would do if he knew that? I wonder what Carlos would do if he knew he might be next?

CHAPTER EIGHT

ANGEL

Sunlight shined through my window and I woke up feeling good. I rolled over and looked at the clock; it was 10:30 a.m. I picked up the phone. *It's time to make the donuts.*

Ring. Ring. Ring. Ring. Ring.

"Hello, is this Pretty Lady?"

"Who's this?"

"My name's Angel. I'm Tony's girlfriend."

"What Tony are you referring to?"

"Tony Bills. God bless the dead."

"This is she."

"I need to talk to you about some business, trust me, it'll be worth your time. Can we meet, say, in an hour or two? I would greatly appreciate it."

"Well, I did have other plans. But since this is business and you're on Tony's team, money's always worth more than eggs from a bunny." Then she laughed.

I didn't know what the hell she was talking about with the bunny eggs and shit, but I laughed too.

"Can you come to Henry's Soul Food Café on Indian Head Highway, say around 12 o-clock noon?"

"Sure, I know the place well. What do you drive?"

"I'll be in a burgundy Benz truck. Bye."

My cell phone had a few missed calls on it and one of those was from J-Rock's number. I called him back and he said he talked to Wack and everything was a go, they were ready and waiting on me.

Angel

That was good news. *So far so good, four down and twelve more to go.* Since it was hot outside I dressed cool for my meeting with Pretty Lady. I threw on a form-fitting Iceberg stretch shirt, Iceberg jean shorts and Iceberg tennis shoes.

I pulled into Henry's parking lot at 11:55 a.m. and saw a woman standing next to a blue Toyota Avalon. She was my height, middle-aged, and very attractive. I pulled into a space and parked my truck. She watched me the entire time and then walked over to me. She greeted me as if I were an old friend, giving me a hug and then we walked inside the café. We both ordered, making small talk as we waited for our food.

"So, what business is it that you have with me?"

"That's what I like, straight to the point. Like I said earlier, my name's Angel. I was Tony's business partner and lover. As you know, Tony's gone. He was my heart and I miss him dearly. Even though you never met me, I was always around. I know that you buy 2 ½ to 3 keys a week and Tony fronted you one. I also know that you owe Tony 20,000 for that last brick.

"I want us to continue to do business together in the same fashion that you and Tony did. As far as the 20 gees go, you can keep 10,000 and just put up the 10 with the money that you usually bring. And I'll leave y' all deal intact. In fact since you're a woman, in a minute, I'll give you a better deal. Tony spoke real highly of you and I'm confident that you'll remain with the family. If you wish to do business elsewhere, that's fine. But then I'll definitely need that $20,000 from you. So, are you with me or against me, Pretty Lady?"

"Angel, you can call me by my real name Deborah, if you like or Pretty Lady if you want. Girl, I'm glad you got in touch with me because I swear I didn't want to deal with Robbie or Duck up at the Gangster Gear Shop. They have the nerve to want twenty-five a key for that so-so shit they over there selling. And I got that ten for you whenever you want it. I would love to do business with you."

That was all I needed to hear. It was time to go. Valley Avenue was my next destination, so I paged the dude Ves and waited to see if he would call me back. He did. I introduced myself and told him I needed to speak with him. I remember Tony telling me about Ves, Dee-Mo, and Moosy. They were childhood friends in Valley Green and later became business partners. According to what Tony said, they were the 'go to' dudes on several strips, but their strongholds were Valley Avenue, Wahler Place, Wheeler Road, the Geraldines, and Brandywine Street.

I pulled into a parking space and dialed Ves's cell phone. He asked me what I was driving and how I looked. I walked down the middle of the court and discovered that I was talking to him as I walked right past him. We smiled at one another, and then hung up our phones. I shot my spiel to him hoping he would come on board. He expressed his condolences about Tony then cracked for my private number.

"I never mixed business with pleasure."

He looked so disappointed, but accepted my offer to cop coke from me on a weekly basis. Dee-Mo was in another building in another part of Valley Green. I spoke to him and Moosy. I found myself walking all over Valley Green like I owned it. I wasn't even scared and Valley Green wasn't no joke. Niggas wouldn't even walk around that motherfucker and here I was, acting like I was strolling through the park. I don't know if it was the Ruger that I had in my purse or just plain stupidity. By the time I was done, I had Moosy, Dee-Mo, and Ves on board. My talk game was impeccable.

I left the Valley and drove straight to Congress Park, which is only ten blocks away. I used to date this guy named Buck, he was from Congress Park. After Buck got locked-up, his brother Squirt took over the neighborhood. Squirt was the top dog but he deferred his power to two dudes, either Marcus or Dip. So, I pulled behind Dip's candy apple red Mercedes Benz SLK. As I approached his car I could see that he was inside playing video games on a Sony Play Station two.

"I'm single with no kids and I love to eat pussy" Dip announced as soon as he saw me approach. "I'm bullshitting, baby. What's up though? You say you need a moment of my time and Squirt told me to give you a moment, so I'm all ears."

I was running my spiel down so much I was tired of hearing it. But the rewards would be greater later. I told myself. Squirt, Dip, and Marcus were buying 6 keys a week so I needed them like a junky needed a fix.

"Angel, I believe Squirt will do business with you, but he has the final say. I don't see why he wouldn't because we need that situation like yesterday."

I told him to holler and peeled out.

******

I heard through a broad name Sherry, that Anthony Blackman, the dude that was 'big' on Elvans Road, got killed. So, I had to go holler at his man Jay Jay. We talked and he was down with my struggle. So was Juvenile from Wellington Park. I was starting to feel like Christopher Columbus or somebody with all the voyages that I was going on. I drove down South Capitol Street to see if I could catch Antwan or Pooh.

Antwan and Pooh ran a small part of the Southwest section of the city. They supplied the Wingates, Oak Park, Galveston, Forrester, Elmira, and Danbury. They owned a store off South Capitol Street called the SAHNA Gear Shop. SAHNA stood for Smash All Hot Niggas Association. I loved it. I can't stand a snitch myself. I guess that stems from me being around hustlers for the last four years. I still remember when the vicious hot dude Playful Edwards told on damn near everybody in the whole city while I was in school. I remember thinking he was weak for doing that.

I went into the store and purchased a sweat suit and asked for Antwan and Pooh. I found out that I was talking to Pooh and that Antwan was in the back room. I introduced myself, gave them my credentials, talked my talk, and sold them on the idea of doing business with a female. It turned out that they really didn't know Tony and that they got hooked up through J-Rock and Wack. They were only buying 2 keys a week but that was cool. I left there feeling like I was on top of the world. I was getting everything I wanted from everybody I wanted it from. I decided to go by my family's house and see my mother and little sister.

I parked in front of my house and went inside.

"As-Salaamu-Alaikum." I said as I crossed the doorstep.

CHAPTER NINE

DETECTIVE SEAN JONES

Detective work is hard. Somedays I wish I would've stayed a patrol officer. It's less stressful writing traffic tickets and helping old ladies cross the street than homicide. Homicide is a cruel business. It takes a certain kind of person to investigate death, work around death, and work with dead bodies. I've been doing this shit for twenty years now and I must say it has taken its toll.

I joined the Metropolitan Police Department Academy in DC in 1982 after I graduated from high school. I always wanted to be in law enforcement ever since I was a kid. I can still remember Captain John Dixon who came to my elementary school and spoke to my second grade class. I remember every word he said. He really inspired me and I decided right then and there at the age of seven that I would be a police officer. It was ironic because when I went home that day and told my father, he looked at me like I was crazy.

"Boy, is you crazy? A police officer, Lord, you must've bumped your head." And he laughed with his friends and ushered me on inside the house. Little did I know, but my father was a street hustler and back in the 1960s and 1970s heroin was the drug of choice. My father sold a lot of it and took good care of his family until he was killed in 1974.

I later learned that my father was killed by a young stickup kid named Kenny Spade. I vowed to find Kenny Spade once I became a police officer and either kill him or lock him up. I graduated from the Academy with honors and got assigned to the 7th District Police Station in the decadent and turbulent southeast section of DC.

I was raised in the Northeast section of Deanwood and man, did life seem rough back then. I remember my life as a kid and I often laugh because I was one wild dude. I remember breaking into the bakery on Addison Road in Phairmont Heights. I stole cars, burglarized a few homes, destroyed and defaced millions of dollars' worth of property and fought all the damn time. I did all of that and still wanted to be a cop when I grew up. That's crazy, huh? You'd think I was a good guy, but I wasn't. I was bad as hell just like everybody else.

I remember jumping people at the Go-Go's up at the Coliseum, the Howard Theater and the Blackhole. I remember running trains on several unsuspecting females; back then we called it running a 'G'. I was in everything but a hearse. So, to now be a police officer and have almost twenty-years under my belt, it's jive funny, but I'm the only one who's laughing.

When crack hit DC in the early eighties, I watched my city turn into a hellhole; a cesspool of drugs, thugs, automatic weapons, and major money. I watched women I had lusted after and had crushes on, turn into walking fucking zombies right before my eyes. DC became *'Night of the Living Dead'*. In my career, I've seen just about everything. I patrolled the streets in the Anacostia area. I broke up fights, settled domestic disputes, chased suspects, and got shot at. In my twenty years as a cop; I shot several people, but I've only killed one.

In 1991, when the country declared DC the murder capital of our great nation, I was twelve feet deep in gang wars, drug deals, rapes, and murders. And I was sick to my stomach every day. I thought I could make a difference, but the crooks, killers, and thugs were smarter, better, and faster than the whole police department.

It seemed like the DC underworld was in control. I put in for a promotion for detective. I was eventually promoted to sergeant in the homicide division. Over the years I've seen babies burned alive, cooked in ovens, and beat to death. I've seen parents kill their children, children kill their parents, children kill their grandparents, and grandparents kill their children. I've seen all the drug-related deaths, execution style murders, every kind of killing one's mind can fathom and a few that the mind can't.

I built a pretty good reputation in the homicide game. I was one of three detectives who maintained a 75 percent closure rate. But DC politics and DC's burgeoning budget woes forced me out of the department after seventeen years. However, I was immediately hired by the Prince George Police Department. I was given the carte blanche in PG's homicide branch. It felt good to finally be appreciated for my years of hard work and dedication.

Today, I'm the lead detective in charge of a forty-member squad. I'm the 'Boss'. The 'Big Kahuna'. Which puts me in the position to delegate the case and action, so I take on a few cases myself. The case that I'm working on right now is a nagger. Everything seems to be in order, yet something is out of place. My gut instincts have never lied to me in the twenty-years I've been a cop and my gut instincts are telling me that this Tony Phillips case is suspicious.

Anthony J. Phillips, a.k.a Tony Bills, a high-level drug dealer in DC, was slain in the apartment of his girlfriend, Kareemah El-Amin. Apparently there was a home invasion. Three masked men allegedly broke into the ground floor apartment via the patio door. They allegedly tied up Tony; took Kareemah into the bathroom; emptied the safe; shot Tony in the head, killing him, and then let Kareemah live to tell the story.

I'm naturally analytic and cynical by trade, so I have several questions in my head that just don't add up.

How did the robbers know when to enter the home? Then why break the patio glass door and risk being seen or heard? And where are their footprints from the mud? It rained, the house should have had muddy footprints all over it. Was music playing? If this guy was a drug dealer, why wasn't he armed, there was no struggle and no fight. What was in the safe? Had to be something to kill for.

Did this Kareemah chick have the combination? She had to, it was in her house. She wouldn't just let this guy put a safe in her home and not know its contents. Why did they leave a witness? Why wasn't she killed as well? Why take her to the other room? Why not just kill her too or better yet, use her to get what they wanted by threatening her life? And if Tony complied with the robbers and they were masked up, why kill him? It just doesn't add up, something about this puzzle has missing pieces.

I pondered all the likely scenarios in my head. One thing about the killing field, you can never rule out anything. The impossible is possible and the least likely scenario might be the one that's true. I'm a stickler for details. I try to break the situation down into pieces and then put it all back together again. I spoke to his girlfriend on two occasions and her story is still exactly the same.

Either she's a sincere victim or she's a cold-blooded killer. I spoke to several neighbors and no one seems to have heard anything that night, not even a gun-shot. Did the killers use a silencer? No one saw any suspicious characters camped out or walking around that night. No one saw or heard anything.

I spoke to the family members and a few friends, and aside from the fact that Tony was the DC version of Pablo Escobar, no one could believe that someone would kill him. Most feigned ignorance when asked about the man who would be king. No one could put a finger on anyone who they knew of, who'd want to kill Tony. But a man like Tony would've been a high-profile target to everyone in the robbery and killing field. The whole city, plus the DC Police Department, the FBI and the ATF, knew that Tony was the front man for the elusive Carlos Trinidad. At the time of his death, Tony was the subject of two investigations and about to be indicted on

Federal Rico and CCE charges in Maryland and Virginia. But all the police agencies really wanted Carlos Trinidad. He was the big fish everyone wanted to fry. He was too slippery to catch though. He never talked on the phone, he never dealt with anyone outside of his circle, and he never touched anything. He was smart, calculating, methodical, patient, ruthless, and mega rich. Carlos Trinidad owned several businesses in the DC area. He contributed large donations to all the right campaigns and is rumored to have access to the ears of several bigwigs in the government, judicial system, and police force. And he happens to have the best lawyer in the country, billionaire lawyer J. Alexander Williams. Tony was, to everyone's knowledge, the closest person to Carlos in the DMV and now he was dead.

Maybe Tony crossed Carlos and it was Carlos who murdered him. Maybe Carlos knew through the political contacts that Tony; was going to be indicted and didn't want the possibility of Tony snitching him out. That's something I should check out. But, still there's something with the girl, Kareemah. She definitely isn't telling me the whole story and she still hasn't returned my call. Maybe I should pay her a visit at her home, catch her off guard.

My twenty years of police work has taught me that people tend to relax in their own environment where they feel safe. If she's relaxed and safe, then she'll let her guard down, and she'll make a mistake. And when she makes a mistake, I'll be waiting to take her down.

CHAPTER TEN

ANGEL

I had to take a break from politicking on the streets, so I stayed home yesterday. I caught up on my reading, watched some television and got my beauty rest. But today I'm back to business as usual. I'm going to meet Sam, an old-timer who did a twenty year bid for a youth offense. Now, Sam runs a crack house on B Street off of Minnesota Avenue that rocks around-the-clock. Tony told me that between him and his nephew Mike, they move about 4 keys a week even though they only buy two. What they do is put a rack of bake on their coke and double their product, thus doubling their profit.

I pulled behind a burgundy Caprice Classic SS with dubs on it. The car was full of dudes smoking weed, which rushed out the windows of the car and past my nose as I stepped from my truck. I called Sam on his cell. I made my introduction then met him across the street from the crack house. Sam and Mike actually ran a whole row of crack houses. Sam told me that it was hard for the police to catch them because they move their headquarters every day. The cops never knew which door to kick in.

I could tell that he wasn't really feeling me or what I had to say. I understood, male hustlers are chauvinistic pigs. They seem to only respect other men even if they're cold blooded punks. Men think women are too emotional for dirty games like drugs and murder. And for me, that's my ace in the hole, that's how I have the advantage, because I am a woman. I know what all these niggas are thinking. They think I'm a big fat pussy that needs to be stroked. No one has a clue I'll kill them, their family, and their pet dog if I had to.

Angel

To my surprise, it worked out and Sam agreed to cop bricks from me at the same price Tony offered him. I drove around for a while and thought about the twins from Saratoga, trying to figure out how to approach them. The twins, Deandre and Dearaye, were small-time hustlers, turned big boys overnight. The inner-city grapevine had it that back in the day, the twins were connected to some major Ethiopian dudes who moved big dope up and down the East Coast.

The streets say that Deandre, the more ruthless of the two brothers, became disenchanted with the breakdown they were receiving from the Ethiopians. He allegedly hooked up a fictitious drug deal for twenty-seven keys of dope and the Ethiopians bit. Deandre allegedly shot and killed two of the Ethiopians and came off with the twenty-seven keys, plus three extra and a rack of money that was hidden in the hotel room.

From then on, the twins were major players in the DC drug game. I heard that Deandre was a real serious dude who was cynical about everybody except his brother. Tony told me about the tattoo that Deandre had. It's a tattoo of a cobra that wraps around his forearm and bicep, and then comes out at his neck, biting his jugular. Rumor has it that he's dangerous. His brother Dearaye deals with the business side of things, while Deandre conveniently removes all threats and potential threats from their midst. Dearaye is the one who dealt with Tony.

Tony always spoke highly of Dearaye. Deandre knew that Tony was hooked up with Carlos Trinidad, so that's all the assurance he needed to know that Tony was legit. Carlos is legendary in all the drug circles in DC. Folklore has it that Carlos runs everything. I could get Carlos to holler at the twins, which would be easier. But then I run the risk of Carlos thinking that I can't handle my business, causing him to renege on our deal. Plus, I already told Carlos that I talked to everyone. I think I'll have to approach Dearaye and work from there.

I put my left blinker on and waited for the traffic to subside. I turned off of Sheriff Road onto 48th Street. Romeo was next on my list. Sheriff Road was known for its weed. You could cop purple, blueberry, and strawberry haze. There were about thirty young dudes on the block selling weed as I pulled up. But neither of them was Romeo. Romeo was the designated heavy hitter in the area and I knew very little about him. All I knew was that he was in his early thirties, loved, respected, and feared. I spotted a black Mercedes G500 wagon and figured it was his and that Romeo was somewhere in the area. Romeo had one of the only G500 Benz trucks that sat on twenty-four inch Sprewell rims. The problem was I didn't have a number for him. I had checked Tony's phone, but had no luck. So, I would have to use the streets to get to him. I'd have to try my hand with one of the roughneck youngins on the block. I walked across the street to where a crowd of guys were standing.

"What's up lovely, what you lookin' for?" asked a dude with zigzagging corn-rowed braids in his hair.

Before I could respond, everybody pulled out bags of weed. They had all kinds of hemp. You could smell the assorted flavors in the air. I singled out the dude who spoke to me first and pulled him to the side. I pulled a $20.00-dollar bill out of my purse and purchased a bag of weed.

"I'm looking for Romeo. Do you know where he is?"

Corn-row looked up and down at me suspiciously.

"I got whatever you need, boo, you don't need no Romeo."

"I have business with Romeo that I need to discuss with him."

"If you and slim have business together, then why don't you know how to reach him?"

I was starting to get annoyed with Corn-row.

"I lost his number; that's why I'm out here trying to find him. Are you going to help me or not?"

"I'm sorry boo, I don't know anybody named Romeo. And I don't know you. Who are you?"

I kinda figured that Corn-row was wasting my time, plus I was fed up with all the questions. I didn't say another word; I just turned and walked back toward my truck. I was pulling my car keys out as a hand grabbed my arm. I turned around so fast with the Ruger in my hand that he never saw me pull it. I pointed the gun at Corn-row's head. I think he realized that it wasn't in his best interest to put his hands on me.

"Damn boo, you heated?"

"Listen champ, I'm in no mood for games. I ain't no cop and I come in peace. I just need to speak to Romeo, that's all. I do the same thing you do. You said you don't know Romeo right? Okay, then just back up and join your men on the curb or I swear to God, I'ma put your face on a shirt."

I thought I might have to make Corn-row an example, but he laughed.

"Any bitch, brave enough to come on 48th and pull a hammer on a nigga, while he's with a rack of other niggas, is definitely a down ass bitch."

He backed up across the street and hollered toward the middle building.

"Aye, Rome. R-o-o-o-o-o-m-m-me-e-e! Aye Rome, come to the window, moe."

Curtains shifted in a window on the top row and the window opened. Then a head popped out.

"What's up Tay? What you want, moe?" the light-skinned dude asked.

Corn-row pointed at me. "Do you see that fine ass honey over by the Benz truck?"

"Yeah, I see her, why? What's up with her?"

"She tryna holler at you, moe. She said y'all got business together. Be careful though moe she's heated." Corn-row rejoined his men on the curb.

About ten minutes later Romeo came out of the building. He was about 5'10 and 170 pounds, depending on whether or not you calculated the extra weight that he carried from what happened to be a Mac hanging from a strap on his shoulder.

"What's up sweetheart? What business we got?"

Oh God this nigga is really fine. He got nice hair. I like his hair and strong manly looking features. I know these hoes is all over him. Romeo, Romeo, I bet you got Juliettes all over the place. He was a light-skinned version of Shemar Moore. *Damn, this nigga is fine. Did he just ask me a question?*

"Naw." I said, recovering quickly. "We never met before. But I was Tony's girlfriend before he got killed and he always spoke highly of you. He said you were a good man. Tony was hooked up with my relatives on the business tip. You and I both know what I mean. I'm here to let you know that, even though Tony's gone, if you still want the same product and price, I can provide that. If not, then all you lost was a few minutes of your time. I know what you buy from Tony weekly and for how much. I want your business to go on uninterrupted."

"Boo, I don't even know who the hell you are."

"I know, I know, but you can check me out. Nome and Black from Condon Terrace can vouch for me. I'm good peoples just check me out. Take my number and if you need me, just call."

Romeo pulled out a cell phone and put my number into it.

"Call me anytime. If you tryna rock, I'll be ready to roll in a few days. Holler!"

Angel

I jumped into my truck and bounced. *I hope he calls. He will, even if it's a booty call, he'll call.* Unfortunately, men always think with their little heads when it comes to a fine woman and that's what makes them weak.

Before I could pull off, I heard laughter. The dudes on the sidewalk were telling Romeo how shook Tay was when I pulled the gun on him. They clowned him something terrible. The strongest thing I have in my corner is the fact that men always underestimate me. They seem to think that they can get over on me because I bleed once a month, but like the Joker said in Batman, *"Wait until they get a load of me!"* Those were my sentiments, exactly.

CHAPTER ELEVEN

TINA

Ring. Ring. Ring. Ring. Ring.

I looked at the clock on the wall and it was almost 2:00 in the morning. *The phone can just ring until the person on the other end realizes that everyone in this house is sleeping.* I hate late night calls. I've had dreams of police officers knocking on the door late at night or someone ringing the phone to tell me that my baby's father is dead.

A woman's intuition is more powerful than you think. I'll never forget the night Tony's mother called me and said that Tony was dead. DEAD! My Tony, dead? How could it be? I know that you live to die, but Tony was so young. I always saw us as old people in rocking chairs or at least that's what I hoped. I know, I know, drug dealers only have two means to an end and that's jail or death. But I still never thought that someone would kill Tony.

Tony was introduced to me by his sister Terri. His sister and I went to high school together. Tony always tried to holler at me, but I was always with someone else. Then Tony went to jail and he wrote me. I wrote Tony off and on for a while and he would call me every now and then. He was nice and always talked and said things to me to make me feel special.

But, I had a boyfriend. Kenny. Now, Kenny was my heart, but he had anger management issues. When he got mad, he became abusive. But, he took good care of me. Unfortunately, Kenny got caught cheating in a crap game and was killed by one of the players over seven hundred and fifty dollars. I guess people get killed for a lot less.

Then as if on cue, Tony started writing and calling me from Lorton. I started going to Youth Center One every weekend to see him. I was so enamored of Tony. The boy had a silver tongue. I think he could talk grapes into pressing themselves into wine. It wasn't long before he talked me into bringing drugs into the jail for him.

I would meet his friend Carl and get the drugs already packaged. All I had to do was bring them inside the jail in my vagina. Inside the visiting hall I'd pull the drug-filled condoms out of me and Tony would swallow them or on a few occasions he's 'slam' them. Slamming was when a dude stuffed drugs or money into his rectum to hide them. I felt safe with Tony; it was a love that rivaled the one portrayed in the movie Titanic. And the funny part was that I had strong feelings for him and we never even had sex. But then Tony took care of that too.

Tony was in jail under what DC corrections called a Youth Act. He had a ten-year sentence and had to do four years before he could be paroled. Tony had two years in and two left to go. Tony convinced me that we should consummate our relationship while he was still at Lorton. I wanted to wait until he got out, but as usual; he talked me into it. Like I said, he was a smooth talker.

"Boo, I need some loving bad. I've been down for two years and I'm tired of beating my dick. You know I don't mess around with no faggies or none of that gay shit so I need some, bad." Tony said.

"Boy, I'm not doing nothing in this visiting hall in front of all these people. Why you can't wait?"

"Wait! I'm supposed to wait two more years to make love to my baby. I love you girl, heart, mind, body, and soul. If I can work my mojo and get us a conjugal visit, are you with that?" he asked.

"Put it together and I'm with it." I replied.

The next time I came to visit a week later, Tony told me that one particular officer at Youth Center One would be working the visiting hall next weekend and the dude had agreed to let Tony and me use the room set aside for shakedowns for about forty-five minutes.

Tony was excited; I was scared to death. What if something went wrong?

I was filled with trepidation all week. When the weekend came I was nervous as hell. I wanted to smell good for my baby, so I splashed on some Victoria Secret body perfume that smelled like strawberries. I dressed in a sexy outfit and drove the thirty minutes it took to reach the Youth Center.

Once I was cleared to visit and processed in, I was escorted to the visiting hall where the officer took me to the little side room. I had about two hundred butterflies in my stomach, but they all died down when Tony walked into the room about ten minutes later. In seconds, Tony was all over me. The room was empty except for two chairs. Tony sat me down in one of them and opened my legs. He pulled my thong off one leg at a time and then dropped to his knees.

Tony gave me the best head I ever had in my life. I was sprung. I came about five times. Then he undressed. He wouldn't let me suck his dick. He said that his wife-to-be didn't have to do that. We knew we'd get married one day. He sat down in the chair and put me on top of him. I rode that dick like a wild Indian on horseback. The experience was extra exciting because of the situation, the rushed time period, and the fact that someone could walk in on us at any time. I orgasmed about three more times before Tony stopped moving and released a lot of pent-up hostilities.

The fact that he came inside of me didn't bother me either, except I wasn't on birth control. I should have brought some condoms, but what the hell! I wanted to feel Tony's dick inside of me. That was our first sexual encounter while he was in jail, but it wasn't our last. We made moves like that for the next year or so. Then I discovered I was pregnant. I went to my gynecologist for my regular checkup and was told that I was three months pregnant.

Angel

I saw no physical change in my body at all. Since I had been moving fast, taking care of Tony's business, and running my daily errands, I never slowed down long enough to realize that I missed two periods. At first I was devastated. I was pregnant before, three years ago, when I was seeing Kenny. But I never told him I was pregnant. I borrowed $300 from my mother and quickly went to Hillcrest Abortion Clinic and terminated the pregnancy. But, this time was different. I loved Tony so much there wasn't anything I wouldn't do for him, having his baby was just the tip of the iceberg.

I was apprehensive about telling Tony at first. *What if he doesn't want the baby? What if he gets mad and doesn't want to be with me anymore? What if he thinks I'm trying to baby trap him?*

That weekend I went to see Tony and I decided to tell him I was pregnant. To my surprise Tony started crying. In between sniffling and tears he told me about his son who he didn't know. Turned out when he was fifteen he got some girl pregnant, but when she told him, he denied it. She turned around and told two other dudes that the baby was theirs.

He was locked up when she had the baby, but heard that the baby looked just like him. He tried to reach out to her, but she wasn't having it. She had a new boyfriend and he claimed the baby was his. She moved and wouldn't let him see the boy. She told Tony, that the boy believed someone else was his dad and it was no need in confusing her situation. She hung up the phone, days later the number was changed and he never spoke to her again.

"I cry sometime thinking about my son." He said as he stared into my eyes. "So for you to tell me your pregnant is the best news I could hear. Don't worry, Tina, I'll be the best father in the world."

Tony was so sincere, he brought tears to my eyes. He was mad he wouldn't be home when the baby was born, but both of us were so happy that day, we cried together, laughed together, and prayed for a healthy child together. Our baby would make us a family; our baby would make us one. I was eighteen years old, pregnant and in love with Anthony Jerome Phillips. I had my daughter May of 1990 and Tony was due to be released in November, six months later. We named our daughter, Honesty, because we vowed to always be honest to one another.

Honesty Shanae Phillips became the light of my life and I doted on her hand and foot, until Tony came home. Tony was living with his mother at the time and I was still at home with my grandmother. Every night I would spend the night with Tony at his mom's house or I'd sneak Tony into my basement. We did everything together and I could really tell that Tony loved me and our daughter. I sat back and watched Tony struggle to be accepted in a society that put a stigma on black men with criminal histories.

I always saw the frustration in his eyes as he tried to provide for his family. Things just didn't seem to ever go Tony's way, so I wasn't surprised when he told me he was going back to the streets to make his living. According to him, the street life was all he knew and besides, no one was breaking their necks to hire twenty-year old ex-con. So back into the fast life Tony went.

With months he was reestablished in Congress Park as the one to watch. Tony never smoked, did drugs, or drank. His rise to the top was inevitable. Once Tony started to gain influence and affluence, then came the females. How long the cheating had been going on or when exactly it started, I don't know. All I know is that I could see the signs. Tony started coming home early in the a.m. He was always tired and we started having sex once a week, if that.

He was secretive and stayed hiding his cell phone. If he didn't hide it, he'd turn it off and he barely answered it when it did ring. When will men realize that looking at the number of the display on cell phones and pagers and ignoring them is a dead giveaway that it's a female? He'd get pages in the middle of the night with codes like, #01, #69, 911, or Hi boo and all that booty call type stuff. I got into the habit of monitoring the numbers on his beeper and cell phone.

If I crossed-reference those numbers with the ones already stored in his cell phone, usually I'd come up with the name and number of a female. Sometimes I'd ignore the obvious and then often times I'd call the female back and ask about her relationship to Tony. But Tony had his girls well trained and I never learned much from them. Tony would always placate me with lies. I knew they were lies and he knew it too, but he just kept right on telling them.

The females were always his relatives, platonic friends, customers, and business partners. But knowing Tony's freaky ass like I did, he was fucking all of them. I knew it and he knew it. Things got to the point where he'd be caught and he'd just come clean, apologize, and swear that it meant nothing; then he'd do it again.

I remember one day when I went downstairs to wash clothes. I found some of Tony's boxers balled up with some other clothes. The boxers had red lipstick smeared all over the crotch. I was upset because his ass was too trifling to wash his own clothes; that way he could hide the evidence of his betrayal. I started to feel like he just didn't care anymore. To make a long story short, we argued, we fought, we cried, we separated; and then we always got back together. Call me stupid; but I love his cheating ass with all my heart.

I decided to accept him for who he was with all his imperfections. Rationalizing with myself; I came to the conclusion that all men are dogs and that when they get in heat, they cheat with any bitch they can find. I told myself that as long as he didn't bring any diseases home and he took care of our home first; then I wasn't worried about him getting his dick sucked on the side or whatever else he may be getting from the broads in the street. To be honest, at first I thought it was me. But after many days of self-reflection and contemplation, I decided that no matter what I did, how I did it, or how often I did it, he would still cheat.

I'm not one of those females who ascribes to thinking that if a man cheats, it's because there's something at home he's not getting. Because a woman can fuck and suck her man's dick three times a day, and five times on Sunday, give him anal sex on call, make love to him in every position imaginable for as long as he wants it, that man will still go out in the streets and fuck some other woman. That's just the way it is. So, I stopped beating myself up about Tony's infidelity and moved on.

Tony was moving up the ladder slowly but surely. Over the next five years his reputation and stability grew. To have a five-year run in the game was pure luck or either skill. With Tony, I'd opt for the skill part. One day, Tony came home all excited rambling on and on about some dude named Carlos and how the dude was this big time drug-dealer that was going to help him blow up.

He never went into much detail about Carlos, but Tony told me that he was like those dudes you read about in the newspapers. Dudes like Fabio Ochoa, the Blanco brothers, the Arelleno-Ruiz brothers, and Pablo Escobar, serious drug lords. I thought he was exaggerating, but sure enough, as time went on Tony got larger and larger in weight and stature. Tony moved us into a brand-new duplex house out in Kettering, Maryland. Then he went and bought me a Mazda MVP minivan and he got a Cadillac Eldorado ETC, a Crown Victoria, a 300ZX, and a GMC Yukon SLT.

Our whole life changed. The house was laid out lavishly from wall-to-wall. I opened a bank account in my name and in my daughter's name, and made regular deposits. Tony was making so much money, it actually scared me. For the most part Tony tried to keep me out of his business; but since we lived together; he couldn't hide it from me. All-night long he would count his money. That was in the beginning before he bought a money-counting machine. He would be in the kitchen cooking cocaine into crack.

I stumbled into boxes in the basement that contained taped up bundles. I knew exactly what they were. I grew up in Arthur Capers, so I know what keys of coke looked like. With all the newfound wealth came a totally different disposition. Tony started carrying two guns, a glock 17 and a Beretta 9 millimeter. Tony collected guns and had them strategically placed all around the house where our daughter wouldn't find them.

Tony counseled me on survival techniques, on how to check for cars that maybe following me, cars that didn't belong on the block, and about keeping my gas tank full so that I wouldn't have to make unnecessary trips to gas stations. He cautioned me about stopping at malls and stores in remote places. He stressed to me that he was a figure now and that dudes will try to get him through me. I understood completely and played my position at all time.

Then Tony bought his mother a house and a Lincoln Town Car. He sold all our cars and trucks and bought me a Lexus LS430 and a BMW-X5. He bought himself a Cadillac Escalade, a Lexus 470 truck, and Infinity Q45, and a Dodge Viper. And we had a backyard full of dirt bikes, motorcycles, and four-wheelers. I guess Tony thought all the material possessions would keep me quiet, but what he never realized, was that all I really wanted was him. I would've give up everything just to go back to the days when it was just me, him, and Honesty.

All the money, the cars, the big house in Kettering didn't matter to me. I loved Tony with all my heart and I continued to tolerate his little flings on the side. I have never known Tony to have feelings for any one woman for a long time, so obviously I was caught off guard with the broad named Angel or whatever he name is. I found her phone number in his pants pocket, and saw her number on his pager everyday so I decided to give her a call. I didn't know the extent of their relationship, but my instincts told me that there was something serious about this broad. I called her and questioned her about Tony. She shot me some lies about her and Tony doing some business together. *Yeah right, this ho thinks I don't know my own fucking man. Whatever!*

Then I left it alone until I found some receipts in Tony's truck that came from several money orders that were made out in his handwriting to J. Mortgage Company. Apparently, Tony was paying the rent at someone else's house, too. I confronted him about it and he told me he was paying bills for his man Dontay. Dontay allegedly took a charge for Tony and Tony was obligated to take care of his family while he was away. I didn't believe a word he said. So I followed him a few times.

Tony always went to the same apartment and I noticed that he had keys to that apartment on his key chain. Later, I found out that the apartment in Glen Willow belonged to Tony's other female. I investigated further and was rewarded with the information that I suspected. The apartment was leased to Kareemah El-Amin. I had two telephone numbers for Angel and they both were billed to Kareemah El-Amin.

I figured that if I just look the other way; Tony would eventually get tired of her, do the right thing and break it off. As long as home was alright, I wasn't tripping. Tony still came home very night unless he was out of town. I know that the broad had a burgundy ML55 Mercedes Benz truck; Tony probably bought it, but I'm not sure. She works at some company out in Lanham so she can probably afford it, especially since Tony was paying all of her bills.

But now my Tony is gone. My Tony! I don't know what went down at that bitch's house, but the police think something is shady. I talked to the detective on the case, a Detective Jones, and he gave me all the details. He spared me no details and I couldn't help feeling stupid, because it was evident that I was a fool all along. He told me the shady evidence that made him think that maybe Angel was involved in Tony's death. I called her and gave her a piece of my mind, and told her that I wanted whatever she had, that belonged to Tony.

The brave bitch had the audacity to come to the funeral. I swear I wanted to choke her ass, but it wasn't the time or place to go Rambo on her. She gave me the keys to the Escalade and I went and got it. The box in the trunk contained Tony's papers, clothes, and knickknacks. Even in death I couldn't be mad at Tony for his cheating ways. I loved him so much, I just accepted his hoes. I can't explain it.

My daughter Honesty took Tony's death the hardest. Tony was a wonderful father and he loved his little girl like nothing else in the world. I still look into my child's eyes and cry because I feel her pain; I remember when my father died when I was ten years old and how I felt. She's a smart girl and she understands that her father's in heaven, but she can't accept it, and she cries for him all the time. I might have to get her some counseling if she doesn't move on. I just don't know what to do to make her feel better.

We talk all the time and I always tell Honesty the truth. She knows that she is mommy and daddy's love child. But, she also knows that about his death. She knows Angel was with him when he died. I told her that Angel was his friend. I figured she'd learn the truth one day, so why not keep it real with her now? Besides, she's twelve years old and she's mature for her age. I just hope she learns to accept the fact that he father is gone. And if that detective comes back and tells me that Angel bitch had something to do with Tony. I swear that bitch will wish she never met him.

CHAPTER TWELVE

ANGEL

Today might end up being a good day, depending on how much I can get accomplished. But then again, like the saying goes, 'any day above ground is a good day'. I woke up early this morning and cleaned up a little. I rip and run so much; my housekeeping needs some attending to. I cleaned up the junk that as all over the place. I washed a few loads of laundry and folded my clothes.

They're on the same type of grind, I'm on. I sat back and formulated my plan for the rest of the day. I crushed a bomb breakfast of cheese omelet; fried lamp chops, home fries, and biscuits. I thought about the remaining dudes on my list and silently hoped that I could hurry up and get all the pieces in place. I want everybody to be ready before I start playing the game. There are only four dudes left who I need to see. I talked to the dude Faceman yesterday and I plan to visit him later on today.

I walked out into the complex parking lot and noticed that my truck was the dirtiest one there. I decided to get my car washed before I started my recruiting mission for the day. I went to my old neighborhood, on 46th and Hillside and let my crack head buddy Otis wash the truck. Otis might smoke crack, but hands down, he was the baddest car detailer around. He be having niggas cars showroom floor worthy. I dropped the truck off to Otis, while he put what he calls the 'smack down' on my truck, and went to my mother's house while I waited for the 'smack down'.

"Assalaamu Alaikum, mom." I said, giving my mother the greeting in Arabic.

Angel

"Wa alaikum Assalaam." She replied. "Child, what brings you to the ghetto twice in one week? Why aren't you out somewhere enjoying this beautiful day that Allah has made?"

"My truck was filthy, so I brought it over here to Otis. Then I figured that I'd come see my mother for a little while. Is that okay?"

"Of course, I'm just washing dishes and straightening up. Is something wrong?"

"Naw, Umi, I can't come and talk to you without something being wrong?"

"Sure you can baby; sure you can. But it ain't like we see a whole lot of you these days. I worry about you girl, especially after that episode with your boyfriend."

You would really be worrying if you knew the truth, I thought to myself.

"I'm hanging in there mom. I'm okay."

"I don't know how you do it, baby."

Me neither, honey child, killing ain't easy, but somebody's got to do it.

"Have the police arrested anyone yet?" My mother asked me.

"Naw, they're still investigating. I'm in contact with the lead detective on the case. He keeps me updated on new leads and so forth."

"Oh, you've been keeping in touch with the detective. I hope he's not upsetting you too much."

"No, I'm okay."

"Well, just be careful out there, honey, and try to get your life together, Angel. I know you don't like to hear it, but I don't want anything happening to you."

"Mom, don't worry about me; I can take of myself."

I got a fully loaded seventeen shot Ruger P.98 in my purse. I'm good.

We talked about a little bit of everything for the next hour until Otis beeped me and told me that the truck was ready. I gave my mom a kiss and left.

A Novel by Anthony Fields

I drove over the South Capitol Street Bridge and turned left onto M Street. I made a right on Delaware Avenue and spotted Gambino, Ron and several other dudes congregating in the first court on K Street. I knew of Gambino through his sister Vicky and I was with Tony a couple of times when he served Gambino.

I blew my horn and called Gam and Ron over. They jumped in my car and we talked for about thirty minutes. They agreed to buy three to five keys a week. Gam and Ron handled all the traffic in Southwest from P Street, Half Street, Delaware, and 3rd to James Creek. They covered the whole area like a blanket. And in the streets, it was said that they commanded a young army proven to be more than formidable in times of war.

Gambino tried to holler at me before and today just like that day, I shot him down. I was tempted, but he played hisself right out of position. He always runs his mouth about this girl and that girl who he's been with, and the other thing I hate more than a snitch is a talkative nigga. I hate 'em.

I left Gam and Ron and hit the highway. Going Uptown, I remembered how much I hated NW growing up. There was always this NW-SE hate thing going on and I grew up smack dab in the middle of that. Being from SE, we were conditioned to dislike everyone and everything from Uptown. DC had crews back then, not to be mistaken for gangs. Every section had their little crew and when people crossed paths they went at it. That was before the influx of guns, so people were allowed to live to fight another day. All the best parties always heard how the NW broads would jump the SE broads and vice versa.

Everybody living in SE was considered dirty. The other three quadrants-NE, SE, and SW, were also looked down upon. Riding up Georgia Avenue, I couldn't help but reminisce about all that and laugh at how things had changed. Who knew that the government would revitalize SE, tearing down several projects and rebuilding them with townhomes and private homes, while NW slowly but surely fell to the wayside. Now, NW is like the projects, and SE residents turn their noses up at NW residents. It's crazy.

In route to Morton Street, I talked to Face, so he wasn't hard to spot standing beside a canary yellow Hummer. Not the new H2 joint, the big bulky Hummer H1. How in the hell are you going to avoid the long arms of the law while moving major weight in the hood, when you drive a big bright ass truck? All I could think to myself was that this nigga is going to jail and it'll be soon. But as long as he's on the streets, I'll make sure that he had bricks to buy. I blew my horn and Face dismissed the hoodrat broad he was talking to.

"Angel, what's up, boo boo?"

Face is the type of dude who flosses too much, talks too much, and does entirely too much. He's that 'center of attention' type character. He always reminded me of this kid from New York, named Alpo I know. He's conceited, braggadocious, and plain fake as hell. I've seen his kind a thousand times. Face is not a gangsta type dude; he's the manipulator, the brain that puts it all together type. The fact that he won't hesitate to drop a nigga where he's standing, is the main reason why niggas tolerate Face. Along with money brings influence and Face had several ruthless cats under his influence.

"Face, it's been awhile, but it's always a pleasure to be in your company." I lied. "You're the ghetto P. Diddy around here."

"Naw, boo, I'm just little ole Face around here. Local boy made it big type situation. These are my people. I was raised right here and I never pull pretentious stunts on my people. When I slide over Southeast or something, then I'm that nigga Faceman."

Face offered me a ride in the Hummer and since I never rode in one, I accepted. We rode around and talked.

"Angel, I need a constant supply of yack, to supply the demand up here. I'm moving joints all the way up to Kennedy Street. If I start skinning more birds, I want less feathers. Right now I'm messing with some major dudes from Glenarden, Maryland. They're charging me twenty-two a key. I'm buying 5 keys a week but they're not consistent. They run out of work a lot. Tony was my man. Slim had a consistent work at twenty a brick, I miss that. I need to buy at least eight joints a week now, maybe ten. You say that you and Tony's people are the same people. Okay! Tell them that I say if we do business on ten keys a week, I need the price to come down. Tell them that and then holler at me. If they at least go down to 19 a key we're in business. Can you do that?"

"Look here Face, I represent the same people Tony dealt with, but I'm just the middle person. Let me get at my folks and see if I can get you ten keys for 19 a joint. Nobody, and I do mean nobody, is paying nineteen a key. I'll let you know something tonight, though."

I said that for the benefit of secrecy, but I had already decided to give him his 10 joints at 19 a key because I needed him and the region that he supplies. The 10,000 a week wouldn't really hurt because I can always make it up on the back end. Every now and then when a dude wants a single brick, I'll sell it for twenty-five or twenty-seven depending on how I feel that day.

Technically, I'm ahead of the game by over $100,000 and I can renegotiate my contract with Carlos in the future. Face can turn out to be a star running back, so whatever he wants, he gets. It's like in fast food, 'the customer is always right'. I left Face and decided to hit Trinidad Avenue from there. The Trinidad Avenue projects were home to some of the most notorious gangsters ever to come out of DC.

My maternal grandmother had lived on Montello all her life. I spent several weekends in her house, so I'm familiar with the hood and some of its residents. I used to look forward to visiting my grandma's house because as a young girl I was in love with all the cute dudes who hustled on Queen Street. People didn't understand Islam on this side of town, so I got teased a lot. But the hustlers were always nice to me. I was the little Muslim girl to them, and they respected me. I have very fond memories of this place.

I drove down Montello toward my grandmother's old house. The streets were pretty much run by the young dudes. Gone are the days when the older dudes used to regulate the strips and squashed all beefs in the name of getting money. Nowadays, all beefs end with hundred round clips. So, I'm not surprised when I hear that Trinidad is beefing with several hoods. The dude, Russell, I'm going to see is basically, young, wild, and running a profitable drug business with this other dude named Fred. They got Trinidad locked.

On 16th Street there's a Chinese store that everybody hangs in. That's where I'll find Russell. Russell is about twenty-three years old, but he's one of the precocious youngins. He came off the porch early. I heard that he's been around since the late eighties when Lil Man and Calvin ran Trinidad. Back then he was a rumored to be jive crutty. They say that he'd sell a person weight and then get them robbed to get it back. But I heard he's no dummy and only crosses you if he thinks he can get away with it. If he knows you'll bring heat to his ass, then he plays fair.

From what I was able to learn; Tony and Russell had a good relationship and Russell never tried anything slick. I just hope that he values his life and doesn't decide that he can try me because I'm a female.

Like Pretty Lady said, "There's no honor amongst thieves."

But to some degree there had to be trust and that's what my team will have to have, because in this male-dominated field, I have to take certain precautions as a female. I'm no punk bitch but at the same time I'm not a female Steven Segal. I bleed, too and I can be tricked and killed. I can't let the fact that I'm strapped make me go into a situation half assed. My game has to be extra tight.

What I plan to do, is meet each dude and get their money, take it somewhere and count it, and then meet them in a public place and deliver the product. All that will be done after carefully making sure that I'm not followed. And everything will be done using Fatima's home as my headquarters. Fatima agreed even though I don't think she wanted to.

I vaguely remember Russell from my childhood, but it was only in passing. I still could pick him out of a crowd though and I did. Russell was one fly dude. He was wearing an All DAZ sweat suit with Gucci tennis shoes. He had a tattoo across his neck that read 'Thug Love'. He was about six feet tall, bald, and jive built. I walked over to Russell and asked to speak to him outside. He obliged, looking me up and down like I was Philly Cheesesteak. I shot my spiel.

"My name's Angel. I grew up around here with you. You probably don't remember me, but my grandmother lived in the house that used to be over there." I pointed to the vacant spot on Montello Avenue.

"Who was your grandmother?" he asked.

"Mrs. Ruby Jones. She had the old blue and gray house over there." I replied.

"I remember old Mrs. Jones. She always hit a nigga off with brownies and cupcakes and shit like that. So JR and Chris are kin to you?"

"Yeah, they're my uncles." I said.

"Okay, I think I remember you, short stuff. So now that we've gotten reacquainted, what's on your mind?"

"Well, you and my late boyfriend were business partners."

"Who's your late boyfriend?"

"Tony Bills." I told him and watched his facial expression change.

"Yeah that was my man. We did business. I heard that Slim got smashed. What's up with that?"

Before I could answer he said. "Hold on cutie; I don't have anything to do with that if that's what you think. Tony was good folks and I respected him. I know people talk dirty about Big Russ like I can't be trusted, but I never crossed anyone who didn't reserves it. Tony Bills was a good muthafucka. I fucked with slim and…"

I cut Russell off before he got long winded.

"Ease up, Rus, I never said that you had anything to do with that. I know who was involved and before the week is out those dudes will be dead. My reason for coming to see you today is strictly business. I was a silent partner in all of Tony's business affairs. I know about your deal with Tony for four bricks a week at twenty-five a key. His connect is my family and I'm here to offer you the same deal, so you'll be dealing with me. The coke is the same product; fish scales all the way uncut. So are you down or what?"

"Boo, I've seen bitches rape niggas before. I've seen bitches fight niggas and whip their asses. I've seen bitches knock out dudes and their bitches. I've seen bitches ride for niggas on enemy niggas and I've seen bitches do some of the most scandalous shit ever, so why wouldn't I buy good coke from a bitch? No disrespect of course. As long as you're not a cop and a rat, I'll buy coke from you. You can take my number and call me in an hour and then we can dance."

I programmed Russell's number into my cell phone. We reminisced about my grandmother for a little while longer, and then I bounced.

The twins are the last holdouts on my list. Once I get them onboard, I'll be ready to roll. Everything is looking good from where I'm sitting. I figured it was time for me to call the big man. I hit the voice dial button and my phone said, "Call Carlos."

In two rings, I heard a thick, heavily accented Spanish voice.
"Hola."

"Can I speak to Carlos, please?"

"Esperato un momento."

I heard some static on the line and then Carlos's voice.

"Angel, what can I do for you?"

How in the hell Carlos knew I was on the phone without me even saying my name, was beyond me?

"I just wanted to let you know that I'm almost ready. Give another day and we'll meet."

"Just call this number when you're ready, okay."

"Okay."

I hung up the phone and started turning some thoughts over in my mind. The best way to get to the twins was through Dearaye, that's common sense. If I put the clamp on him, he'll convince his brother to spend his money with me. I thought about approaching Dearaye out in the open like I did everybody else, but my gut instincts told me that might not be a good idea. Since Tony is gone, Deandre may balk at dealing with someone he doesn't know, especially a female. Technically, I could proceed without them, but I'd rather have them copping from me. Tony had once said them niggas spend damn near a half million a month on coke. I definitely need that money.

So Dearaye is definitely my key. I found out through a friend of mine, that Dearaye is a clubber. He goes to all the DC nightclubs, Club U, the Classics, Tradewinds, the DC Tunnel, the Dream, the Legend, and a rack of other hot spots. He's rumored to be a big Chuck Brown fan.

One of the things I learned in history class is that man's greatest weakness is women. Women using sex as a weapon to control men is as old as prostitution. So like they say, "If it ain't broken don't fix it."

Angel

I'll have to bait Dearaye in with a little sex and then shoot my shot from there.

I'll make it my business to go out to Legend tomorrow night and catch Dearaye there, if he shows. *Me and Fatima need an excuse to go out anyway. Let me call her and tell her to be ready.*

CHAPTER THIRTEEN

Angel & Fatima

I called Fatima to see if she was ready to go. She was, so I'm on my merry way. I'm dressed to kill, no pun intended. I'm giving them the new Donatella Versace ensemble; dress, shoes, and bag. And I'm iced out in accessories. *Halle ain't got shit on me. Donatella just don't know, but if she did, I'd be the new Versace chick.*

I looked at myself in the visor mirror. My hair's cut and styled perfectly. When I blow up, I'ma have to open me a shop and steal Stephanie from that beauty salon. I checked my nails, proper.

Fatima lives about twenty-five minutes from me, but since I drive fast, I made it to her house in fifteen minutes. I blew the horn. Seconds later my beloved sister in crime stepped out her front door. Girlfriend was killing them, too, with what she had on. I smiled to myself as I thought about all the clothes and shoes she owns; it's ridiculous. As Fatima approached the truck, I got out and walked around the passenger side.

"You're driving tonight, sista girl. I been driving all day and I'm tired."

"Oh yeah! Now I'm the chauffer, huh? I'm Mrs. Farnsworth Bently, huh? You got that, sweetheart, but I'ma get you back. You looking good as hell in that dress too, boo. You brought out the big hooks to snag the big fish, huh?"

"Girl, please! Dearaye ain't no big fish. Russell Simmons, naw, better yet, Robert L. Johnson's a big fish. Bill Gates, Steve Jobs, and Mark Zuckerberg are big fish. Master P and Puffy are big fish. Kevin Garnett and Lebron James are big fish; feel me? Dearaye 'the ghetto fabulous drug dealer' is a guppy, swimming in a pond full of big fish. You look like you just came back from Paris or something, Ms. Givenchy."

I hit the remote for the CD changer. Jay Z's CD blasted in our ears. As I listened to Jay, I sat back and thought about everything that had happened in the last three weeks. A small inner voice nags me sometimes, but then my rational voice steps in. "The end results justify all means."

"Angel."

"Huh?" I replied.

"How's everything going with the takeover, as you call it?"

"Everything's going good. After I bring this nigga Dearaye and his brother onboard, all my pieces will be in place. But then again, I can proceed without the twins, which I probably will do, but I still want them to cop coke from me. I'll call Carlos tomorrow and arrange to get the coke from him.

"After I get everything in sync, I want to branch out a little. I want to eventually supply everybody who's buying coke in DC, no matter whose toes I step on. The dudes in the Gangster Gear Shop, the Spanish Boys uptown, whoever, they all can get it, if they in my way. I want to supply all demands, corner the market, and rape the town. When I'm satisfied, I'll take my earnings and roll.

"Then I want to move to California. I want you to come with me Fatima. I'll have enough money for us to lay back and live it up. You can quit that dead end job you have. We can get into the Hollywood way of living and hobnob with the people who make shit happen until my big break comes. That's why I'm putting so much pressure on myself. I want to be outta here in five years, tops."

"Girl, it sounds like you've given this a lot of thought. I believe that you'll do what you say you will. Just be careful, boo. You're making deals with some dangerous dudes."

We pulled into the Legend parking lot. I could hear the band cranking from outside. Go-Go music is so rhythmic you automatically start to dance when you hear it. Since I don't know Dearaye or his brother, I asked Doodie to come to the Legend and point him out. Doodie is my heart and he knows that I'm in a position to repay his gratitude. I see his Yukon Denali on dubs over there in the cut. We paid, showed our ID and walked into a crowded room of sweaty black people.

Instantly, I remembered why I hate going to clubs. All the dudes in the club are trying to get their mack on. I'm sick to my stomach trying to get rid of these scrubs and their weak ass pickup lines and disrespect. Every dude with hands tries to grab you and feel on you. The bold dudes will just grab you and take you to the dance floor. As Fatima and I made our way to the bar, we were groped, squeezed, and fondled. That's why I never party at clubs. You leave a club feeling like you've been molested and I should know what that feels like.

Most men don't know what a woman has to go through in a nightclub just to have a good time. I wish that we could turn the tables and let men see how it feels to have their nuts squeezed from one end of the club to another. I bet they wouldn't like it.

At the bar I ordered a Cosmo and Fatima opted for a soda. Girlfriend be tripping me out. She still holds fast to certain laws of Islam but compromises others. For instance, she won't smoke cigarettes, do any drugs whatsoever, drink any alcohol, and she offers her salat and goes to Jumah. But, yet and still she dresses whorishly, fornicates often, practices oral and anal sex, and goes to Atlantic City to gamble, all of which is forbidden in Islam.

Islam is a strict religion. You can't skirt the fence; either you're on the right path or you're not. That's why I refuse to be a hypocrite. I hope Allah forgives me one day, but I have to be my true self and being true to myself makes me do a lot of things I know are wrong. I like to drink on occasion and if the mood strikes, I might puff on some trees.

If a dude pops a Viagra and puts that work in all night long, I might smoke a cigarette to calm my nerves and hormones. Marriage is one half of our faith and you can only sex with your spouse. I don't see any husband in my near future and I need some hard dick when I feel like it. I don't mean none of that plastic dildo stuff. I know in my heart that I'm not finished sinning, so why ask for forgiveness every day when I know that I'm going to do the same thing again?

I spotted Doodie across the room talking to a couple of dudes. I swear we must be subliminally connected because he spotted me at the same time and brought the two dudes over to the bar. He introduced us and I finally got the chance to meet the illustrious Dearaye.

Fatima was engaged in conversation with Dearaye's friend Wop, who I had also heard of. He was a big drug boy from a spot called 'the Circle'. Dearaye sat on the stool next to me and then Doodie made his exit. To my surprise, Dearaye was incredibly good-looking. If I had to compare Dearaye to someone famous; I'd have to say that he looked like Nelly. He just had cornrows instead of a tapered haircut. I instantly liked him. He was dressed in Prada apparel from head to toe.

Dearaye never actually spoke to me; at first he just stared at me. I started to feel self-conscious like I had something on my face or a booger in my nose.

"Why are you staring at me like that?"

"I'm sorry. I know that it's rude. But you're absolutely beautiful and I don't know what to say out of fear of sounding foolish. I meet females all the time, but there's something different about you that's intoxicating; and that's without any drink from this bar. See what I mean? There's one of my foolish lines. Is Angel your real name?"

"No, my name's Kareemah. It's Islamic. My father nick-named me Angel. I've heard about you. You have a twin brother, right? And you be in Northeast somewhere?"

"Yes and yes." Dearaye said. "I hope what you heard wasn't bad. People tend to lie. Some people call me Twin. You can call me Dearaye or Twin, just as long as you call me. See there I go again with the stupid lines.

He smiled a pretty smile. I returned the smile as I thought to myself that niggas are all the same. They're like dogs that smell pussy and they come around sniffing. And this one is easy prey. If I was trying to kill him, he'd be dead. But I'm only trying to get his cash. I shot him a fictitious story about my life and listened to him do the same. He totally downplayed the fact that his brother and him are big players in the game and that they're rumored to be rich. That was good, because I don't like dudes who brag.

We ended up exchanging numbers and dancing a bit. Fatima seemed to be enjoying herself with Wop, so I just chilled with Dearaye. When the club let out we said our good-byes and left. I crashed at Fatima's house. The next morning Dearaye called my cell phone and invited me to breakfast. I declined, acting like I had to work. I promised to call him later. I was ready to see Carlos and make my move. I called Carlos. He picked up on the third ring.

"Hello Angel, what's up?"

"When can I see you?"

"I'm tied up at the moment in a meeting. I should be available soon. Do you know where the BET Soundstage Restaurant is in Largo?"

"Yeah, I know the place."

"Well, meet there around 2:00 p.m. Is that good for you?"

Angel

"Perfect. I'll see you then. Bye."

Fatima and I talked while eating breakfast.

"Angel, I dig Wop. He's smooth, cute, and cool as hell. And he's real. He was up-front with me about all the females who he deals with. He claims to be searching for the right person. When most dudes try to run game and lie, all that you can tell is that they're faking. I have a good feeling about Wop. His real name's David and underneath that rugged veneer there lies a kindred soul. You know I believe in Karma. I feel something about him that I can't explain. Girl, I swear I feel giddy like a teenager with a crush. We're supposed to hook up sometime today."

"You really like slim, huh?" I asked Fatima.

She nodded.

"That's cool. If you feel good about the dude and dig him that's all that matters. He's cute though. Plus, he has that thug swagger like he toting a big third leg. Just take your time, boo, and feel the situation out."

"I'm not about to do anything stupid like elope. I'm just saying I like the dude. I dig his style."

"Like I said, go for it. But if he does anything to hurt you, I'll have to pay him a visit."

I smiled at Fatima as I got up from the table and she smiled back knowing exactly what I meant.

CHAPTER FOURTEEN

Angel & Fatima

I spent the rest of the day on the phone. I had to touch base with my hood fellas. I talked to my mother and tried again to sell her on the idea of letting me pay for Adirah's private school. She wouldn't bite so I left it alone.

At 1:30 I left to meet Carlos. It took me twenty minutes to get to the BET Restaurant from Fatima's house. I looked around the parking lot trying to recognize a car that possible belonged to Carlos. I found none. But knowing Carlos, he's already inside the restaurant sitting beside a window watching me.

I heard a lot about the BET Restaurant, but I never bothered to come here. The place is nice though. At every booth there's a TV screen that plays BET or whatever live entertainment that might be featured that night. Today was gospel day. While a live gospel group shouted their praise, Carlos and I discussed drugs and money in whispered tones.

"Angel, how are you? You look well. I'd like you to eat something. Please don't decline my invitation a second time." Then he motioned a waitress to our table. Carlos ordered the stuffed chicken and I ordered the fried catfish.

"Carlos, I'm feeling pretty good. But let's get down to the nitty-gritty. I'm ready to roll. I spent the last week making sure that everything's ready to go. I've been networking and politicking like I'm running for public office. All my peeps are ready. I'm ready. I have fifteen dudes lined up to buy all fifty bricks as soon as I get them. Honestly, I need about fifty-five. I have the fifty thousand for you now and I'll give you the other fifty grand when I drop off the million. If you add the extra five bricks, that will make it 825 grand that I have to pay. It's up to you."

I never sold the two odd keys but that still didn't matter because I'd just give him fifty out of my stash and then the other fifty when I move the keys.

"The fifty-thousand is in my car so however you want me to get that to you, is cool. So when can I get my bricks?"

"The fifty-thousand that you brought with you is already in my possession."

"What?"

"I said," Carlos replied as he expertly cut his chicken into sections. "The fifty-thousand that's wrapped in a McDonald's bag is already in my possession.

I'm quite sure he noticed the look of confusion on my face so he continued.

"When you drove up, I had a man in the parking lot watching you. While you walked across the lot into the restaurant, he was searching your truck. He found the fifty grand under the driver's seat. When you sat down I was on the phone, right?"

I nodded.

"I was talking to him. He also found your gun that's in your purse. A seventeen-shot Ruger. Listen to me Angel. Always remember that I'm the man. I'm like God, because I know everything and I create life and take life. I'm the one who people hear about but can't figure out. I deal with people all over the world. I never play games and I never joke. I might laugh, but I never joke. I take care of large business on a daily basis. No one crosses me. You cross Carlos you die. It's as simple as that. Not the next day, not two or three years later, but the same day. Within twenty-four hours they're dead. I'm still searching for answers to what happened with Tony at that apartment. So far, nothing has turned up; but I have some ideas. If someone robs Tony or they rob you, they're robbing me and again, no one robs Carlos and lives.

"You enter the marriage at your own risk. I don't expect excuses and I don't tolerate fuck ups. If you get popped, stay quiet and you'll be taken care of; that's on my word. Work with the feds and your whole family dies. For you Angel, that means your mother, the Islamic teacher and your little sister who goes to school on MLK."

Carlos paused to let his words take effect. My blood was boiling. I don't like it when people threaten my family. *That's a no-no. This motherfucker don't know who he's playing with.*

"Angel." He said. "I mean no disrespect. I'm just letting you know how serious this shit is. That's why there's no women in the game at this level. Most women can't stomach the rough side of the game. Very few women have the balls to play the game at this level but I have a feeling that you do. Never deal in emotions Angel, never. Emotions and business do not mix. Since I've been in your company, I've grown to respect you and I like you as a person. I may even grow to love you, but that point is Angel, that if the need arises I wouldn't hesitate one second to kill you. And that goes for everybody I employ. Never mix pleasure with business and never get high off of anything. If you smoke weed, stop! From what I hear, you only drink on occasion, so that's good.

"And don't be surprised that I know about you family. I know everything about you. It's my business to know everything about my associates. I told you I'm like God. I could tell you things about Tony you never knew. And speaking of Tony, he was like a son to me. Tony knew the streets; Tony knew the people. He could be strong, yet humble, aggressive but fair, and smooth yet dangerous. Most of all he was smart and loyal. In this game Angel, loyalty goes a long way, especially with me. We'll be dealing with millions of dollars and money had been known to create greed where greed never lived before, that's why loyalty is so important. Messing with me you'll get rich. You can quit at any time and someone will be in position to take your place the same day. So with all that said, now we can do business. Listen to me carefully and always follow my instructions to the T. Tomorrow at 1:00; go to Iverson Mall. Take your friend Fatima. I also know about her; she's your closest friend. Go and do some shopping. Park your truck on the ground level under the garage. Stay inside for a little while. When you come out of the mall, a black Ford Explorer will be parked next to your truck. Let your girlfriend drive your truck while you drive the Explorer. The keys will be in the ignition. Drive the truck to wherever you want to unload the stuff. Then take the truck to Sam's Car wash on Branch Avenue and leave it. Leave the keys under the driver's side doormat. Do you understand everything I've said?"

I nodded.

"Okay. Each time you pick up the product it will be in a different location. Never keep a routine. When everything's complete and the truck is at Sam's, call me and say, I can't make it to dinner. And I'll know everything's okay. When you finish scrambling and you have all the money, call me and tell me that you need to see me. Wherever you decide to meet, I'll have an associate there to unload the money from your car and move it. So again I ask you, do you follow me?"

"Yes, I follow you." I replied. "And Carlos, it's definitely a pleasure doing business with you. I'll never do anything to cross you for any reason. But let me make one thing clear—never, and I mean NEVER, threaten my family again!"

I left the food untouched and got up to leave the BET Soundstage.

"I'll holler tomorrow."

I got to get out of here before I say something that can get me killed. Maybe I shouldn't have spoken to Carlos like that. I don't want to piss him off. I need him. But fuck that, I don't care who the hell he is or what he can do, kill one of my family members and it's on like shit.

I called Fatima and told her I needed her to go shopping with me, no butts about it. She was too busy rushing me off the phone. *Probably doing the nasty with Wop. She sure is a sucker for those thugged out pretty boys.*

"Hello?" I said as my phone started ringing.

"What's up love; are you busy?"

"Naw, I just left work." I lied. "Why what's up?" The caller was Dearaye.

"I'm trying to see what's up with you."

"Well look, I'm free later on. I'm going home to shower and get some rest. Call me later around 8:00."

"I'll call you then. One."

When I'm feeling good about myself I treat myself to a long hot bubble bath where I can relax and unwind. When that white broad made that Calgon commercial she wasn't bullshitting. I also do my best thinking while relaxing in a hot bath. I'll have to do a rack of driving and counting tomorrow, but I can handle it. I'll take the fifty keys to Fatima's house and basically work from there. Under no circumstances will any men come to my apartment. That ain't happening.

I might have to start carrying both of my hammers, twin Rugers. As I laid in the tub, I thought about the last time I had sex. It was with Tony. *I killed him afterwards though, poor guy.* I've been doing so much, I forgot about sex. I could always give Dearaye some today, but naw. I decided just to release some tension myself. My legs were already open, one foot on both sides of the tub. I rubbed my clit until I felt those familiar stirrings in my bones. I dried myself off and laid across my king-size bed, naked. I grabbed the remote to the DVD player and pushed play. In the DVD player was my triple X freak movie called Superfreaks 6. I have all the Superfreaks DVDs, 1 through 10; but 6 is my favorite. People can hate porn all they want, but me, I love it.

Tony introduced me to freak movies and I've been hooked ever since. Honestly, I like to watch the double and triple penetration one, gang bangs, and women getting their pussy sucked. When I watch that stuff my pussy be soaking wet. I love Janet Jacme, Kitten, Obsession, Crown Princess, India, and Menaja. Those are my girls. They represent real whores all day long they don't give a fuck.

And as far as the dudes, I love Mr. Marcus, Jake Steed, and Lexington Steele. Them niggas can get my pussy anytime, anywhere, barefoot, and naked in a snowstorm in the middle of Alaska. And how could I forget Sean Michaels. That nigga got dick for days. I could visualize myself fucking all of them at the same time. By the time I realize what I was doing. I was cumming all over my fingers. And like a true superfreak, I licked my fingers and tasted myself. Then I fell asleep.

When I woke up, it was 7:39 p.m. I got dressed in jeans, t-shirt, and tennis shoes. When my phone rang at 8:10 I knew it was Dearaye.

"Hello? Angel?"

"Hey, what's up?"

"Nothing, what you doing?"

"Nothing, I just woke up and I'm hungry. I'm on my way to get something to eat; why don't you meet me?"

"Okay, cool, where're you going?"

"I'm leaving in a few minutes I'm going to T and T. Do you know where T and T is?"

"Come on boo, who don't know where T and T is. T and T's fish, ribs, and seafood is legendary."

"Cool, I should be there in like twenty minutes. I'll probably be there before you. I bet you don't even remember what I look like?"

"That's a bet you would lose. How could I forget you? I'm on my way. One."

I pulled up in front of T and T and tried to find a parking space. The dudes that be vending out here always have some good DVD movies. I hollered at one and bought X-Men 3 and Mission Impossible III. I watch action movies too. I also copped three X-rated movies; Back Dat Azz Up 27, Booty Talk 10, and Anal Gang Bangs in the Amazon. I can't wait to watch them. I put all the DVDs in my truck and walked into T and T. I ordered two pounds of Alaskan crab legs, sat down at the raw bar, and waited for Dearaye.

Dearaye walked in exactly as my melted butter was being served to me. I stood up and we hugged.

"I swear you're going to be my wife. Damn you're fine. I'm in love."

"Boy, sit down and order something. I didn't know what you wanted so I already ordered some crab legs as you can see; you can get your own or share these with me."

"I don't be fucking with them crabs. They stink like hell and they break me out. I'm on them steamed oysters and clams hard." He ordered twelve oysters and twelve clams, steamed. "So, Angel, where's your boyfriend at?" he asked me.

"I don't have a boyfriend. My last boyfriend died. Where's your girlfriend, and don't start lying."

"I have female friends." Dearaye said as he put the melted butter and cocktail sauce on his clams and oysters that were served on half shelves, "but no one special. As fine as you are, there's a man in your life somewhere. Women always say that they're single and then 2:00

in the morning when the dude comes banging on the door because they won't answer the phone, that's when they remember they have a boyfriend."

"Well not me. I'm happily single. I'm doing a whole lot in my life right now so I'm just chilling."

"Doing a whole lot like what?" he asked.

"Damn, you sure are nosey!"

"True, true."

"You'll know more about me when I choose to let you into my world, if I choose to."

Dearaye methodically put Old Bay seasoning and other trimmings on his seafood and I watched him punish his twenty-four clams and oysters before saying another word. He wanted me to try one. I did and actually like it, so I ordered some for myself.

"Angel, you know people say that clams and oysters are sexual stimulants; hint, hint."

"Boy, ease up, you ain't getting none today, so kill that noise. You remember that Chuck Brown joint that said, 'We just met; we can't do that yet'?"

"Sure, you're right."

We both laughed. Then we ordered our meals. I ordered the barbeque chicken dinner and Dearaye ordered the fried catfish dinner. After I finished eating, I was ready to roll. Dearaye must've thought that we were locked in for the night, but I had to bust his bubble.

"Well, thank you for the hospitality and for the meal. I'ma go on home and finish cleaning up, and get ready for work tomorrow." I lied with the straightest face.

"Okay, at least call me tonight. Can I get another one of those hugs?"

"Sure!" We hugged and then we left. I ended up at Fatima's house. But she wasn't home. I figured she must've been with Wop. I figured I'd wait. I have to get her ready for tomorrow. I popped my Mission Impossible III movie in and watched my boy, Tom.

I fell asleep on the couch and woke up to find myself still alone. It was 3:00 in the morning and Fatima still wasn't home. *Where the hell is she?* I called her cell phone and got her voicemail. *She must be somewhere getting her freak on. You go girl.* I called Dearaye on the cell, but got his voicemail too. *He must be getting his freak on too. I ain't mad.* I had plans for him that could wait. My goal is to persuade Dearaye to talk to Deandre into buying at least ten bricks a week, who cares who he's stickin' it to, as long as I get that dough.

Fatima slid through the door around 6:00 a.m. I was like a mother relieved to see her child come home.

"Damn girl, you must really like that nigga Wop, huh? You pulling all-nighters and stuff like you're seventeen years old. Come on, spill the beans. What the sex like?"

Fatima looked at me like she had really been through an all-nighter. She sat down on the couch and kicked off her shoes.

"Angel, that nigga is all of that. He wore my ass out. He had me seeing spirits and stuff. I must've come like ten times. We went to the Econo Lodge off of Branch Avenue, lounged in the Jacuzzi and talked, then he started eatin' my pussy. Girl, I swear, then he fucked me, all night, Angel, all night. I think I love that nigga. Girl, I'm still shaking. So, how was your dinner date?"

"I was alright, nothing like that shit you talkin' about. I met Carlos though and we got to be at the Iverson Mall at 1:00 o-clock, okay."

"Okay, what we doing?"

I ran the whole plan down to her. Then we both decided to get some rest.

Angel

It was 11:15 when I rolled over and looked at my Rolex. I woke up Fatima, showered, and dressed. Fatima did the same. We were out the door by 12:30 and at the mall on time. I did as Carlos said and went shopping. I spent about forty-five minutes looking at shoes, bought a pair of sandals then left. Just as Carlos said, a black Ford Explorer was parked next to my truck. I jumped in the Explorer as Carlos told me to do and Fatima jumped in mine.

At Fatima's house I unloaded the boxes in her garage. There were five boxes containing eleven bricks in each one. The 55 keys of cocaine were at the end of my fingertips. I felt like I was in Columbia or something. The sight of all that coke made me nervous. Just one of those bricks could put me in jail for life and I had 55 of them. I couldn't help but feel like I had finally arrived. I dropped the truck off at Sam's and got in the passenger seat of my truck as Fatima drove off. We stopped to grab a bite to eat and I phoned Carlos.

"Hello Carlos? I can't make it to dinner, boo. I'm going to have to reschedule. Okay, bye."

With that said, I was ready for the world that waited for me.

Wait until they get a load of me.

CHAPTER FIFTEEN

Angel & Dearaye

The first person I called was Doodie. We met at the barbershop and I hit him with three bricks and he hit me with sixty thousand. Then I went to Condon Terrace. That visit with Nome was worth 95 grand. Fatima dropped off the coke after I left with the money. Then I hit Congress Park, Park Chester, Barry Farms, Evans Road, and Wellington Park before calling it a day.

When I got back to Fatima's house, again she wasn't home. I decided to go to Run and Shoot. I haven't been there since Tony died. I changed into sweats and hit the road. I paid the eight-dollar entrance fee while chatting with Tish, who runs the desk at the front of Run and Shoot. I jumped on the treadmill programming it for forty-five minutes on level six and at a level 10 incline. I put on my headphones and listened to Keyshia Cole's CD as I ran. Forty-five minutes later I was exhausted and drenched with sweat. Next to me was a white woman, running just as hard as I had been. *What's a white woman doing out in PG County this hour of the night?*

I showered and got dressed and went back to Fatima's. *Where is she, she's still not home.* I went over to the walk in closet in the bedroom where I had a regular sized four hundred pound safe installed. I pressed my code on the electronic key pad. I looked inside at all the money I had made. *Wow, my plan is working faster than I expected.* I closed the safe and got in Fatima's bed and went to sleep. The next morning, I got up to go meet Demo and Company, Pretty Lady, Sam, and Romeo.

Angel

A lot of people knew that I carried a gun, but for those who didn't know, I let it be known by sitting the Ruger in my lap as I counted their money. The sight of a gun almost always threw dudes off. They never think about girls and big guns. The following day, I successfully hit Face, Gambino, Antwan, and Poo and Russell from Trinidad. With the exception of Nome who owed me $5,000, everybody came correct. So I was two hundred and forty-five thousand dollars richer and I had all the money for Carlos. *If I hustled at this rate, this consistently for the next two years, I could have twenty to forty million dollars. That's what I have to do.*

I called Carlos and told him that I couldn't make it to dinner. I packed the money into a large duffle bag. I met Carlos at Applebee's Restaurant on Donnell Drive in Forestville. I put the bag on the backseat floor and locked the doors. I went into the store and found Carlos as usual, at a booth by the window.

He smiled, stood up, and embraced me.

"Angel, What's up?"

"Hey Carlos."

"How's life treating you Angel?"

"Life's treating me pretty good. I'll call you when I need to see you again." I said and rose to leave. Carlos motioned for me to sit back down.

I knew Carlos was stalling for time so that his associate could get the money out of my truck and leave without me seeing him. I never knew why I wasn't supposed to see him. But, I thought it was better if I didn't ask too many questions. I hadn't really eaten all day so I ordered the chicken and broccoli fettuccine. Sure enough, the bag with the money in it was gone when I got in the truck. *How the hell does he do that?*

I unlocked the door and got in my truck. *I have to find a way to launder my money. Stashing safes everywhere isn't going to get it and I can't fuck with no banks. Mmm, maybe I should open up a beauty salon. Mmm, maybe open a couple of businesses. Yeah, that's what I'm going to do.*

I picked up my cell and dialed my dealership.

"James Smith speaking can I help you?"

"Hi, James, this is Ms. El-Amin. You sold me a car last year, do you remember me?"

"Of course, of course, I remember you. What' can I do for you?"

"Well I was wondering if you still did real estate stuff on the side?"

"I sure do; as a matter-of-fact I have several properties on the market right now. What do you need?"

"I need a house that I can turn into a beauty salon. Can you help me?"

"Ms. El-Amin, don't I always look out for you? Of course I have something for you. It's perfect for what you have in mind. Give me a day or two and I'll set something up so you can see the property I have in mind.

"That sounds good to me. Thank you."

"No, Ms. El-Amin, thank you."

I met Dearaye at Fatima's house. He pulled up in a white Range Rover; it looked like it was on 23's. We went to Annarandel Mills Mall to a spot called Jillian's and then to the movies.

As the day wound down into the night, I decided that the time had come for me and Dearaye to take our relationship to the next level, if you know what I mean. I was ready and I was long overdue. It hadn't been since the night Tony died. I was definitely ready.

Back at Fatima's house I invited Dearaye inside. We lounged on the couch talking until Dearaye asked me to do his hair. I took Dearaye to the bathroom, washed his hair, conditioned, and then blow-dried it. He didn't seem to mind that his hair smelled feminine and fruity. I sat him down on the floor between my legs.

Angel

It's been a long time since I braided some hair, but once you do it, you never forget it. I greased his scalp and went to work. While I plaited his hair, Dearaye had my legs up over his shoulders. He started massaging my toes. Why did he do that? *Does he know about my foot fetish? Lick my toes, lick em.* I wanted to scream the words, but I couldn't, not yet anyway.

After I was finished braiding his hair, I took him upstairs and undressed him silently. I'm not a selfish lover so I don't mind pleasing a man first. I licked him all over and paid special attention to his midsection. I kissed his dick but never put my tongue on it. That drove him crazy. I stood up and undressed for him. Then I did a little striptease dance for him.

"Girl, you look good as shit. Come here, I want to taste you. Come here!"

He didn't have to tell me twice. In a flash, I was laying him down so that I could straddle his face. I run a lot and my calves and thighs are in good shape, so I rode Dearaye's face like I was in a rodeo. Every so often I'd lift up and he'd pull me back down on his face. He had an experienced tongue and he made me come several times before he grabbed a condom from off the dresser and opened it.

I took it from him and put it in my mouth and used my lips and tongue to put it on his dick. I had to relax the muscles in my throat and sort of deep throat the whole dick to get the condom fully on. Dearaye started moaning as I gave him a little neck and throat. I didn't want him to come so I stopped my oral assault, laid him back, and sat on top of him, swallowing his dick inside me. I worked the muscles in my kittykat so he'd feel the tightness.

"Oh! Angel! Oh my God Angel. It feels sooo good; don't stop. Oh Angel! This pussy is like that. Shit!"

Then he came after shaking violently like he was having a seizure. He said something I couldn't understand and went straight to sleep.

The dick was trash to me. I mean, don't get me wrong; I came and everything but the test comes from how long you can put that work in.

The dick can be big and thick and all that good stuff, but if you can only work for ten minutes; the dick is garbage. At least to me it is. I lost all respect for him as I listened to him snoring. It's times like these when I regret killing Tony. He really knew how to please a bitch, tongue, dick, elbows, whatever. I was horny as hell so I played with myself until I came. Then I took a shower and went to sleep.

Then next morning, Fatima and I sat in the kitchen as I told her all about Dearaye.

"Angel, the only reason you gave him some was because you want to get in close with him to manipulate how much money him and his brother spend on coke, right?"

"Yeah, but it was all over so fast. I guess I can't be mad though, huh?"

"Exactly, he's a means to an end, remember that."

"Yeah, you're right. My job is to get him and his brother."

"Exactly, so if you want to throw a little pussy his way in the meantime, so be it, just stay focused on what you're using your pussy for. It's not to marry the nigga; it's to get his money."

"You're right. I'll let him hit the kat a few more times and start whispering in his ear about a nice connect I got for him with a good price and even better product."

"Well do what you do. Me and Wop are going to the Poconos this weekend; are you trying to roll with us? We can get two cabins and do it up."

"I don't know right now. I'll let you know soon. I'm about to go wake Dearaye's weak ass up and put him out."

Angel

"Dearaye! Dearaye! Wake up, boo. I got breakfast on the table for you. Come and eat while it's hot. There's an extra toothbrush in the bathroom medicine cabinet. Get yourself together and I'll see you in the kitchen."

Dearaye tried to grab me and pull me down on the bed.

"Come on boy; food's on the table. I, like most black people, never play games when I'm hungry."

I went back into the kitchen with Fatima and started to eat my French toast, cheese omelet and turkey sausage. A few minutes later Dearaye walked in.

"Fatima, I hear you and my man Wop are hitting it off real well. I hardly see slim anymore."

"Yeah, Wop is my boo." Fatima replied.

"This food is the bomb. Who cooked this, you or Angel?"

'I did, why?"

"I was just asking because it's good, that's all."

After we ate I couldn't get rid of Dearaye's ass fast enough. He kept trying to get a round two in, but I wasn't having it.

"I told you that we'll hook up later. I have some things that I have to do. The sooner I get started, the quicker I'll be done and then we can hook up."

"Okay, boo, I have to handle some business myself. Call me when you're finish." We kissed and then he finally left.

"Girl I think you got that nigga hooked. Damn, I thought he wasn't ever gonna leave. You keep it up and you gonna have that nigga stalkin' you and shit."

"You think he'll buy coke from me?"

"I think he gonna do whatever you want him to."

I decided to take my little sister to the mall to shop and to catch a movie. I haven't spent much time with her so today would be as good as any. I know I need to start spending more time with Adirah because she's at that age where she'll have questions about stuff. She'll need to be around someone other than my mother who is only going to give her the Islamic side of the coin. Adirah needs to know both sides of the coin so she can make the right decisions.

"Angel?" Adirah said. "How come I hardly ever see you anymore? How come you change your number so much? Can we get some snicker doodle cookies? And what mall are we going to?"

I forgot to mention that girlfriend can talk a mile a minute.

"Whoa! Calm down, baby. I have to work and take care of grown folk's business; that's why you don't get to see me often. I change my number all the time because people be playing on my phone and I gave my number to people that I shouldn't have. We're going to Pentagon City and yes, you can get some snicker doodle cookies. Do you want to get something else, like some shoes or clothes?"

"Mommy already bought me all that stuff. Angel, are you Muslim like the rest of us?"

"Yes." I replied.

"Well, why don't you cover your hair and wear clothes that cover your body anymore? What Masjid do you go to and do you have a boyfriend?"

I have to be real with Adirah, so I looked her right in the eye and told her the truth.

"I'm a Muslim because I bear witness that there's no God but Allah and that Muhammad is his messenger and the seal of the prophets from Allah. But right now I'm not on the siratal mustigin. Allah knows my intentions. I'm fighting a jihad within myself, so right now my nafs are getting the best of me. That's why I'm not wearing my hijab and coverings. I don't go to Jumah anymore, but I'm still Muslim. I'm just sinful right now. And no, I don't have a boyfriend. But I will be sure to let you know when I get one Ms. Growny Pants. Adirah, listen, don't use me as a role model because

Angel

I'm not living right. Look up to Mom. Always listen to Mom and when you become old enough to make your own decisions, you can decide what's best for you. Do you understand where I'm coming from?"

"Yeah. Don't tell Mom, but I have a crush on this boy at school named Dawud. I think he likes me too."

"Oh yeah?" I said as I laughed.

Me and Adirah talked about a lot. She's a beautiful little sister who's slowly coming of age. She's very precocious and intelligent. I bought her four pairs of shoes, and several outfits that she'll probably never wear. Then we went to the movies. Afterwards, I dropped her off at home.

"I had fun. Thanks, Angel." Adirah said as she gathered all her shopping bags from the mall.

"I had fun, too. As-Salaamu-Alaikum."

"Wa-Alaikum As-Salaam."

CHAPTER SIXTEEN

Angel & Dearaye

I made good on my word to chill with Dearaye and I let him pick me up from Fatima's house.

"Where're we going?"

"Let's go to Henry's and get something to eat, then we can go to my house. I figured I'd let you into my world, so you can see how a brother's livin'. Plus, my brother should be around so you can meet him. His name is Dre."

Oh I know his name and I've been waiting to meet him.

We went to Henry's on St. Barabas Road and ate a scrumptious soul food meal. Then we went to his house out in Fort Washington, Maryland. It was amazing to say the least, a Dynasty looking mansion located in the affluent part of PG County. I knew that homes like this existed, but I would have never guessed club-hopping, thugged-out Dearaye owned one.

"Do you like it?" Dearaye said as we pulled into his five car garage.

"Like it? It's unbelievable. How many acres do you have? Do you really own this house?"

"Damn, a young black man can't own a big house and some land?"

"That's not what I mean."

"My brother and I bought this house for our mother. She got diagnosed with cancer and we thought this would be nice for her. See that garden, my mother planted that garden by hand. She really loved this house. She died two years ago. The doctors told us that chemotherapy and radiation worked, but they were wrong. The cancer came back."

He paused for a moment as if in deep thought.

"Come on inside. You'll like the inside, let me show you."

Boy oh boy was he right. The house was absolutely beautiful and had everything you could think of, including two kitchens, a home theatre, a wine cellar, indoor heated swimming pool, twelve bedrooms, and sixteen bathrooms.

They must be doing something besides five keys a week for all this. This is some other shit they got going on in here.

Dearaye excused himself and left me in the family room watchin' BET and the new Beyonce video. *Beyonce, Sasha whoever the hell she is, she sure can shake her ass and sing to top it off. Go, B, go!*

"And who might you be?"

I turned around and looked into the most intense hazel brown eyes that I've ever seen. I couldn't respond because I totally mesmerized by the essence of the most gorgeous man I've ever seen in my life. From the contours of his shirt I could see that he was muscular, whereas Dearaye was a little flabby. I knew exactly who he was when I saw the tattoo on his arm and the cobra head biting his neck. He was seven-thirty sexy and confidence lived in his eyes.

"Earth to woman, where's your head at? Who are you?"

"I'm Angel. I'm a friend of Dearaye's. You must be Deandre?"

"That would be me, the infamous me. You can call me Dre. Ray mentioned you, but he didn't tell me you were supposed to be on the cover of a magazine."

I smiled not knowing what else to say. And I'm used to compliments all day and running, it was just that hearing the compliment come from him made me blush and I never blush. *The last guy that made me blush was Andre from college. Snap out of it.* I've come too far in the game to be starry-eyed over a man. But if I did believe in love at first sight, this would be it.

"Alright Angel, I hope to see you again sometime."

Then he left as quickly as he had appeared and a few minutes later, Dearaye came back with photos in his hand. *What the fuck is he doing with pictures?* The nigga had a bunch of photo albums and shit. *Let me find out I got to sit here and look at this nigga's memories.* I guess this was his way of letting me into his world so I looked at his pictures, asked who the people were, and appeared to be interested.

Then Deandre came into the room and Dearaye introduced us. Now for whatever reason this nigga acted like he didn't just see me a few minutes ago.

"Oh, it's nice to meet you." Deandre said shaking my hand like a stranger.

"Nice to meet you too." I answered back.

Before you knew it, a whole conversation had blossomed. I don't know where Dearaye went, it was like he just vanished in the presence of Deandre and we talked for what seemed hours. Dearaye tried to involve himself in our conversation but couldn't gain control of the situation. Finally, the phone rang and Dre went to answer it.

"Hey, my brother can be a real chatter box, if he's getting on your nerves…"

"Oh no, it's fine, I'm use to people who talk a lot."

"Well, we can go if you're ready."

I knew he was trying to get me the hell away from his brother. And I understood.

"Okay, no problem, I'm ready."

"Alright, let me go upstairs and get my baseball cap and keys, I'll be right back."

As soon as he turned the corner, that damn Deandre came out from nowhere like Sneaky Sneaky in Mr. Deeds.

"Oh God, you scared me half to death."

"Sshh." He said as he pressed his finger to my lips. Then he grabbed my hand, kissed it, and put a piece of paper in it. Then like a ghost the nigga just seemed to disappear. I put the paper in my purse and waited for Dearaye.

******

I rushed inside Fatima's house after Dearaye dropped me off. I immediately went to the kitchen, sat at the table, and found the piece of paper Dre had handed me. *Call me. It's important, 555-3235.*

I couldn't help myself. I grabbed the phone and dialed the number.

"Hello?"

"What's so important?" I asked.

"Angel? What's up?"

"What's up? Deandre what kind of games are you playing?"

"I was hoping you would call. Did you feel the chemistry between us today?"

"Deandre, please. Run that weak ass game on somebody else."

"Angel, I'm a grown ass man. I don't play games. I just go after what I want. I didn't get to this point in my life by being passive. So, what you mess with Ray. I still want you. My brother will understand; he's a player. He'll respect the game. It ain't like y' all bummed up. Do you have a commitment to each other?"

"No we don't. But…"

"But what? Y' all had sex, is that it? If y' all did Angel, so the fuck what. That doesn't stop from wanting you. I'm not tripping off that. I'm real. I'll take care of Ray. So tell me right now what's it going to be? Want to go out for dinner or a movie?"

Dinner or a movie, is this guy nuts? What the fuck kind of set up is this? I can't go out with him, they're brothers for Pete's sake.

Deandre, look, boo, I can't lie and say that I didn't feel something when we met. But I don't even know you. I just met you and I don't want to hurt Dearaye."

"Hurt Dearaye? Angel, do you think you're the only woman who Ray has? I know you're not that naïve."

"I'm hip to what you're saying but you're his brother not the next nigga out here, you know what I mean?" *Can't you just cop from me and stop trying to make the game so complicated?*

"Angel listen to me. Fuck society's standards and double standards about females messing with brothers. If you meet one brother, and fall in love with the other, does that mean that you have to stay with the one who you don't want? White women don't. And who says it's wrong for us to be together just because you've slept with my brother? I'm secure with myself. If you don't love Dearaye but you stay with him knowing that you want me, then that would be wrong!"

"I'll tell you what, Deandre, we'll play this thing by ear. Let me break the news to Dearaye then we'll talk. Is that good enough for you?"

"Cool. Make sure you call me back later. Don't make me come looking for you, Angel."

Nigga, you need to look for yourself. This crazy motherfucker is getting ready to put a monkey wrench in my whole plan. I can't do brothers, can I?

Before I could decide exactly how to proceed, my phone rang. It was Dearaye. As soon as I answered, he exploded.

"Bitch, you fucking with my brother! Damn you ain't shit. I brought you up in my crib and you in here hooking up with my brother. You don't even know my brother like that. You fucking me and now you wanna fuck my brother? You're a vicious ho. Who the fuck do you think you're playing with? I should've treated you like the ho that you are. You're a hooker in disguise. I should've busted nuts all in your face and pissed on your ho ass…"

Why didn't Deandre let me tell Dearaye? Why did he tell him? What is wrong with him? Now, he got me in the middle of him and his brother's bullshit. I couldn't believe that Deandre told his brother about me. He wasn't supposed to. But who cares? I had heard enough. I hung up the phone on his punk ass. *Tell it to the dial tone nigga. I don't know who he thinks he's calling a ho? Fuck him!* The dick was trash anyway. Now I can whisper sweet nothings into Deandre's ears and pick his pockets until I get tired of him. He's the main catch of the day anyway. Dearaye will get over it; besides he doesn't have a choice in the matter.

CHAPTER SEVENTEEN

Dearaye

I can't believe this shit. I can't fucking believe he did this shit to me again! He always takes my girl from me. It's all my fault. I should have known better. *Why did I introduce him to her?* All my life my brother has always found a way to end up with whatever it was that I wanted. He always took whatever it was that I had that I cared about. As far back as I can remember he's always done shit like this to me. Take sixth grade, I had the biggest crush on Erica Winslow, somehow she became Dre's girlfriend and he'd play with her at the public park. Without me.

Then, he took Carlena Bowman from me in high school. I had asked her to the prom and everything. I got my suit and shit and I even had a corsage in a box with a yellow bow on it. I got to her door and her parents said she had already left to go to the prom. I was devastated and so hurt, I didn't even go. Later, I found out that Dre had taken Carlena to a motel and they had sex with each other. She was supposed to be my girl and she was supposed to go with me that night to the prom and then we were supposed to go to the hotel and she was supposed to have sex with me, not him.

I remember Dusty, my golden retriever. I loved that dog so much. Dre knew it, too. That's why he was always mean to him. When I wasn't around he abused the dog, kicking him and pulling his tail and doing a bunch of mean shit to him. It got to the point that Dusty wouldn't go near Dre and would only come to me. Dre hated that. He hated Dusty. One day when I came home from school, I found my dog dead in the backyard. Dre laughed at me and called me a cry baby.

"Why you cryin' over that dumb dog anyway?"

"I know you did it. I know you did it. I hate you!"

I charged my brother with all my might knocking him to the ground and throwing blows. My mother had to break it up.

"He killed Dusty! He killed Dusty!"

"Deandre did you harm that dog?"

"No, mom, I swear I didn't kill Dusty."

And that was the end of it, as usual my mother let it go and Dre got away with killing my dog. He swore up and down that he was innocent. But I knew better. I buried Dusty in the backyard and even made him a tombstone. I took two pieces of wood and made a cross out of them with a hammer and some nails and I wrote Dusty's name on the cross. One day I came home and found the cross had been pulled from the ground and was gone. I knew that someone had taken it and in my heart, I knew who that someone was.

Over the years, all the girls that I had a crush on liked Dre. For some reason, everybody like Dre over me and they thought he was my big brother. Maybe that's because I've always let Dre be the big brother when in all actuality I'm the oldest. It's true. I'm older by five minutes. I'm the firstborn son. I'm the one who inherits the birthright and the covenant, like all that biblical stuff. But Dre has always stood out more than me. He was the better athlete, the better dresser, and the better go-getter. In high school, he was voted most popular, best dressed, and best athlete. I was only voted most likely to succeed.

A few years ago, my mother was diagnosed with cancer and I brought in a home health care nurse to take care of her. My mother had 24 hours, seven days a week round about care. I wanted her to be at home, surrounded by her things and all her loved ones in her final days. But Dre didn't want that. According to him, he couldn't stand to see our mother wasting away. One day when I came home, I found my mother gone. Dre had fired the home health care nurse and placed our mother in a nursing home for the terminally ill. My mother died alone with no one around her but strangers. Inside, I never forgave Dre for that, still don't.

You know, I'm out here in these streets trying to make sure that everything's taken care of on the business tip and he calls me with that bullshit. Talking about how he likes Angel and she done chose him. *Chose him? Who the fuck does he think he is, Bishop Magic Don Juan? Chose him? Whatever!* She chose him. To Dre, everything to him is a game. But like everything else, I accepted what he said. I played it off like it was no big deal.

"Hey man, go ahead, run with that bitch. Her head game is phenomenal. Do you."

I couldn't bring myself to tell Dre my true feelings, because I didn't want to seem weak. I could hear him now.

"I know you ain't catch feelings for this bitch? How? Let me find out nigga yousa pussy."

That's a good question, though. *How did I catch feelings?* I think I had feelings for Angel before we even had sex. But, after we had sex, I was really digging her . I had big plans for me and that girl. *Why did she have to choose Dre? I really liked her. I trusted her and everything, took her to my house and showed her my picture book, why?* That was my second mistake. My first mistake was thinking she was different. Now I see that she's just another no good ho like all the rest of 'em.

I called her after I hung from Dre. I shouldn't have done that. I tried to curse her out, but she hung up on me like I was nothing. No female disrespects me like that and gets away with it. This ain't high school, anymore. I think she needs to be taught how to respect her superiors. And one day, Dre is gonna answer to me too. He thinks he's Mr. Untouchable. But he can be touched. Dre thinks that just because he's always handled the dirty work, that I won't get my hands dirty too. Well he's wrong. I'm tired of being his yes man. I've helped to build our empire just as much as he has. I was the one who put in the footwork, all over this city. I was the one who sold all the keys of dope to that nigga Craig Williams. I introduced Dre to those Ethiopian niggas. I introduced him to Rob and Duck and them niggas fuck with me, not him. I was the one who hooked him with Tony Bills and brokered the deal that we had until Tony got killed. I'm the one who makes sure everything runs smooth.

I pay everybody, meet and placate everybody, and drop off and pick up everything. I'm the one on the front line who niggas plot against and hate. I'm the one on the front who niggas are gonna tell on. I'm the one riding dirty with all kinds of shit in the car with me. If the police stop me and search me, I'm gone for life. But Dre doesn't respect that; he doesn't appreciate that. I guess that's not enough to make him recognize the 'G' in me. All he does is reap the benefits of my hard labor and treat me like some kind of flunky. If he's the so-called brains and backbone, then what the hell am I?

Dre got bitches galore. Dime bitches, fine bitches, fly top of the line bitches, but he still wants mine. I could be datin' Minnie Mouse, Dre gots to have her. Why does he always want mine? When our roles reverse, and they will reverse one day, I'll ask him. One day. Until then, it's cool. He can have Angel. I hope he sticks his dick so far in that bitch's throat, he chokes her to death. But, today's a new for Dearaye James and my brother is going to have to learn that the world is not his alone, even if he has to learn the hard way.

He thinks he can just take Angel from me and I'll roll over and play dead like I've always done. Well, baby brother, today is a new day and he has another thing coming. It may take while; but time is always of the essence.

'Patience is a virtue, but if you wait too long, it's cowardice' that's a George Jackson quote and I ain't no coward. He'll see and so will Angel, fucking whore.

CHAPTER EIGHTEEN

ANGEL...

Cooking up coke is a hard job. Especially since new age cooking has taken over. I remember back in the day when coke was coke. Back when there was no such thing as a number system for crack. But when you cooked up 28 grams, you automatically lost 3 grams, but that 25 grams sold out in a minute. No matter how many grams you cooked, you always lost grams but the coke was the best and the prices were high.

Nowadays you can go into the kitchen with 125 grams and some Pyrex glassware and put 40 grams of baking soda on coke with very little water and bring back 160 grams easy. I know dudes who can take one brick and cook it, bring back two brick but the quality of the coke would register high on the dookie scale. And it's hard to move coke that's on the dookie scale. You'll be known as the garbage man or in my case the garbage woman. That's the only drawback of stretching coke; you lose out on the quality, and these day's people want quality not quantity.

But here I am, putting 20 grams on 125 grams. I cooked 4/8. An eighth is 4 ½ ounces, depending on how you sell it. But either way, 4/8 adds up to ½ a key. I decided a couple of weeks ago to break two bricks down and give them out to my lil' homies so they can get some money. I grew up with dudes on Hillside, Simple City, Alabama Avenue, Benning Park, and 54th and D. I looked out for all the youngins I knew so that they could come up. I knew that some of them were real young like 14, but I never felt bad because a fourteen-year-old growing up in the ghetto has no chance of survival out here and that's real. The only thing promised to these young cats is death and jail, so if I can help this nigga eat, then so be it.

I'm making major moves so it's all love. I've branched out to 49th and Call Place, 57th Street, Central Avenue, and Fort Chaplain. I got some good men stomping down on those blocks. I have to swing by there when I leave here. I talk to Deandre a lot, but for the most part, we haven't hooked up yet. I dropped a few lugs into his ear about me having some people with good prices and bomb coke. The bricks that I set aside for him, I've been breaking them down and flipping. I'm almost up to moving a 100 brick a week. I'm doing things that Tony never accomplished. I got all kinds of dudes hollering at me.

I'm the epitome of the new black millennium woman. I'm maintaining a multimillion-dollar drug business while masquerading as the average Jane. After I did all my drop-offs and pick-ups, I had to go meet James. He wanted me to look at a house that I'm interested in buying. He said it would make the perfect store front beauty salon.

Driving down Benning Road, I noticed the same black Caprice wagon was still behind me. I always work my mirrors to monitor my surrounding. At first I thought nothing of it because all my side stops were basically in the same area, but then I noticed the wagon again up by 54th and D, and by Benning Park. The windows were tinted so I couldn't see the passenger. Maybe I'm just being paranoid, maybe not. I turned off Benning Road and went toward Bladensburg Road. The wagon kept straight so I eased my mind a little. I must've been lunching.

The house that James wanted to show me was located off of Queens Chapel Road around the corner from the DC Tunnel Nightclub. That's a good location. I pulled up to the house and saw James's red Ford Expedition outside. I looked at the house; it was perfect. It was a sturdy, three-story brick building. It needed quite a bit of work, mostly painting; wiring, minor repairs, a good cleaning, and modern fixtures and appliances.

It was perfect.

"I'll take it."

"That will be easier said than done. Kareemah. You have no credit, no job, and tax returns.

I ended up paying James some cash under the tables and he ended up hooking everything up for me. At twenty-four, I Kareemah El-Amin, became a first time home owner. I named my beauty salon, Angel's Beauty and Barber Palace. The first floor would be renovated and restored to be a barbershop while the second floor would operate the beauty salon. The top floor of the three-story building would be like a private club or lounge room and the basement would be recreational and that's where I'd put my office.

I had everything all laid out. Once the Palace gets off the ground, I plan on opening a communications outlet store. I want to feature all the top of the line gadgetry in communications from companies like Nextel, Motorola, Verizon, Erricson, and MCI.

First things first though and the first thing is the Palace. My plan is to have it opened in the next ninety-days. Fatima will be the manager of the hair salon and run things for me. It will be good for her because she can set her own hours and have more time to spend with that damn Wop. And that's exactly what she wants anyway. All she knows is that the sun rises and sets out of his asshole.

Since she has so much free time on her hands, I had her contact a plumbing company to lay new pipes and fixtures. Then the electricians and electronic people came in and ran wires for me for everything from electric to internet, sound, and security. The carpenters and drywallers were next, then roofers and window installers. Finally, the painters and carpet installers completed the interior. I contacted a company called Sign-A-Rama and they came out and mounted 'Angel's Beauty and Barber Palace' on top the of the first-level roof in front of the house.

I paid people to pass out fliers for the grand opening and paid for commercials on 93.9 WKYS and on 95.5 WPGC the most popular radio stations in DC. I even paid for a commercial on Channel 32, the Howard University station. I was ahead of schedule and excited because everything was on track for my legal and illegal operations. Over the last two months I done moved more bricks that you could talk about. I finally convinced Deandre into copping from me, so he's buying ten to fifteen keys a week at twenty-three a piece. It wasn't easy, but I got it done. Thank goodness for my goodies.

Fatima, Wop, Deandre, and I all went out to the Poconos about a month ago for a weekend getaway. We rented separate cabins next door to one another. But, I didn't see them niggas the whole time we were there. Dre had me held up like a hostage and shit. Me and Dre lounged around all day and made love all night. All we did for three days was have sex.

Nobody has ever made me feel that good since I don't know when. Don't get me wrong, Tony was great in bed, but Deandre was intense, creative, and totally uninhibited. Those three days in Pennsylvania were like being out in the wild. Believe me when I say that I cried, laughed, moaned, shook, fought, and love hard that weekend. I did things to Dre that you would never think of, things that I got off the freak movies.

I experimented, enjoyed, and experienced a whole lot in those three days. I gave Dre the forbidden fruit that Tony had taken from me. Ever since we went anal, Dre and I have been together almost every day. He was the one who dealt with most of the contractors and workers who worked on the Palace. He's so bright in business and so smart. He gave me the best ideas and really helped me with the grand opening. I hired my friend, Tamara as my accountant. I had

Fatima managing and Tamara doing all the counting. It took a lot out of me to woo her away from her day job at TD Waterhouse, but I did it.

About two months after the shop opened, I was sitting in the salon watching one of the flat screens on the wall as the hairdressers and patrons moved about when my phone started ringing.

"Hello."

"Angel, these niggas out here just tried to kill me."

"What? Are you okay?"

"Man, these niggas tried to get me at the Amaco. I got out the trunk, paid for my gas, and when I came from the cashier booth, a burgundy car was parked at the pump behind my truck. As I reached for the gas nozzle, three dudes got out of the car and pulled hammers on me. One said, "you better not run." And another said, "Come here." Man, I hauled ass so fast you would've thought I was Carl Lewis. Them niggas started shooting at me and chased me into Capers Projects and I hid in the bushes."

"Then what happened?"

"Nothing, I laid on the ground and tried to cover myself with leaves and shit and I called Ray."

"Then what happened?"

"I stayed in the bushes until he got there, then we went back to the gas station where my truck was. Shit was still sitting at the pump. My hammer was still under the seat and I had like $23,000 in the glove box that was still there. So, they weren't trying to car jack me or rob me, they were definitely trying to murk a nigga. I can't believe this shit, I got lady bugs and shit still crawling on my ass."

I know he's not complaining. Nigga, you are a drug dealer, what do you think these motherfuckers out here will do to you? Play fair? Let me find out this nigga is really a pussy.

"Well, I'm just glad you're okay."

"No, I'm really not okay. I'm dirty, I got bugs crawling on me, niggas trying to get at me and my head is killing me."

Dre was definitely shook. But I managed to calm him down. We discussed different scenarios about who was behind the almost abduction.

"I bet them niggas wanted to kidnap me and hold me for ransom. I bet that's what they was trying to do. That's why they said 'come here'. If they wanted to kill me they could have right there at the gas pump. But, they didn't, I'm telling you, they was trying to kidnap me."

The question wasn't what were they trying to do; the question was who was trying to do it? And truth was; it could have been anyone. His lifestyle was too high profile for a small city like DC, actually both of us were. Truth was we both had to be careful. We were in the most dangerous business, in one of the most dangerous towns. And honestly, the last thing I wanted was to be abducted. So, I made sure to be extra careful.

With that all that said and done, I focused back on expanding the drug business in the streets. My youngins from Hillside had stepped up their game and were moving two keys a week. As long as I kept the coke buttery, they kept all the clientele happy and we made all the money. It wasn't just them either, everyone was prosperous and everyone kept coming back to re-up.

Then I got a call from my little homie, B, from Hillside. He said three dudes in a Caprice wagon pulled up on the strip and robbed him. Then Lil Butch called saying his mans and them got robbed by three niggas in the same kind of car and Donte from Alabama Avenue called and said his man had just been robbed and gunned down and the getaway driver was in a Caprice wagon.

Wasn't that a Caprice wagon that was following me that day and parked outside my house? Damn, now my money is gonna be fucked up. Fuck a duck, when it rains it pours. And who the fuck is behind the wheel of this Caprice wagon? I got to get to the bottom of this and real quick.

Then two weeks later, I go to see Sean and Chris and they tell me about a Caprice wagon that pulled up on the block, but they peeped the move and sent over 50 shells in it's direction. It sped off and never came back. But one thing is clear, these niggas is trying to knock everybody I'm down with. *I wonder if I'm next.*

Just as I was leaving Sean and Chris, Dre calls me with his panicked ass.

"Somebody done robbed my workers."

Shit, they robbing mines too. But, I didn't say a thing. Dre still didn't know I was the one serving him keys of coke. He thought I got the coke from my uncle. Dre didn't know where I lived. He thought I lived at Fatima's house and at the end of the day, that's what he needed to keep thinking. I digested everything he was saying and all the while I couldn't help thinking that there was a strange connection to everything that was going down; a very strange and unusual connection. I just couldn't figure out what it was.

Ring. Ring. Ring. Ring. Ring.

"Hello?"

"Yo' Tommy?"

"Yeah, this is me."

"Start putting phase two in effect."

"I'm on it."

I was on my way from Run and Shoot when I got the call. Things were starting to get nasty.

"Angel, what's up? This is Marvin."

"Ain't nothing Marvin; what's up with you?"

"Bad news, boo, bad news. Can I talk on this phone?"

"Nooo, never talk on no phone! Give me a minute and I'll be right there."

I hung up the phone. It took me twenty-two minutes to be exact before I pulled up on Marvin's block. I hit his cell phone and he emerged from a building and hopped in my car and started running the day's events down to me.

"About two hours ago a beige Crown Vic pulled into the circle and caught everybody off guard. Four dudes pulled out hammers and started robbing the strip. So, Lil' Chucky, he starts running and one of the dudes shoots him in the back and then they left. Then my man, Pac, grabbed Lil' Chucky and took him to DC General. Man, these niggas is fucked up about that shit; everybody ready to ride down on whoever they got to."

"Did you recognize them?"

"Man, I ain't recognize shit, two of 'em had on masks and the other two were barefaced. Didn't nobody look familiar to me. Man, I don't know, Shorty ain't nothing but fifteen years old and he don't even be hustling, he just be out here with us and they sayin' he not gonna make it."

"Alright, listen, I got to go, but I want you to call me if you hear anything."

"You know I will."

I don't know what's going on, but something's cooking. I can smell it and taste it. I don't want to involve Deandre because I knew he had problems of his own. But, I know that I have to do something. So, I decided to enlist a few good men to be in position to move out, if and when I say so.

Although, I wouldn't hesitate to bust my gun, the smart thing to do is to pay somebody else to put the work in, and I know exactly who to holler at. I thought about two thugged out gangsta niggas that

I knew from high school because their names were ringing bells all over the city. These two niggas had been crushing shit since their teens. And I knew exactly where to find Stink and Boochie.

On my way to Sayles Place Projects, Marvin called me and told me that Lil' Chucky didn't make it. *That poor young kid. He wasn't even in the game. Why don't these niggas go to a gun range and learn how to aim if they want to run around with guns?*

I pulled up on Sayles Place and saw Stink outside with some other dudes knee-deep in a crap game. I jumped out of my truck and was held up under a million eye balls. I called out to Stink, who looked up, and did a double take and threw up one finger as if to say, 'wait a minute'. A couple of minutes later Stink walked up to me. I hadn't seen him in a while, but he still looked the same- grimey.

"Sister Kareemah Muhammad Akbar, what's up or should I say, As-Salaikum Salaam or whatever?"

"Knock it off Stink; you know my name ain't no Muhammad Akbar. And the greeting is As Salaamu Alaikum. But that's neither here nor there. A simple hello will do." I replied.

"Fuck that shit. What's the difference anyway?" Stink asked. "Muhammad, Akbar, El-Amin, it's all the same Farrakhan Mooslim shit ain't it?"

I didn't like being put in the position of defending my beliefs when I was violating all the articles of my faith myself. What could I tell a babbling fool, anyway?

"Look Stink, I don't care what you call me; I'm here because I need your assistance."

He looked me up and down with a contemptuous look. "You need my assistance. Hold a minute. I saw you over at Barry Farms about a year ago. You was with that nigga Tony Bills, acting like you was God's gift to the world. I spoke to you and you acted like you didn't even hear a nigga. Now you pop up over here out of the blue talking about you need my assistance. Picture that with one of those digital camera. If you'll excuse me, I have money over here to win."

He turned around and walked away. I couldn't give up because I needed him.

"Whoa, hold on a minute, Stink. Just hear me out. If you don't like what I'm saying, then you can go back to your small change crap game. I'm trying to put you down with some serious money. Just hear me out."

"You got three minutes, Kareemah, and then I'm gone." Stink said as he walked toward me.

"I'm really sorry for the way I came off at the Farms or wherever. I must've been mad at Tony or going through PMS and I took it out on you. But honestly, I don't remember the day you're talking about. I would never have purposely thrown you shade. You should know that. You, me, and Boochie go back to school days when people were wearing S-curls and hi-top K-Swiss. So why would I fake the funk on you? But like I said, if you took it that way, I'm sorry. Now what I need from you is those things that you do so well. I want to hire you and Boochie to be on my team."

"Your team?"

"Yes, my team. I made some strong moves after Tony got killed. Now there's a lot of people in my business. At the present, everything's kosher, but if the need arises, I need a few good men to put in that work. I'm paying cash and a lot of it. See, I think I'm being followed and a lot of dudes I'm supplying seem to be getting robbed. I don't really know if all the things that are going wrong right now are connected. I'm just trying to look ahead. If and when I need you and Boochie, I'll call you. I'll meet you, fill you in on what needs to be done, and bring a down payment. I know how y' all ride and I respect the way y' all get down. I have $10,000 in the truck for you, right now. Sort of like a retainer's fee. You and Boochie trying to get paid or what?"

Stink looked at me like I was the one who was crazy.

"You really have changed little Kareemah Farrakhan Bey. When I knew you last, you were the little Mooslim girl at school. Now you're the female Nino Brown, huh? I can dig it. Who am I to make waves? I'm feeling you on that money shit, though. For the right amount of money, I'll go at the pope in Rome, while he's riding his Popemobile. I'll catch the bus to kill a preacher at Sunday school. I'll dig a hole and wait for Bin Laden's ass just to smoke him. It's no problem. As long as that cheddar is proper, holler at your boy. I know that Boochie is down for whatever. So yes, you can rest assured that if you need us, we'll come running."

"Where's Boochie, anyway?"

"He got a broad in the spot. He's getting his nuts out the sand right now. But I'll surely holler at him and let him know what's up."

"It's all good. I'll see him next time I come through. Come and get the ten gees." Stink followed me to the truck. I gave him the $10,000. "Give me a number for you and one for Boochie in case I can't reach you."

I programmed both numbers into my cell phone, then made a quick getaway in case I was being followed.

I put the conversation I had with Stink in the back of my mind as things slowly returned to normal. I paid for Lil' Chucky's funeral and tried my best to calm down a rack of buck wild youngins who wanted revenge. After the Simple City youngins rode down on a few of their enemies and killed a couple of dudes in Lil Chucky's name, they were straight. Life moved on eventually and money started to flow again. I lost a lot of money that month, but in this game one has to expect a couple of losses. My pockets were too deep to even feel the pinch.

Things took off at the Palace. The Washington Post did a small article about the Palace in the business section. James called me one day and showed me a storefront property that was up for leasing. It was perfect for the communication store. Again James took care of all the paperwork. Over the next couple of months; I went through the same renovating process that I did when I first opened the Palace. I couldn't do a whole lot because the space was leased and not bought. Once the store was ready, my friend Roy came through with all the contacts to all the big communications companies and before you knew it, I had contracts with everybody. I offered Roy a managerial position at Angel's communications Outlet and he accepted.

I was still seeing Carlos every week and supplying everybody as usual. It was time for a vacation so me, Dre, Wop, and Fatima went to Jamaica then hopped over to the Caymen's Islands. Of course I opened a bank account while I was there. What can I say, life is grand.

CHAPTER NINETEEN
ANGEL

Ring. Ring. Ring. Ring. Ring.

I opened my eyes and looked at the clock. *Who on God's green earth can this possibly be calling me at 3:26 in the morning?* I thought as I reached for the phone.

"Hello?"

"Why haven't you been answering your phone? I've been trying to reach you all day." The caller shouted into the phone. I could hear her sobbing.

"Mom, is that you?" I shot up out the bed like a bullet. "What's wrong? Why you cryin'?"

"If Fatima wouldn't have given me this number, I wouldn't have been able to…"

"Mom, you're scaring me; what's wrong?"

"It's Adirah, baby. She's gone!"

"What do you mean she's gone?"

"She's gone! We can't find her. She didn't come home from school yesterday. Please tell me you know where she is. Please tell me that Adirah's with you!"

"Mom, please calm down! It's hard for me to understand you."

"Don't tell me to calm down! My baby is missing and you tell me to calm down. I'm losing my mind."

"Mom, where are you?"

"I'm home, where you think. Your uncles are out lookin' for her. Can't nobody find her. I just came back home from the 6th District Police Station filling out a missing person's report.

"Mom, I'm on my way."

I hung up and got dressed. In seconds I was headed out the door. I must've run every light from Marlboro Pike to Benning Road because I got to 6-D in like, three minutes.

What the fuck is going on? Something's not right with this picture. I felt like a heavy weight had been thrown on my head. Adirah kept flashing through my head and for some strange reason I knew deep down inside that Adirah being missing had something to do with me.

I parked the car and ran up the steps to my mother's door. I rushed inside and heard my mother in the kitchen crying. She was sitting at the table, with photos of Adirah scattered all about.

"I had to give the police a photo, so I gave them this one." She said holding up the most recent head shot of Adirah from school.

"Mom, what are the police saying?"

"They talking about there's nothing they can do because she has to be missing for twenty-four hours before they start to investigate. But, they let me put in the report anyway and if she doesn't show up tonight a detective will be here in the morning because the last time I saw her was yesterday morning when she left out for school. I called her little friend, Monica, and she said the last time she saw Adirah was after school got out and she was headed home, walking up E Street as usual. Angel, I'm scared. She was in school, everybody saw her leave school and walk him like she does every day."

I held my mother as she broke down again. It broke my heart to see her so distraught. I couldn't help myself and I began to cry too.

"Have you checked with all her friends, Mom? You sure she didn't go over to anybody's house on her way home?"

"I've checked with everybody. She's just gone; vanished into thin air."

"Naw, she's got to be somewhere. Don't worry we'll find her mom. We'll find her."

"Angel, no, I'm telling you something ain't right. Adirah wouldn't do nothing like this. She's too responsible. She would've called me. She doesn't do stuff like this. Something's wrong."

"Have you checked all the hospitals?"

"I've checked, Angel. I've checked everything you could think of. She's not there." Then my mother raised her hand toward the sky. "Oh, Allah! I seek refuge in you from Shaiton. Oh Allah, please protect my daughter and bring her home safely." Then she fell to her knees and threw her body on the floor.

I watched my mother pray in the middle of the kitchen floor and I was helpless. What could I do to comfort my mother? I wanted to tell my mother that everything was going to be all right, but I couldn't. I didn't want to leave my mother but I had to. None of this made any sense. Adirah wouldn't just up and run away. I'm sure of that, so the only conclusion that I could come to was that somebody snatched her, but who? I decided to wake up Deandre.

"Hello?" he said sleepily.

"Somebody snatched my little sister!" I still couldn't believe it, even as I said it.

"What?" he said. "Hold on. Who dis, Angel?"

"Yeah, it's me. Did you hear what I just said?"

"You said something about your little sister. What time is it?"

"Somebody's snatched my sister! She's gone! She never came home from school." I shouted into the phone.

"Who snatched her? Where are you?"

"I'm riding around trying to figure that out. I just wanted to let you know what's going on. I..."

"Where are you right now? I'm coming to you..."

"Naw, I need to be alone right now. I need to think. But let me ask you something. Have you noticed that in the last couple weeks, niggas tried to snatch you and shot at you, both our workers been getting robbed, Lil' Chucky is dead, and somebody been following me and now my sister's gone. Isn't all of this too much of a coincidence?"

"I feel you, boo." Dre said. "Do you think all that shit is related?"

"Yeah, I do. I know my sister, and she just didn't run away. Somebody has my sister and when I find out who, I'ma kill 'em. Let me get off this phone. I'll call later."

"Angel, let me…"

I hung up on Dre and drove back to my mother's house. My four uncles were distraught. And my mother was still crying. You could see the hurt and pain in her face. I felt helpless, and I never feel that way. The phone rang and everybody jumped at the sound. My uncle's Samir's eyes lit up like a Christmas Tree.

"It's Aminah, she wanted to know if we found Adirah yet." My uncle Hassan said hanging up the phone.

Then the phone rang again and Uncle Hassan answered it.

"No, please don't hurt her. We'll do whatever you wanted, just don't hurt her."

Then he hung up the phone and turned to everyone in the room.

"Adirah's been kidnapped. Why, I don't know, but the voice on the phone said that she's safe, all praises due to Allah, and that he wants a lot of money for her return. The voice said he'll call back with instructions."

My mother passed out.

I couldn't take no more and I left the house. Tearfully, I drove around until I got tired, then I drove to my apartment and ran bathwater. I sat in the tub wracking my brain for answers. In my heart, I knew that no matter what my family did, Adirah was doomed. The El-Amins are poor, my family doesn't have any money to pay a ransom for Adirah. But I did. And whoever snatched my sister knew that. Plus, in my heart of hearts, I knew that the money wasn't really the issue because whoever was behind this could've snatched me or Fatima. But, they didn't, they snatched a little girl. *Why Ahdeerah? Why?* I just wish I knew who it was. Who the fuck was behind kidnapping my little sister? *Maybe it's one of the dudes I deal with? Carlos? It can't be him; I haven't done anything wrong.* I'm going to track down the motherfuckers that's behind this caper and when I do, they are gonna know that they fucked with the wrong bitch.

And it was at that very moment, I felt my heart get heavy for my sister. I knew I'd never see her alive again, not in this life time anyway. Tears began to stream down my face and I sunk my head under the water in the tub to wash them away.

Angel, stop it! What the hell are you doing? You're sitting in a bath tub. Get up! Get up now and save Adirah. What is wrong with you? Pull yourself together and go get your sister.

I jumped up, grabbed a towel, wrapped it around me, then I reached for my cell phone. I dialed a familiar number.

"Hello?"

"Stink, It's me Kareemah. I need to see you and Boochie right now. Can y' all meet me at Horace and Dickies on MLK in like fifteen minutes?"

"We'll be there!"

I hung up the phone, dressed, and was out the door in less than five minutes.

When I pulled up to Horace and Dickie's fish market, Boochie was sitting on the hood of a BMW wagon, eating a fish sandwich, while Stink stood nearby talking on a cell phone. I walked over to both of them then led them to the back of the alley behind the market. The butt of my .45 automatic Colt hung casually out of my waistband.

The gun must've had an effect on both dudes because they kept staring at it. Then their eyes met mine as I spoke.

"The situation is this. Somebody's snatched my little sister. Whoever's behind this shit called my house and requested a ransom. They said they'd call back with instructions. In my heart, I already know I'm never gonna see my little sister again.

"I'm not waiting either for them to make a move. Fuck that, I need to know who is behind this and I need to know now. I have $100,000 with me now for you two to split as a down payment. I want you to find out all the niggas that's known kidnappers and serious gunslingers for hire, question them, then kill them.

"I want so much blood to run in the streets that motherfuckers think it's the Red Sea. I think the only way, we might be able to save her is if we start killing these niggas out here and these motherfuckers realize this shit ain't no game. They might just let her go with a paid ransom." A tear fell down my eye despite my effort to hold it back.

"Maybe you'll come across someone who knows about my sister. When the job is completed I have another $100,000 a piece for both of y' all. Just be smart and don't get caught. Once the word goes out that dudes known for kidnapping are dying in the streets, maybe these niggas will bow down and not want a war. Before you kill these dudes don't forget to ask questions. Call me in a few days with your progress. And if you find anything; let me know soon as possible."

"We on it." Boochie said. "I'm sorry about your sister, Kareemah. I'm a ride for you, Boo. I hate when dudes bother kids. I'd kill these dudes for free."

"Thanks, Boochie. Holler back."

CHAPTER TWENTY

THE NEWS

"**G**ood evening, this is Maria Wilson, reporting live to you from the corner of 13th and Congress Street, Southeast where three black men, who appear to be in their mid to late thirties, have been found dead with gunshot wounds to the back of the head. The bodies were found by two nine-year-old students on their way home from school. All three bodies were pulled from a trash dump container in the alleyway of Congress Street.

"All three bodies seem to have been shot twice in the back of the head at point-blank range. The police have ruled out robbery as a motive as all three men seem to still be wearing hundreds of thousands of dollars in jewelry. These three murders bring the total body count to twenty-eight for the past two weeks. That's right, twenty-eight people murdered here in Congress Park in only two weeks.

"Officials indicate that Washington, DC is on the fast track to becoming the nation's murder capital. I've just been told that we have DC Police Chief Arthur Ramsey standing by and in a few minutes, we'll speak to him live.

"For all those who've just joined us, this is Maria Wilson of City Under Siege Fox News reporting live from the corner of 13th and Congress Street, Southeast, where three men were found dead just hours ago. All three men were killed execution style and the authorities have ruled out robbery as a motive. We now go live to the Municipal Center where Lauren Horner is standing by live with DC Police Chief Arthur Ramsey. Lauren!"

"Good evening everyone. This is Lauren Horner reporting live from the Municipal Center, the headquarters of Chief Police Arthur Ramsey. I have Chief Ramsey here with me who can hopefully shed some light on the high rate of murders that have brushed through the city like a wild fire. Chief."

"Hello Lauren. What we are experiencing right now in DC is a spate of execution style murders. The last time we saw this many murders in one week, was back in 1988 when we had an influx of out of town drug dealers like the Jamaicans, New Yorkers, and Miami gangs that came to the district and literally went to war with local drug dealers over trafficking and territory. Not since then have we seen a time like this. These recent murders are barbaric, gruesome, cold, and calculating and we promise that whoever is behind these murders will be caught and brought to justice."

"Chief Ramsey, what can you tell the viewers about these murders?"

"Well, Lauren, we don't have a lot of leads at this time and what information we do have, I'm not at liberty to discuss at this point because these murders may all be related and are part of an ongoing investigation."

"Chief Ramsey, do you have any suspects or anything that you can give the public to reassure the residents of DC that this blood bath will come to an end?"

"Well, like I said and I say again, at this time we don't have much to go on in regards to motives or to any possible suspects, but I can say that no one has been arrested for these murders. Right now we're comparing evidence gathered at each crime scene and hopefully we will be able to see whether or not these recent executions are all related.

"I've put more officers on foot patrols and in police cruisers. I've personally talked to the mayor who's very concerned about the number of homicides in the past several weeks. I've assured him that the Metropolitan Police Department is doing everything possible to keep the streets safe. Our number one priority right now is to make arrests and stop these murders. Whoever, is behind these brutal attacks must be brought to justice and our streets be made safe."

"Chief Ramsey, is there a number that people can call with any information about these murders?"

"I'm glad you asked that. Yes, there's a number that people can call if they have any information that may assist us in stopping these horrific and brutal murders. The number is 202-679-0074. Again the number is 202-679-0074. We're urging anyone with information about the murders in the past several weeks to give us a call. We are going to need the public's help and any information we receive from the public will be kept confidential."

"Thank you, Chief. This has been Lauren Horner reporting to you live from the Municipal Center, back to you Maria."

"Lauren, what's the atmosphere like down there?"

"Maria, let me just say that this current wave of homicides has everybody on edge. I've been here for maybe twenty minutes and you can feel the tension in the air. I witnessed the chief in conference with several top officials in the Police Department and a liaison from the mayor's office has been here all day I'm told. So Maria, there's definitely a lot of activity going on and decisions being made about what to do to stop these brutal killings.

"Thank you, Lauren. For anyone who has just tuned in, this is Maria Wilson reporting from City Under Siege Fox News, live in Southeast where three dead bodies have just been pulled from a dumpster. We will have more details for you tonight on Fox News at eleven."

CHAPTER TWENTY-ONE

ANGEL

Every news station in the metropolitan area has been broadcasting stories about the recent onslaught of homicides in DC. I just finished watching one and I must say that Stink and Boochie are doing a wonderful job in the killing field. The streets are watching and everybody's listening. The word on the streets is that somebody is killing crutty dudes who kidnap and kill for a living.

You can literally see the fear in people's eyes as you drive through the streets. You can read the 'am I next look in niggas' eyes. The killings are so brutal and accurate that even the hustlers are paranoid. When the streetlights come on, everybody goes inside. It's been a week since Adirah was taken and we still haven't been contacted again by her captors.

My family is torn apart and we are all holding onto the hope that Adirah is alive and will return to us, safe and unharmed. But, the truth is, I know better. I already know she will never ever return. Ever since the night my mother told me, I felt the cold hand of her death. I know I will never see her again in this life, I know and my heart is broken because she's gone. I can't explain the pain that aches in my heart for my sister. You know I'd kill my own father, if it meant saving her life. I'd die for her, without a second guess and now I wish I could trade places with her, my little sister, sweet, sweet, Adirah. She had so many dreams and aspirations. She had all of her life in front of her, to just be taken is so meaningless and her life had meaning. The worst of it all, is that she is gone because of me, because of my life style. I know the truth. I need not seek anything except revenge at this point and vengeance shall be mine so sayeth the Lord. Then I'll be that, but I will revenge her in this life or the next. I will not stop, until I find her captors and I will not stop until they pay, and I promise you, they will.

Exactly, nine days after my sister was taken, what I already knew to be true, became a reality. The police contacted my mother to advise our family that a young black female who fit the description of my sister had been found in Fort Dupont Park. My mother collapsed and she fell to the floor.

My uncle called and I met him at the city morgue to ID the body. It was her. It only took one glance to see that it was her. She had been found bound at the ankles and her wrists had been tied tightly behind her back. She was completely defenseless. Her mouth was gagged with her own panties and duct tape had been placed over her mouth. She had been severely, beaten, raped, sodomized, and then strangled. She was found only fifteen blocks from my mother's front door. All that searching and she was only fifteen blocks away.

My heart ached at the sight of her. My mind tried to imagine the pain she had endured and I couldn't help to think of my beautiful little sister being brutally tortured to death. She'd never know love, she'd never grow up, she'd never be a mommy, she'd never be with me again and I couldn't hold it back. The sight of her broke me down and I couldn't stand anymore. I dropped to my knees in front of the table that she laid on. I couldn't do anything to help her and I cried for her. I cried for her pain and I cried for all the love I had for my sister.

I'm so sorry Adirah, I'm so sorry. It's all my fault this happened to you. I'm so sorry, but I promise I will get them. Do you hear me? I will get them.

The sound of my cell phone ringing brought me out of the silent reverie I was in.

"Hello?"

"Kareemah, this Stink. Can you meet me? I got something you need to hear. You alright?"

"Yeah, Stink, they found her body, she'd dead, Stink, she's dead."

"Kareemah, I'm sorry to hear that, but this is gonna make you feel better, trust me."

"Okay, where you at?"

"Meet me at the HOBO Shop."

"Ten minutes."

The line went dead.

I hadn't been to the HOBO Shop in a long while. I pulled up on Southern Avenue and saw Stink's BMW wagon parked out front. I walked into the shop and saw Stink and Boochie. They led me outside and we got back in my truck. Then he dropped his bombshell on me."

"We snatched up this chump from 18th and D, named Baby Daddy. Him and a dude named Rick be putting in work on that side. After I shot the dude in both legs and both arms, he broke down and spilled the beans on your little sister. Not only that, but he said his partner was talking to some other dude about a broad named Angel that was moving a lot of weight. He said his man Twin told his partner that you stayed heated and you barely slip. You were the target, but they couldn't get at you, so this nigga Twin set it up for them to snatch your sister. They thought they was snatching her for change, but that was just a set up. Once they snatched the girl, the nigga Twin told his partner to kill her. The Baby Daddy dude told me everything, how they ran trains on her for days, and then they killed her. And the most important thing this Baby Daddy nigga said was that his man Twin is a twin and he wants to kill his brother too. Do you know who this nigga Twin could be, cause Baby Daddy said he don't know the nigga's real name and I clucked this nigga in his head for hours, but that was all he could give me."

My blood ran cold and I couldn't believe what I just heard. All this time, I never thought that Dearaye was my enemy. I never knew that he was fucked up that much about me and Deandre. Another one of the principles of the Art of War is to know thine enemy. I violated a major principle of the Art of War and now I'm paying dearly for my mistake. But how could I have known that a piece of pussy would drive a sane man to unthinkable acts? Who knew that he took my relationship with Deandre's as the ultimate betrayal? I knew that he was mad because he called me and cursed me out, but I had no idea he was homicidal.

"I know who he's talking about. The twin's name is Dearaye. He was mad at me because I cut him off and started fucking with his brother, Deandre. But I had no idea that he'd pull some shit like this. Okay. Dearaye's the target now. He doesn't hang in any one spot, but he grew up on Saratoga Avenue. Start looking for him there. I haven't seen him in a while, but I know he owns a deli on St. Barabas Road. Find him in the next twenty-four hours and I'll have another $100,000 for both of y'all. I want him alive and well. Call me when you have him. You got that?"

"No doubt." Stink said.

"What did you do with the dude, Baby Daddy, who gave y'all the information?"

"I blew his muthafuckin' brains out."

"Good."

CHAPTER TWENTY-TWO

ANGEL & DEARAYE

I sat in my apartment and patiently waited to hear from Stink. *That punk ass nigga Dearaye did all this shit. I can't believe it. All because I didn't wanna fuck with his three-minute ass. I couldn't believe it was him who was responsible for my sister's death. What the hell was this nigga thinking? Is he fucking stupid or just crazy?* I couldn't believe it, just didn't want to believe it. *They ran a train on my little sister.* I wiped a tear; I'm so tired of crying I don't know what to do. But I can't help it. Every time I imagine Adirah being gang-raped by them niggas, I cry. I had a nightmare about Adirah once. It was the day after I identified her beaten and bruised body. I haven't slept much since. My sleep will never be peaceful until I get my hands on Dearaye and on all the dudes who played a part in her death.

Keeping with Islamic tradition, my beautiful little sister was cleaned, anointed with oils, and then wrapped in shrouded sheets. Forty-eight hours after she was found murdered, she was buried. Although I hadn't bumped my head in prayer in years, I made Janazah salat for my sister. I prayed for both our souls.

The police told my mother that they had gathered a lot of clues, but as of yet, still had no suspects. Fuck the police. They don't have to worry about doing their jobs. Deputy Dog here is already on the case. I wish I could tell my mother not to worry, but I couldn't. I have to deal with everything quietly. And I have it all figured out in my head.

I'ma make Dearaye tell me everybody who was involved in my sister's rape and murder. Then I'ma kill him and everybody else who he names. Then I'll have to kill Deandre. *Why does love hurt so much? Every dude who I love, I have to kill. Why?* But, if I let that nigga live and he finds out I killed his brother, he'll come after me. It's the law of retribution. So, that nigga gots to go too.

Then the thought came to me about what Baby Daddy told Stink. He said that Dearaye talked about killing me and his brother. He wants to get rid of Deandre, maybe I should let him pop Deandre for me. Naw, I can't do that because what if he comes for me first and not his brother. No, the best thing to do right now is stay focused. And the best weapon that I have right now-is the element of surprise.

I hope Stink and Boochie find Dearaye before he tries to do something to Deandre. I started working on my sad faces. The ones that I'd have to give Deandre once he finds out his brother is dead. He'll never know how lucky he is because my wrath has not called for his blood-or at least not yet, anyway. Plus, unbeknownst to him, I'll actually be saving his life.

I was laying down trying to rest for a while when my cell phone rang. I knew that it could only be either my mother or Stink and Boochie. I grabbed the phone.

"Hello?"

"Kareemah? It's me Stink. We got a present for you."

"I own a beauty and barber salon on Queens Chapel Road called Angel's Beauty and Barber Palace. You hip to it?"

"You talking about the new joint over there by the DC Tunnel?"

"Yeah. It's on QC Road in the middle of the block. The sign on the house is lit up. Meet me there."

"That's a bet. Give us about twenty-five minutes to get there. I'm gone."

I got dressed and did about ninety mph all the way to my shop. I beat Stink and Boochie there, unlocked the door and deactivated the security system. Then I sat on the front porch and waited. About five minutes later, a dark-colored Caravan pulled up and Stink jumped out. He opened the side door on the van. There laid Dearaye, duct taped up, struggling to free himself. When he looked up and saw me; his eyes got as big as teacups. He knew why he was there.

"Bring him upstairs." I said and turned to lead the way into the Palace. Dearaye struggled and it took both Stink and Boochie to carry him inside and up the stairs to the third floor. My lounge area was still under construction. I took a big piece of plastic and laid it on the middle of the floor. To my benefit, the workers had left tool boxes and all kinds of equipment. I would use it all on Dearaye's ass. Stink and Boochie threw him on the floor. I looked down at him, helpless and thought of my sister and I spit in his face.

"Motherfucker, what the fuck is wrong with you. You thought you would get away with this bullshit? What the fuck you hurt my sister for?"

"What are you talking about? I haven't done anything to you." He replied. "What's going on?"

"Twin, lying to me will get you nowhere. You might as well come clean and I might let you live."

"I-I-I don't know what…you're talking about. C-C- come clean about what?"

"So you wanna do this the hard way, huh? I tried to give you an opportunity to make it light on yourself. But naw, you wanna be all tough and shit. That's cool. I know it was you who put them dudes on me and your brother. It was you who arranged for my sister to be snatched. Then, for no reason at all, you ordered her death.

"You don't have to tell me that because I already know that. Did you know that she was only fourteen years old? She was beautiful, wasn't she? Why did she have to die for my sins, Dearaye? Why did they have to beat her like that? Did you fuck her, too, Dearaye? I know you niggas ran a train on my sister?

"She was a special. She survived being raped by our father. Only to be raped again by you and your men. You fucking asshole. I saw her, Dearaye. I saw the way her face was swollen and bruised, both her eyes were black. I saw the missing teeth and the gashes in her scalp. How long did she lay in that ditch, Dearaye? In the fucking cold, naked, and lifeless, and decomposing?"

Tears dropped from my eyes. I made no attempt to wipe them as I continued my interrogation.

"It was you, Dearaye. You sent the dudes in the Caprice wagon and the Crown Vic. Did they tell you that they killed a fifteen-year-old boy for nothing? He wasn't even a street dude. The money that they got from my workers was nothing, small change. I wasn't even mad about that; it happens you know. But you had to hurt me, right? You had to really hurt me.

"You found out about my family and you targeted my little sister. Not me, but my fourteen-year-old sister, my only sister. Now that's fucked up. You've caused me permanent damage. You've succeeded in hurting me and most of all, you destroyed my family. Why didn't you just kill me? You knew where I laid my head. You knew about this shop and the other store.

"Why not me? Huh? You told them dudes that I kept the hammer with me, didn't you? And that I'd bust with no hesitation, didn't you? You even put a hit out on your own brother. What did Deandre do to you that made you that mad?"

Dearaye had the look of a defeated man in his eyes. I think he knew then that he was going to die. I guess he decided to face his death with dignity because he wouldn't speak. I got mad.

"Now you're speechless? You had so much to say when you put them dudes on me. You had a lot to say when you decided to kill my sister. You had a lot to say on the phone that day when you called me and cursed me out. I was all types of bitches and hoes. The cat got your tongue now, huh? You ain't got no words for me? At least answer this. You did all this shit to me because I dumped you?"

Dearaye never said a word. I looked around the room at the tools and decided to enjoy myself a little. I went and got a chair.

"Pick him up and put him in this chair."

I went and got one of the tool belts from across the room.

"Tape his mouth back up."

I took a Phillips head screwdriver and stabbed him in the fleshy part of his left leg. He tried to scream, but couldn't.

"You ain't got no rap for me? Huh? We'll see about that."

I stabbed Dearaye in both of his thighs and calves. Then I took the big flathead screwdriver and stabbed him in both of his butt cheeks. He squealed, cried and tried to scream. Blood dripped on the floor beneath him, but I wasn't worried about him bleeding to death. He'd be dead long before that.

"I'ma take this tape off your mouth again, Twin. If you scream, I'ma shoot you. If you tell me what I wanna hear, I'ma let you go." I pulled the tape off his mouth. "Talk to me Dearaye. Tell me who was with you. If you give me your buddies; the ones who raped and killed my sister, I swear to God, I'ma let you live."

Dearaye looked at me with a defiant look and then to my surprise, he started to laugh at me. I put a fresh piece of tape on his mouth. I grabbed the hammer out of the tool bag. I beat both of Dearaye's kneecaps until you could see parts of the bone coming from his pants. He passed out from the pain. I told Stink and Boochie to watch him while I left the shop for a minute. Twenty minutes later I returned and Dearaye was still out cold.

I put smelling salts under his nose and he came to. He tried to scream, but the tape muffled his tried. I kicked him and smacked him in the head with the tape measurer. Then, I beat him over the head with the leveler. Blood was everywhere. I kicked Dearaye until my toes started to hurt. I walked into the bathroom and washed my face and hands.

"Dearaye, let's try this again. I want you to tell me who the dudes were who raped and killed my sister, everybody who laid a finger on her. I want the names of everybody, from beginning to end. Either way, I'ma find out what I wanna know. I can keep you here and torture you every day. Is that what you want? How do you think I found out about you, Twin?

"Your man gave you up, Baby Daddy from 18th and D. He gave you up before he died. All the dudes who've died in the last ten days, died because of you. And a lot more dudes are gonna die, including your brother, until I'm satisfied. Do yourself a favor; tell me who those dudes were and I'll leave you alone; let Deandre live and I won't even tell him that you put them dudes on him. Come on Dearaye, your wounded pride will heal and so will your wounds, if you're alive."

I pulled the tape off his mouth again and listened carefully as he broke it all down for me.

"Please don't hurt me anymore. I'ma tell you whatever you want to know. I was upset, Angel; with you and my brother. He took you away from me. I loved you! I fell in love with you! I thought you loved me, too. Please don't kill me."

"Just keep talking Dearaye and you'll live."

"I paid three dudes to follow you around. I wanted to know where you lived, where you worked, everything. I didn't pay them to kill you or Deandre. They were only supposed to rob you, rob your runners; hurt the pockets, that sort of thing. Never did I say kill anyone. I wanted to hurt both of you; just like y'all hurt me. I never paid anyone to kill anybody. I didn't know that they killed a kid.

"I didn't pay for that. I did tell them, to snatch your sister, but it was for the money. I called your house and spoke to some man. But Tommy said that we should kill her and forget about the money because you'd probably never pay it. I told them that they were wrong. I told them, that you had a rack of money. I knew that it was you supplying the coke.

"I knew about you the whole time we dated. Our mutual friends can't keep their mouths shut. I knew that you were Tony Bills's old girlfriend and that he left you money and drugs when he died. I wanted to hurt your pockets, not you. I begged them to let your sister go, but things got out of control. They started to believe the hype about themselves. They called themselves 'The Murderers'.

"They didn't listen to me. I didn't want your sister to die. Do you really think I would kill my own brother; my dead mother's flesh and blood? I just wanted to make him take a fall for a while to see that the world doesn't revolve around him. He's always running everything. He's always in control. I wanted him to feel my pain; to be the yes-man.

"He always act like his shit don't stink. He's always taking everything I've ever loved, including you! How do you think I felt, knowing that you and him were together? Huh? How do you think I felt seeing y' all together? Did you ever consider my feelings? I wanted to hurt you, but I never ordered or paid for any killings.

"You have to believe me! Angel, I swear I didn't do it. The three dudes in the black Caprice and the ones in the Crown Vic are the same. They robbed your workers and killed your sister and your friend, the little kid, Chucky. It wasn't me. Please don't kill me. I'll pay you all the money I have left. Just don't kill me. I'll do anything for you."

"Who are the dudes, Dearaye?"

"Angel, let me go and I'll kill them for you. I'll do that and we can be even."

"Who are the three dudes, Dearaye?"

My patience was wearing thin and I think he knew it.

"Their names are Tommy, Ricardo, and Short-Short. They hang down Sursum Cordus. Tommy and Ricardo are brothers and Short-Short's their cousin."

"How do we find them Dearaye? How do I get in touch with them?"

"I have a cell phone number for Tommy." Dearaye said. "He's the ring leader. He's the one who killed your sister. I begged him not to, but he wouldn't listen to me."

"Dearaye, I'm going to give you a chance to save yourself. I want you to call Tommy and get him to come here. If you get him here, I promise to kill him instead of you. Stink, give him your cell phone. If you call anyone other than Tommy, I'm killing you."

Dearaye dialed a number and connected with someone so I figured it was Tommy. He did a pretty good job of sounding convincing and he talked Tommy into meeting him on Queens Chapel Road. He told Tommy that he was outside my shop and that he was going to kill me as soon as I came out. He hung up the phone. I waited.

Thirty minutes later Stink and Boochie came upstairs into the room with a tall light-skinned dude with curly hair. They had him at gunpoint and he looked like he was about to shit on himself.

"Tommy, what's up? You know who I am, don't you? I'm the one you followed around like a fucking FBI agent. I'm the one who you was scared to grab because I would've blasted my way out of a jam. So, you grabbed my fourteen-year-old sister, beat her, raped her, then you killed her. What do you have to say, Tommy, before I kill you?"

He looked around and saw Dearaye beaten and bloody.

"I don't know what you're talking about."

He looked at Dearaye. "What the fuck did you tell them, moe?"

"He told us everything, moe, so you can cut the bullshit."

Stink smacked Tommy upside the head with his pistol. Tommy dropped to his knees and began to beg for his life. He started screaming at Dearaye about being set up and Dearaye lying on him. Then he started admitting shit.

"Okay, okay listen. He contacted me and put me on you. I did what I was told. He told me to rob all the runners and strips. My cousin accidentally shot the youngin'. We didn't mean to kill shorty. The little girl situation wasn't me. That was my cousin. That nigga is crazy for real!"

Then he started hollering so much we had to gag him, too. I didn't believe a word of what he said. He tried to pass the buck, but it stopped with him. Dearaye said the he was the principle offender so he was going to die for the offense.

"Thank you for bringing Tommy here to me. But Dearaye, I can't forgive you for putting all of this into play. If it wasn't for you, Tommy would never have gotten into my business. You're just as guilty as this nigga right here. It's as if you strangled yourself. I lied to you boo; I'm not going to spare you. You don't deserve to live and that's as simple as that. I want you to watch what I do to Tommy before I kill you."

"Stink strip this pitiful motherfucker." I said pointing at Tommy. "Stop crying and sniffling you bitch ass nigga. You're a gangsta; remember. Did my sister cry and plead for her life? Why did you have to beat her like that? Huh? Did she fight you? Did it feel good raping her, you sick, twisted, fuck? She was a virgin. Did it turn you on when you strangled her? Did it take long for her to die? What was her crime, huh? I saw what you did to her; don't worry about answering my questions; you can save your answers and your pleas for Allah. Tell him." I looked at Stink with hate in my eyes.

"Tie his ass to the chair. Don't sit him down; bend him over the chair."

Boochie and Stink looked at me like I had gone mad. Once I was satisfied that Tommy was held down in the right position, I grabbed my bag. I pulled out my most recent purchase. All eyes widened as I strapped on the dildo. The rubber dick was twelve inches long and fat with veins and everything. I grabbed the Vaseline out of my purse and rubbed a generous amount on the dildo.

"Tommy believe it or not, I'm not a bad person. I can be rather nice at times. I'm going to show you more mercy than you showed my sister. I'm about to rape you, but I'm not going to stuff dick up in you off the dryness. I'm going to lube up so that you can enjoy it. You may even like it to death."

I positioned myself behind him and shoved the whole dick up his rectum. He couldn't yell or holler. All he could do was faint. Not him too, I thought as I kept right on pumping the dildo in his ass. I was a person possessed. Then he let his bowels go and shit got messy, literally. *What the fuck, this nigga done shit all over the place. Fuck!*

I went and got towels and water and cleaned him all up. Then I revived him and fucked him some more. In the corner I saw big crocodile tears the size of pennies come down Dearaye's face. I satisfied my lust for revenge for like thirty minutes or more. I decided to go ahead and kill him. I wrapped a phone cord around his neck and pulled on it. Then I got an idea.

"Stink, Boochie lay him down. I want you to hold one leg and Boochie you hold the other. I want to put him in the buck."

They laid Tommy on his back and held his legs up. He was in the missionary position with me laying on top of him. I put the dildo back in him and said, "I want you to look at me. I want my face to be the last one that you ever see. Open your eyes! Look at me!"

I held onto both ends of the cord and pulled with every ounce of my strength in me. For my sister. For my family. I pulled for Lil Chucky. I pumped the dildo in and out as I pulled the cord. My tears fell on his face as he closed his eyes and breathed his last breath. I pulled until I was sure that no life was left in him. Then I looked at Dearaye.

"Twin, or should I say Ray? You shouldn't have done this to me. I liked you. But I liked your brother more, big fuckin' deal. Your sex was trash and I used you to get at your brother. It was him who I wanted the whole time. I needed you to get at him. I fucked you to do that. It worked, huh? Then I fucked him to get him to buy 10 to 15 keys a week from me. That worked too. Dearaye can't you see? People like Deandre are over you because he's better than you; he's smarter than you and better looking, even though y'all look alike. He would never have pulled this stupid shit that you did. That's what makes y'all different. Stop looking so shook; I'm not going to put that big dick in your ass. That's too good for even you. You get to die quickly now that you've suffered a little."

I turned to Stink. "Stink, turn that music up as loud as it'll go."

I pulled the four fifth out of my waistband and forced it into Dearaye's mouth. He choked on the barrel. I cocked the hammer back.

"I'm giving you thirty-seconds to make peace with the Allah. One-Two-Three-Four-…"

I pulled the trigger and blew Dearaye's brains all over the plastic on the floor.

"Get rid of these niggas for me. Take them and Tommy's car to the Maryland side and dump them. I have $100,000 right here for y'all like I promised."

I handed it to Stink. "I owe y'all $200,000. But I need y'all to end this for me. Find the brother, Ricardo, and the cousin Short-Short, and kill them. I'll bring the rest of the money I owe in cash with a bonus to wherever y'all want after this is done. I want to read about those two dudes. You did good, real good, thanks a million. Call me when it's over."

I walked downstairs to the barbershop. I put all the incriminating stuff like the cord, dildo, and tools in a bag. I sat down in one of the barber chairs and thought about what I just did. I thought that killing Dearaye and Tommy would make me feel better, but it didn't. I guess that was because their death couldn't bring my sister back.

Once Stink and Boochie had cleaned up and removed both the bodies, I locked the door to the shop and went to the beauty salon on the second floor. I sat down in the chair and before I knew it, I fell asleep. No nightmares, just peaceful sleep.

******

"**D**id you see that wild shit, slim?" Boochie asked Stink.

"Yeah, I saw it, nigga. I was standing right next to you."

"I thought we was some dirty muthafuckas, but that bitch Kareemah takes the cake. She pulled out that big ass dick. I was like whoa, what the fuck?"

"I'm hip. I ain't never in my life seen no shit like that, but I know one thing, that was gangsta." Stink said as he started freaking his Black & Mild. "Where the hell should we dump these niggas?"

"Go straight out Bladensburg and hit Eastern Avenue on the Maryland side. I know a little spot by Kaywood Gardens that has a rack of woods. First, stop by the gas station and get some gas so that we can torch the van when we done. I'ma call my girl and tell her to come and get us after we done."

"Aye, Boochie. I would hate to cross that bitch. She don't be bullshitting."

"I'm hip."

CHAPTER TWENTY-THREE

2003
Det. SEAN JONES

Another day, another dollar. I was just called to another crime scene. Two bodies were found on Eastern Avenue and Chillum Road in Hyattsville. Detective work is always hectic. I've seen enough dead bodies to last me two lifetimes. I pulled up to Chillum Road, crossed under the police tape, and flashed my brass to the local brass. The Hyattsville police had the area cordoned off and were doing a good job of preserving evidence. Hyattsville Police Department HPD, although autonomous, falls under the Prince George County flag, which explains why I'm here.

This one is a bizarre scene. Two young black men, which is not unusual in this area, were murdered. I hate to be the one to say it, but when you live in a predominately black metropolis, the people you find killed are predominately black. Every now and then someone may kill a white person, but it's not the norm.

"Detective Jones, PG Homicide. What have we here?" I asked one of the HPD boys.

"Well, what you see is what you get. Two black males in their late twenties maybe early thirties. Both found about an hour ago. The medical examiner places the possible time of death between 3:00 and 5:00 a.m. One of them is partially nude. He appears to have been sodomized and strangled. Affixation may have occurred during the sodomizing. The other stiff was beat-up pretty bad, stabbed, and shot at point blank range. The back of his head is gone. A large caliber gun was used. Both bodies were dumped here. A burgundy caravan believed to be connected to this crime, was found a block away. It was set on fire. The local fire department was called out. We believe the perpetrators dumped the bodies here and then dumped the van, setting it on fire, probably to destroy evidence.

"But why would they dump the bodies before setting the van ablaze? Why not set the van ablaze with the bodies in it? That way you can destroy all evidence, even the bodies?" I asked Mr. Know It All...

"Your guess is as good as mine. It looks like some sort of sex crime to me. Maybe these two were engaged in sex, when the gay lover came in and caught them. The gay lover is probably a thug faggot, who totes, pulls a gun, and ties up one while he humps the other and kills him. Then he beats and shoots the other. I don't know. It looks like a homosexual crime to me. But it's not my job to figure this out. That's why you get paid the big bucks and I don't. you can take over from here. I'm out of here!" the cop said and left.

The forensic technicians and the assistant were all over the bodies. I did my investigation without getting in their way. The first body I examined was the partially nude one. He was sprawled spread-eagle on the ground. His pants hanging from one ankle. He had on socks and one boot, a Timberland. He wasn't wearing a shirt or jacket. He wasn't beaten or bruised, just sodomized and strangled. There was dried blood all over his testicles and rectum. And there were welts across his neck, *Must've been some kind of thin rope or cord.* Results, would be in a few days. *We'll know for sure then.*

The second body was face-up in the grass. This one was beaten pretty badly; he had lacerations to the face and head that were pretty nasty and stab wounds in the legs and butt. *Maybe some kind of icepick?* The legs were turned at such an angle as to denote broken bones and a bone protruded through his pants. The clothes that the second body had on caught my attention. I'm a stickler for details and I'm definitely catching a vibe. The deceased was wearing black designer jeans, no socks, black Prada slip-on loafers, and a black linen shirt. I fished my notepad out of my pocket and read the information that I took while investigating another homicide.

Then all at once all the pieces fell into place. Yesterday, about 7:45 p.m., 911 operators received several calls about a shooting at a deli on St. Barabas Road in Oxon Hill. I was called to the scene minutes later because a man had been found lying in front of the store suffering from gunshot wounds to the chest. EMT workers were unable to revive the man when he lost consciousness. They pronounced him dead at 8:01 p.m. When I arrived on the scene, I interviewed several witnesses, who all gave different stories, but overall, all the facts were the same.

The witnesses reported that several men always hung in the deli. They say that the man found at the scene was one of the regulars. The store was rumored to be owned by two brothers who were big drug boys in DC. The twin brothers were known as the Twins; or Dre and Ray. At around 7:30 p.m., a burgundy van pulled up in front of the deli. Three or four men went inside; and about five minutes later gunshots were heard. The men came out of the store with one man at gunpoint and put him into the caravan.

Witnesses say that the men wore masks when they exited the store with the man at gunpoint. They report that the man being held at gunpoint was trying to resist and was struck repeatedly with blows to his head. The side door was left open as the van sped away from the scene. The second man stumbled to the front of the store and collapsed outside the deli. Several witness, who refused to give their names out for fear of reprisal, said that the man abducted was one of the brothers who owned the deli. Nobody knew which one he was because they were identical twins.

The caravan had DC license plates and one witness could only remember AF-6 and three other numbers.

At the station I talked to several officers on the Drug Task Force because the witnesses said that drugs were sold out of the deli. The two brothers were known to every drug agency in PG. The local office for the Drug Enforcement Agency faxed me a dossier on the twin brothers.

The brother were Deandre and Dearaye James. They were twenty-nine years old, born and raised in the district. The file contained information gathered from reliable sources. The twins were small-time drug dealers who hustled in the Northeast section of DC around Saratoga Avenue. They hooked up with a major foreign supplier and brokered deals for themselves and for other drug dealers. One of the brothers allegedly killed the connect and made off with several kilos of heroin and a large sum of money. So the small-time dealers became big-time overnight. And eventually their long arms reached into PG County.

The deli was legally owned by a woman named Geraldine James, the twins' aunt, but the unofficial word is that the twins owned the deli. The decedent who died in front of the deli was identified as Ronald Fletcher, a small-time thug who hung out in the housing complex adjacent to the deli. Mr. Fletcher was originally from the Naylor Road section of Southeast and was believed to be the lieutenant for the James brothers. The witnesses all said that the man who was abducted wore a black dress shirt, black jeans, and black dress shoes. One witness even notices that the man who was held captive was wearing no socks.

As I finished reading my notes I was willing to wager that the dead man at my feet dressed in all black is the same man abducted from the deli and is one of the James brothers. There was no identification found on either body. I drove down the block to the scene of the burned van. The caravan was burned pretty bad, but a spot of color near the rear bumper indicated the vehicle was in the red family.

Angel

Everything in the van was destroyed in the fire. I poked around inside and saw what appeared to be a charred boot, possibly a Timberland. The sole was melted but enough of the boot remained. *I'll bet money this is the stiff's other boot.*

I'd also wager that this van is the same van that was used to abduct the James brother. I interviewed people from both sides and no one seems to have seen or heard anything. The thing that really boggled my mind was *who could the second dude be? And how does he fit into the deli abduction equation? Were the two deceased men killed together in the same spot? If so, where? Why were they dumped before the van was set on fire? Questions are all that I have. This case will be hard to solve unless I catch a hell of a break.*

I went back to the office to document my initial findings. I was busy reading the 911 transcripts when I decided to call my buddy Rick who's still with the DC homicide division.

"Hey, Rick? What's up buddy?" I asked him when he answered the phone.

"Sean Jones. Are you lieutenant yet?" he asked.

"Hell naw." I said. "I'm still sergeant but I get paid lieutenant money. Are we still on for the summer, hitting the cabin in West Virginia?"

"Nothing besides death can keep me away. How's everything with you? Who's the current lady in your life?"

"I got a new one, Michelle, you gotta meet her. How's your wife?" I replied.

"She's holding on." He joked. "It's rough being married to a man who's married to his job. My wife says this job is ruining our marriage, especially these days. Man, we got so many homicides, the chief is on my ass every day. The Mayor's driving him crazy and he's taking it out on us.

"There's a lot of political pressure to stop these murders because this is the nation's capital. Between us Sean, we're drawing blanks. We don't have jack shit. Whoever is behind all these recent deaths, needs to teach a class at the academy. They're either extremely smart and careful or extremely lucky."

"Hey, Rick, that's why I called. I have three bodies in my backyard, all killed within the last twenty-four hours. The bodies were found in different locations but I'm certain that they're all connected. You worked in the narcotics division before going to homicide, right?"

"Yeah, thirteen-years in narcotics, why?"

"Are you familiar with the James brothers, Deandre and Dearaye?"

"Of course, every officer in vice and narcotics knows them. It's just hard to make anything stick on them. Why you ask?"

"Dearaye James was abducted from a deli that allegedly he and Deandre James owned in Oxon Hill. A man who was inside the deli with Dearaye was shot and killed. Witnesses say that two men held Dearaye at gun-point, that happened yesterday evening. Early this morning the burgundy van was found in an alley in Hyattsville on fire. Dearaye was found a block away dead from a gunshot wound to the head.

"He had been beaten up real bad and both his legs were broken with a blunt object. He was also stabbed several times in the legs and the buttocks, which suggests some sort of crime of passion to me. He pissed somebody off real bad. The funny part is that his body was dumped before the van was ablaze. Plus, his body showed up with another body. We're still trying to identify the other body. I have a file about an inch thick on the James brothers in front of me, but something is missing, so I need you to fill in a few blanks for me."

"Okay." Rick said. "Shoot. I'll see what I can do."

Angel

"Is there some sort of drug war going on in DC or something? Do you have any info that would suggest why someone would kidnap and kill one of the James brothers? And do you think that the killings out here could be connected to the murders there?"

"First, let me say that at this point we're still investigating everything. Like I said earlier, we have diddly-squat, nothing, nada. So there's no way I can give you an honest answer about the murders being connected. There's definitely something going on in the streets, but we're not sure if it's a drug war because we've found no drugs anywhere at any of the crime scenes. Someone is killing people for some reason and by God we're using all of our resources to find out why. We receive so much bullshit information it's hard to tell whether the stories are real anymore. As far as the James brothers go, I'm not aware of anything brewing that would tell you why someone just beat the shit out of one of them and then killed him. Shit, drug dealers kill each other all the time. That's the good thing about them; they tend to help society out by killing each other. But what I do know is that the James brothers are big here in DC; they control a large part of Northeast and Northwest. If someone was brave enough to move against them by killing Dearaye, there's going to be more dead bodies popping up everywhere in retaliation. Deandre is rumored to be the hotheaded trigger man out of the two and somebody just killed his brother. It's about get crazy. He's the real power behind the operation, the gunslinger. He's going to kill people for sure. Like I said, we know everything about both brothers, all the way down to who they're sleeping with. Deandre's the lucky one in more ways than one. Not only is he alive, but he happens to be sleeping with the queen of cocaine. Our agencies are investigating her and her ties to the illustrious Big Willy, Carlos Trinidad. She's probably supplying him, too. She runs major weight in the city and believe man when I say that they're baking a cake for her."

"What's her name Rick?" I asked.

"Her nickname's Angel, but her birth name is hold on for a minute it's a funny name; her family is Muslim."

What he said caught my attention.

"Her name is Kareemah El-Amin."

I almost fell out of my chair. I was speechless.

"Did you just say Kareemah El-Amin?" I asked.

"Yeah, why? Do you know her Sean?"

"Do I know her? *Do I know her?* She's the unofficial suspect in a murder that took place about a year ago. Do you remember when that big time drug dealer Tony Bills got killed out here in Seat Pleasant?"

"Of course I remember the Tony Bills murder."

"Well, Ms. El-Amin was Tony Bills girlfriend at the time he was killed. As a matter of fact, she was with him on the night he was killed. I could never prove it but I believe Ms. El-Amin was either involved in that murder or she committed the murder herself. I investigated her for a while, but couldn't find a thing to back up my hunch. Now you're telling she's involved with another big drug boy whose brother just got killed. Something is real suspicious about her."

"You didn't let me finish." Said Rick silencing me as I listened to him. "Ms. El-Amin just recently experienced death in her family. Her younger sister was kidnapped, beaten, raped, and strangled. The girl was only fourteen-years-old. We found her body down Fort Dupont Park. Twenty-four hours after she was kidnapped, a wave of murders execution style, hit the streets and the blood hasn't stopped running yet.

"Some of the dead guys we positively IDed and ran their prints. A good number of the dudes killed were wanted in DC for kidnapping, murder, or some sort of assault. Whoever killed them did us all a favor, but we still have to find the person responsible. I briefly gave all of the above some thought and wondered if everything is connected or am I just making pieces fit under pressure. Make sure you call me and let me know the identity of the other person. Whatever I find on this end, I'll call you and give you details."

"Hold on sailor, you're in luck. I just received a stack of papers. I'm sure the identity of the other stiff is here. Hold on a sec. Viola! Here it is. The second man has been identified as Thomas J. Murphy, 25 years old, 185 pounds, brown eyes, black curly hair. He has a tattoo on his right shoulder that says, 'The Murderers' several other tattoos…"

"Hold on." Rick interrupted. "Did you say that he has a tattoo that says 'The Murderers' and his name is Thomas?"

"Yeah." I told him.

"Oh shit. I think you may have Tommy Guns out there dead. There's a small clique of youngins who call themselves 'The Murderers', and Tommy Guns is the leader. They're a group of dudes whose occupation is intimidation, witness tampering, and murder for hire. We know that Tommy Guns has a younger brother named Ricardo. They roll with one of their cousins, Short-Short and a rack of flunky dudes who do whatever Tommy Guns tells them.

"We know all about these dudes and we believe that they're responsible for a lot of murders. Fax me the info on Thomas Murphy and I'll make sure that Thomas Murphy is in fact Tommy Guns. If he's Tommy Guns, then we might have big problems on our hands. This is big, I mean huge and if it is Tommy Guns, we got a war going on in the streets right under our noses. I wonder what was his connection to Dearaye James. Look Sean, hopefully we can help each other solve these murders. I'll call you back later."

"Okay, Rick, later."

I hung up and couldn't help but think about Kareemah El-Amin. *Where does she fit into all this? I know her connection to Deandre, but what's the connection to Dearaye and Thomas? I need to have a talk with Ms. El-Amin again and soon!*

We have to notify the next of kin about the death of Dearaye and that would give me the chance to question Deandre. I went through my paperwork and came up with a number for Geraldine James, Aunt Ginny; the aunt who, on paper, owns the deli. She was uncooperative. I told her that I had to speak to Deandre. She was reluctant at first, but then she relented when I told her that he may be in danger and promised I have Deandre give her a call. I was pessimistic though, because most drug dealers don't like to talk to the police. But to my surprise, an hour later my phone rang and it was Deandre.

"Hello? Is this Det. Sean Jones?"

"Yes, it is; who am I speaking with?"

"I was told that you're investigating the murder of my brother Dearaye James. I was also told that you have some information that may be helpful to me since apparently; I'm also in danger. Okay I'm all ears, what's the deal?"

"First, let me express my condolences on the loss of your brother. Second, I believe his death is connected to some other murders that have taken place in the district. Listen, I know all about how the game is played. How dudes on the streets are too thugged out to cooperate with the cops and all that. I'm not asking you to snitch on anyone. I want to ask you a few questions about your brother and your girlfriend Kareemah El-Amin."

"What does Angel have to do with this?"

"At the moment, I'm not sure, but like I said, you talk to me and I'll tell you what I know. Agreed?"

Angel

The other end of the phone became silent. I thought that he hung up; but after a long pause he said, "Alright, agreed!"

"Okay. To gain your confidence, I'll go first with a little bit of what I know, and then you go. Yesterday evening your brother was abducted from a deli in Oxon Hill that I know you own. His companion, a young black man named Ronald Fletcher was killed inside the deli, which I'm sure you already know. None of this info has been released to the public, so you're hearing this from me, exclusively.

"Your brother was taped up with some strong tape, probably duct tape. He was held hostage, tortured, beaten, stabbed repeatedly in the thigh, calves, and buttocks; this suggests to us that someone was mad at him because they took a blunt object like a bat or a heavy hammer and beat his kneecaps until the bone was pulverized. Then someone put a gun in his mouth and shot him. So my question is, do you know of anyone who would've wanted to kill you or him? Somebody he crossed or cheated? Any enemies? A rival drug dealer or ex-girlfriend who was jilted? Anybody?" I was so anxious to solve this murder; that I didn't realize how painful it must have been to Deandre, the way I broke the news of his brother's murder.

"Naw, I'm not hip to anyone who would be dumb enough to bring my brother this type of move. I can't believe this shit. My brother ain't never crossed nobody. He wasn't a crutty dude. He's one of those humble type of dudes always seeing the good in people. I didn't know about any enemies. I doubt it though. As far as rival dealers is concerned, my brother and I got out of the drug game several years ago. We are well respectable business people who owned several businesses in DC. The haters are another story. We invested in a lot of stock and CDs so we are well-off and the haters hate to see someone prosper."

"What about your girlfriend Angel?"

186

"To be honest, I wasn't around my brother long enough to know his friends. Especially his many bitches." Deandre said. "But from talking to him there were no stalkers, crazies, or vindictive ex-girlfriends. Let me ask you something now?"

"Okay." I said.

"Why did you mention Kareemah El-Amin and how do you know her?"

"I've known Kareemah El-Amin or Angel for about a year. Did you know a dude who got killed in 2002 named Tony Bills?"

"Yeah. I knew him. So?"

"Well, Angel was his girlfriend at the time of his death and she was with him the night he was killed. She says that intruders killed Tony Bills, but I believe that Ms. El-Amin is the one who pulled the trigger. How well do you know Ms. El-Amin?"

"I...I thought I knew her well, but evidently I was wrong. Tell me more."

"Okay, I will. But first answer a question for me. Dearaye's body was found dumped in a ditch here in Maryland along with another black man named Thomas 'Tommy Guns' Murphy. Did you know him? If so, what's his connection to your brother?"

"I don't know any Tommy Guns' Murphy, so I don't have a clue as to why they were killed together."

"I never said they were killed together. We don't know that for sure. What I said was that their bodies were dumped together. When your brother was abducted from the deli, he was alone. So Tommy Guns had to come from somewhere."

"Well, I don't know him. I swear. I've never heard of him before today. Now tell me more about Angel."

"Okay. Isn't it strange that Angel was with Tony Bills? He's a drug dealer. He's linked with the drug kingpin Carlos Trinidad. Then he's mysteriously killed. Angel emerges as the premier cocaine distributor in DC after his death. The DEA believes that she's responsible for over fifty percent of the drug flow moving in DC and Maryland. Now she's allegedly linked to Carlos Trinidad. But there's no concrete proof to nail her on anything. What I do know is that Angel El-Amin is beautiful, rich, and extremely dangerous."

"So why do you think that she's connected with my brother's death?" Deandre asked me.

"I never said that she was connected. That's what I'm trying to find out from you. I know she's your girlfriend; I know that her sister was recently abducted, beaten, raped, and killed. The parallel is the other guy, Tommy Guns. Tommy Guns was apparently abducted, beaten, and killed. The connection is that Tommy Guns was raped."

"What do you mean he was raped?" he asked.

"He was raped, Deandre, as in sodomized. He was raped by someone with a big penis, too. His rectum was split in two, literally. Then he was strangled. How was Angel's little sister killed?"

"She was strangled!" he shouted.

"Right, Deandre, are you starting to see what I see?"

"I see it, Detective, but I still don't believe it. All that could be a coincidence. I don't think that my Angel would hurt anyone. In fact, I'm sure of it. Dearaye would never hurt Angel's sister. Why? And Angel wouldn't hurt Dearaye. She loves me. You're cracking up, Detective. I know my boo and she's not the person you think she is. She may be a liar, but that doesn't make her a killer. I'm gonna get back with you if I find out anything. I have your number, I'll call you, if I find out anything."

"Okay Deandre. You do that."

I hung up the phone. I felt kinda dumb. I came away from our conversation with nothing to aid my investigation. I gave him everything and he gave me nothing. But it's cool because eventually I'll get the chance to bring Kareemah El-Amin to justice.

CHAPTER TWENTY-FOUR

Deandre

*M*an, *I can't believe this shit! What the fuck is going on? Somebody killed my brother. My brother! Somebody did all that geeking shit to my brother. Why? Was it about money? Was it an old beef that came back to haunt us? I do know one thing though. It on like a muthafucka. They think these last few weeks been bad; the homicide rate is about to go up some more. DC is about to be declared a straight up war zone. If I find out who did this to my brother, they can all cancel Christmas.*

I'm on my way right now to Lincoln Heights. One of the dudes on 50th Street owed me some money. He pulled a gun out on Ray one day and threatened him. I never took the situation seriously until now. I don't know who killed my brother, but this nigga Ducksauce is about to pay for it. I pulled into the circle in the Heights and saw Wali and Lil Pat chilling, with a rack of youngins. I blew the horn.

"Wali, what's up moe? Pat, what's happening?"

Both men walked up to my car. "Dre, what's up slim?"

"Ain't shit. I'm looking for that nigga, Ducksauce. Y' all seen him?"

Wali looked down into my lap and say my chrome .50 caliber Desert Eagle. "Naw I ain't seen slim, Dre. Why, what's up?"

"That's none of your business. You do know that we mind our business in the two thousands, right?" I told him.

As I looked up at Pat, he looked me in my eyes and smiled.

"That nigga is up the street by the basketball court." Then he turned and looked at Wali. "Fuck that nigga, Wa. He ain't no homie for real, that nigga doing all kind of crud ball shit and then run around here. Plus, I found out that he was the one who robbed Lil Smooth and them." Then he turned back to me. "Dre, that nigga got on some blue jeans and a throwback Boston Celtics jersey with some green and white Air Nikes. He might be in his car. He pushing a black Monte Carlo SS coupe. Handle your business, moe."

And just like that, Ducksauce was caught in the crosshair of serious scope-mine. I rode up to the basketball court and saw the black Monte Carlo parked by the curb. A female was leaning into the passenger side of the car talking to a dude in the car. I spotted Ducksauce behind the wheel. I made a left onto 50th Street and cruised down to the Monte Carlo.

I pulled my Benz parallel to the SS and shouted. "Hey Ducksauce!"

He looked over at me and tried to duck, but he was too slow. I watched the top of his head explode from the impact of the .50 caliber bullet. Blood was all over his man, who sat there in shock. I looked at the broad on the sidewalk.

"Bitch, if you say a word to anybody about this, your family gonna die!" I said to her then sped off. I hit East Capital Street on my way back out of Ft. Washington. I still can't believe that Ray is gone. I know I did a rack of crutty shit to him, but I could do that. I been fucked up in the head since yesterday when Aunt Ginny called me. She told me that a dude got killed in the deli I own. Dudes in the area told her that Twin got snatched. I took the deli from a dude who owed me money and couldn't pay me. Dearaye took over the day-to-day operation of the store; it was like his office. Then he started moving the coke out of the back of the store and word got around. I told him to ease up, but he was a lot more stubborn than people know. How whole thing was the fact that he was five minutes older than me. So therefore, he wanted to be the leader. Since he's was older, he felt that I should listen to him. But it didn't work out that way; it never had.

A Novel by Anthony Fields

I remember when we were like fourteen-years-old. We were running with a crew of dudes called the BM12. Ray wanted desperately to be in charge, so we let him lead us. Every move we made was under Ray's leadership. I did so much time in Cedar Knoll messing with Ray, it was ridiculous. I already knew that Ray wasn't cut out to be a leader, but I had to prove it to him. He just didn't have the head and heart for running shit. So I took over. I started doing a rack of push-ups and calisthenics. By the time I graduated high school I was a beast in all sports. I started wreaking so much havoc on the Northeast side, that the cops were scared to death of me. When I put the hammer in my hand it was over.

One day, I did some stupid shit. I got mad at one of my homies over a bitch. The broad was a whore. Everybody knew it but me. I fell in love with her. Out of all the bad bitches who I had, I fell in love with the slut. Every time I went in and out of jail, one of the dudes in my crew fucked her. People would tell me but I wouldn't listen. One time I was away for a few months, she started messing with some big-tyme homeboy. When I came home, she broke off the relationship. But dude wasn't going for it and wasn't trying to hear that she was back with me. One day, homie just took her pussy by force. She came to me crying. I was hot. To me it was a respect thing. Word got around like a California brushfire. I felt that the streets were watching and I had to do something. It was my defining moment. I felt that the streets were watching and I had to do something. It was my defining moments. I got a 9 millimeter Beretta from one of my homeboys. I caught the dude on Rhode Island Avenue walking toward the subway station. I hid in the cut and waited for him to approach. I jumped from the cut, stepped onto the sidewalk, and emptied the clip into him. Although I got away with murder, everyone knew that I did it. That killing put me on a different status in the hood. My brother never tried to lead again.

Angel

Over the years I went on to kill more niggas out here in theses streets. Including the Africans that eventually made us all rich. Ray made all the moves while I laid low. Shortly, thereafter, we had damn near all of Northeast sewed up.

Ray hooked up our deal with Tony Bills. Now, I find out that Angel was his ex. Did Ray know that? This shit is crazy. Why did the dudes who snatched Ray kill Ronald? What was that all about? I remember Shorty from around the way; he was gangsta. The people at the scene told Aunt Ginny that three or four dudes had Ray at gunpoint. I was waiting for a call to come asking me for money, but none came. I tried to relax, but I couldn't believe that all of this was happening. Somebody just kidnapped and killed Angel's little sister and now my brother gets snatched and killed. Maybe she was right when she said that this was all connected. At least the cops think so, which brings me to my next question.

Why did that cop tell me all that shit? What was his motive behind that?

I knew that the cop found my brother out in Maryland, but I didn't know that he died so fucked up. The people who killed my brother did a rack of crazy shit to him. In my heart I know that Ducksauce was innocent, but he was marked for death anyway. *Who the hell is Tommy Guns? And why was his body dumped with Ray's? Damn. Damn.*

I swiped at the tears in my eyes as I pulled into the driveway of our house; my house now. I looked around at all the things that belonged to Ray. I broke down. *Dearaye what the fuck did you do? I told you to keep a hammer on you. I told your dumb ass to watch your back at all times. You always had to be hardheaded. Now you're gone.*

I looked into the sky to ask God why. Ray never killed a soul. Why did he have to die? Why? I stared into the sky as if answers to my questions would appear. When none did, I became enraged. I started breaking up shit. I ripped all the paintings off the walls. The pain in my heart wouldn't subside. I felt like a major organ had been ripped out.

I took my brother for granted and now I can't even say I'm sorry. I wiped the tears from my eyes as I raised the .50 caliber to my own head. Life without my brother would be hard. He was all I had left, besides Angel. Now the cops think that Angel has something to do with Ray's death. Why? I dropped the gun and paced the floor. Somebody has to know something.

I'm gonna find out what happened to my brother and who's responsible. And God forbid that Angel's involved. Why has she been keeping so many secrets? I didn't tell the cop about her and Ray being together before us. That would've been the connection that he wanted. I ain't no rat anyway, so I don't even know why my aunt Ginny put him in my mix. I don't want any police around Angel if she's guilty of anything.

What if Ray played a part in Angel's sister's death? Ray wouldn't have done that; I'm tripping. But what if he did, and Angel found out about it? I called Angel's cell phone, but again I got no answer. I haven't talked to her since the night that I found out about her sister. *Why is she avoiding me? I have to find out what's what. Right now I need answers and then I'll deal with Angel.*

I changed my clothes and then jumped into my Yukon Denali XL. It took me twenty minutes to get to Northeast. I pulled up in front of the buildings that I used to hang in. I confronted a group of dudes who I grew up with. "Where's Monty?" I asked the group.

"What's up, Dre? Monty's in Lee Lee's house, moe. Want me to go get him?" this dude Shaka asked.

I didn't even respond as I stepped off. I didn't know who to trust. For all I know those niggas out there could've killed my brother. I climbed the steps and knocked on apartment 14 B. Lee Lee opened the door as I bogarted my way into the apartment pushing her aside. I felt her grab my arm.

"Dre what the…"

Before I knew what I was doing, my fist connected with her face. I stood over Lee Lee as she laid sprawled on the floor. I kicked the bedroom door in. Monty was laid out on the bed, in his boxers, smoking a blunt.

"What the fuck, Dre? What you do that for, moe? What's up witchu?"

He asked me so I told him, but only after I pulled out my .50 caliber D.E.

"Bitch ass nigga, somebody killed my brother. You were the closet person to him, so you have to know something. I want to know now. I swear to God, Monty, you better tell me something or I'ma smash you in this muthafucka and then I'ma smash Lee Lee. Hurry up before I change my mind and kill you for the fuck of it."

Monty threw up his hands in a sign of surrender.

"Dre, calm down, moe. Fuck! I just talked to Ray a few days ago. He didn't mention anything about no beef or nothing. But, he was acting strange and shit. He told me that he was making some serious moves. He said that niggas was gonna be on his dick in the end. I pressed him out to tell me what was up, but he wouldn't. He kept talking about hitting heads and running the city. I thought it was just the pills talking."

"What pills? My brother wasn't on pills."

"He was on everything, Dre. Ray started popping pills about four months ago. He didn't do it all the time, but he did it enough. You could always tell he was crunk. Dre, man you can kill me, my mother, my whole god damn family if you want to, cause I don't know nothing about nobody wanting to kill slim, though. That's my man, you know that."

He looked like he was telling the truth, so I eased up.

"Do you know a dude named Tommy Guns and some niggas called The Murderers?"

"I know them dudes. Tommy Guns and The Murderers are from Sursum Cordus. They're grimy ass niggas who'll kill anybody for money. Tommy Guns has a brother named Ricardo. A lot of people call him Rick. Both of them mainly be with their cousin Short-Short. Short has a sister named Daphnie. Ray used to mess with Daphnie. That's how all of us ended up kicking it. They call themselves The Murderers. It's about two or three more niggas that be with them. They shiesty and all, moe, but them niggas wouldn't kill Ray."

"I never said they did. The dude Tommy Guns is dead too. The police found him and Ray out in Maryland in a ditch. Somebody snatched up Ray from the deli and killed Ronald."

"What Ronald?"

"Lil Ronald Fletcher, Quenita, and Faggy Poo peoples. The cops say that the dude Tommy was raped and strangled. They beat Ray bad then shot him in the head. Did you ever hear Ray mention a broad named Angel?"

"Hell yeah! He talked about her all the time. He hated that broad. He never said why, only that he was going to fix her. He talked to Tommy and 'nem about bringing her and somebody else a move. But I thought he was just venting. Because you and I both know that Ray ain't on no vengeful crutty shit. This broad Angel whoever she is, must've really crossed slim, because he talked about getting at her on a regular. But like I said he only got like that when he was crunk off the pills."

I had heard enough for me to believe that Angel may have been behind Ray's death.

"Here, here's a few dollars for the door. When Lee Lee wakes up, tell her I'm sorry. I'm out. One."

Angel

"Dre, hold on moe. I'm tryna roll withchu when you find out who got Ray. That's on my word; I'm tryna smash some shit. Get at me when you find out what's up alright."

I nodded my head and walked out the apartment. I felt bad about Lee Lee, but she got in my way at a bad time. I have to clear my mind. There are too many questions in my head that I can't answer. So the stuff the cop said had a ring of truth to it. Ray must've paid Tommy Guns and 'nem to bring Angel a move. But what did Angel's sister have to do with it? If all this is true, then it must've been Tommy and 'nem who robbed and killed Angel's workers.

Somehow, word must've got back to Angel and she put money on Ray's and Tommy Gun's heads. I flashed back to the night Angel called me and told me that her sister was missing. The words she left me with chilled me to the bone.

When I find out who took my sister, I'ma kill em!

It's time for me to pay my dear girlfriend a visit. I dialed all of Angel's numbers and got voice mails for each phone. *Where the hell is?* I'ma keep trying until I reach her. Then her and I will have a long talk and then she'll die.

CHAPTER TWENTY-FIVE

ANGEL

"**I**n other news today, DC police have identified the bodies of four men killed over the weekend. DC police say that 23-year-old Dontez 'Short-Short' McClain was found dead from gunshot wounds to the chest. He was found in the unit block of North Capitol Street. DC police were called to the scene of a shooting in the 1300 block of Girad Street Northwest; where they believe they discovered 18-year-old Vincent Gamez unconscious. DC police believe that Mr. Gamez was a victim of escalating violence between rival Hispanic gangs. One-five Amigos and Vatos Locos. A 19-year-old man has been arrested in the case; 48-year-old Maurice Featherstone was beaten to death on Saturday. Police have arrested his 30-year-old live in girlfriend Naomi L. Smith and charged her with second-degree murder. The man shot Sunday night coming out of Ben's Chili Bowl, who later died at Georgetown University Hospital, was identified as Ricardo Murphy.

I clicked off the TV and smiled. I counted out $200,000, then put it in a duffel bag. I called Stink.

"Stink what's up?"

"You. What's up with you?"

"I got that money for you. I had to tied up a few loose ends, but I'm ready to see you now, if you're available."

"I'm always available when it comes to big face money. Where you at?"

Angel

"I'm over by Butler Gardens about to pick up my girlfriend and then I'm going to Talbert Street to pick something up. Why don't you meet me at the Tourist Home at the top of Talbert Street. I should be there in twenty minutes.

"That's a bet. We're on Sayles Place, so we'll be there three minutes after you, a'ight?"

"A'ight. I'm gone."

I picked up Fatima from Tameka's house in Butler Gardens and then drove to the Tourist Home. I ran my plan down to Fatima.

"I just need you to keep Boochie busy. I don't care how you do it. String him along, tell him you're thinking about giving him some pussy. I need you to stall him long enough for me to get Stink comfortable. That's the key to me killing him. Don't feel sorry for them niggas, Fatima. They just killed over thirty people; remember that. After I deal with Stink, I'll come downstairs and deal with Boochie."

"Angel, I don't know about this. I've never actually seen you kill anybody. I ain't never seen nobody die. What if I faint or something? Why do you have to kill them anyway? Just give them the money."

At times like these, Fatima really irked my nerves.

"Fatima, listen to me, in this game, you can't afford to leave loose ends. Stink and Boochie are loose ends. They know too much about my business. What if one of them was to get locked up or something? They could broker a deal with the cops to give me up. Sammy The Bull gave up Gotti. Playful Edmonds gave up everybody to free his mother. Tall Eric and Moe gave up Kevin. Need I say more?

"And what if they decided to extort me for more money? Then there's the possibility of them trying to bring me a move. Trust me; I know what I'm doing. In this game, you have to cover all the bases, retrace your tracks, and cover them too. There's no way on Allah's green earth that I can leave both of them breathing. It will hurt me in the end; I know it.

"They know too much, Fatima. I have to kill them. If you're not with me on this, just tell me and I'll take you home. You act like I'm asking you to pull the trigger. I just need you to be nice to Boochie for a few minutes. Stop worrying so much; after this, it's all over. Besides this is all for Adirah. Remember her? She didn't deserve to die like that and you know it."

"Angel, don't even go there with me. I loved Adirah just as much as you did. You can't never question that. And I never said I wasn't with you. I'm always with you, ain't I?"

I didn't answer her question, but I was confident that Fatima saw things my way. We pulled into the Tourist Home parking lot. I saw a charcoal gray Cadillac SLR with paper tags. I figured that it had to belong to either Stink or Boochie.

"I'ma introduce you to Boochie and make some small talk. Y' all stay in the lobby and chill. I'ma get Stink to get us a room. Give me at the most, fifteen minutes to deal with him. Then I'ma deal with Boochie. Got that?"

Fatima nodded her head.

"Are you ready? Don't be acting all shady, either. Like you know something is up. Come on."

The Ruger was in the bag with the money. The .45 was in my purse just in case. The Ruger was fitted with a silencer to conceal the noise; the .45 wasn't. Both Stink and Boochie were sitting in the lobby when we walked into the Tourist Home. I hugged both of them and then introduced them to Fatima. Then I turned to Stink.

"I wanna holler at you about something alone. You can count the money or whatever, but I need your advice. Fatima can keep Boochie company while we're gone."

Stink looked at Boochie and shrugged.

"I'll be right back. Don't start telling Fatima no lies either." He winked at Fatima and then walked over to the clerk. He paid for a room for an hour. The room was on the second floor...room 212. *I'ma play that number later. You never know I could hit the lotto.* It was at the end of the hall, so that was good. Once inside the room, I immediately started my song and dance.

"Stink, I appreciate how you took care of everything for me. If it wasn't for you and Boochie handling that business, I'd still be at square one. When I told you that I would bring the money with a bonus, I meant that. Boochie is alright and everything, but I'd rather give you the bonus." I kicked off my Chanel loafers. "But, I still need your services." I pulled my shirt over my head. "I need you to find the other twin, Deandre. I have a couple of addresses for him." I unsnapped my bra and let my breasts free. I watched as Stink's mouth started to water in anticipation of getting a hold of me. "I don't want his body found at all." I unbuttoned my jeans and wiggled out of them. "Then it's over, there's 200 gees in the bag, like I promised. After y' all hit Deandre and get rid of the body, I'll pay y'all another $100,000."

I stood there in only a red thong and let Stink digest what I looked like. "Are you down with that?"

Stink walked over to me and started kissing my neck. Then he said, "You know I'm with you. Cash rules everything around me. That nigga won't be no problem." He licked my shoulder. "Didn't we find Short-Short for you?" He started sucking on my left nipple. "Didn't we find Ricardo?" he pressed me up against the wall and pushed both my breasts together trying to suck both nipples at once. "Didn't we kill them niggas for you?" Stink dropped to his knees and started to kiss my pussy through my panties. "I got you, boo. You in good hand with me." Then he started to eat me.

I wanted to let Stink eat me, but time was running out. I told Fatima fifteen minutes. I grabbed Stink's ears and pulled him up off his knees. I untied the string on his sweatpants. I pulled out his dick and stroked it. When it was hard, I pushed him back onto the bed.

The bag with the money was at the foot of the bed. I licked Stink for a while until he begged me to put it in my mouth and I did. I sucked him off for a few minutes until I felt him about to cum. I used my free hand to reach for the gun. I grabbed it. Stink's eyes were closed so he never saw the gun flash as the bullet hit him flush in the face.

I pumped three more bullets into his chest for good measures, then I wiped down whatever I may have touched. I got dressed, grabbed the money, and bounced. I carried the bag of money in one hand and the gun in the other. Before I reached the lobby, I dropped the bag of money on the steps.

I put the gun in the small of my back and walked out into the lobby. "Boochie, Stink wants you to help him count the money."

"Call me." Boochie told Fatima and then rose to go to the stairwell.

I bought the silenced 9 millimeter from behind my back and shot Boochie repeatedly in the chest and face. When he hit the ground I walked over to him and put two more bullets into his head. I walked over to the steps and retrieved the bag of money. Fatima started screaming and I looked at the bitch with a 'shut the fuck up' look. But her scream alerted the clerk behind the desk who in turn came out of the office to investigate and that mistake was costly.

As soon as she saw the body on the floor, she looked directly into my eyes. Before she could say a word, I shot her and kept shooting her until the gun was empty. The clicking of the empty clip brought me back out of my daze and I pushed Fatima out of the Tourist Home door. She had a frightened look on her face and was hysterical.

Angel

"Get off me, I can walk. Angel why did you kill that lady, the clerk? Why? Huh? Oh my God! I can't believe this. Angel, what the hell is wrong with you?"

I opened both doors to the truck and waited for Fatima to get into the truck. She didn't. I looked outside and saw Fatima running down Talbert Street. I put the truck into gear and raced down the street to where Fatima was, stopped the truck, jumped out, and grabbed Fatima.

"Fatima, what are you doing? Huh? Where are you going?"

"I...I...I have to get away from you." Fatima said. "Angel, you're crazy. I'm afraid of you. I don't feel safe around you anymore. You killed that lady for nothing! Who are you going to kill next, ME? Let me go!"

"Fatima, calm down and get in the truck. We'll discuss this as we drive home."

I put her in the truck and then walked around to the driver's side and got in. We rode in silence for a while until I spoke up.

"Fatima, I had to kill her. She was a witness to a murder. She saw me with the gun after I shot Boochie. Your scream made her come out of the office. She was gonna call the police and give them our descriptions. We would've been charged with double homicide. Did you want that to happen? Do you want to go to jail, Fatima? You were right there; you did nothing to intervene. So, in the eyes of the law, you look just as guilty as me. She had to die. Her only crime was having a shitty job in the wrong place at the wrong time. Stop thinking about it and pull yourself together. I didn't start this Fatima; Dearaye did. I just ended it. It's over Fatima. No more killing, I swear."

She probably couldn't even hear my words through the heavy sounds of her tears.

******

All the way back to Fatima's house, she was quiet. I could see that she was visibly shaken up. And then a scary thought went through my mind. *You have to kill Fatima.* And I knew that scary thought was true. I didn't want to kill her, how could I. She was my best friend in the whole world. I love Fatima like my own sister, like I love myself. *No, I can't bring harm to her. No.* But, if she keeps flaking out like she did back there on Talbert Street, I may have to consider it. When we got to Fatima's house, she went upstairs and shut her bedroom door. Then I heard it lock. I decided to let her be. *She just needs some time and a little space, that's all.*

I checked the messages on my house phone and there were several; three from Detective Jones, the dude on Tony's case. I had forgotten all about him. *I wonder what he wants. Fuck that, I'm not calling him back.* Five messages were from Deandre's cell phone, all marked urgent. One message was from Charlie T. I knew that Charlie T. was Carlos. He said that he was just checking up on me. I made a mental note to touch base with him later. 'First things first' has always been my motto, so I dialed Deandre back on his cell phone. He answered on the first ring.

"Where you at?"

I was caught off guard by the aggressiveness of his tone of voice.

"I'm out and about, why, what's up?"

"Why have you been avoiding me?" he asked.

"I needed some time to myself. I just lost my sister."

"I need to see you as soon as possible. When can we get together?"

"I have a couple of thing to do right now that can't wait. I'll meet you after that. I'll call you when I'm finished a'ight?"

"Yeah, a'ight."

Then he just hung up the phone. No bye, baby bye, or none of that shit. My thoughts started racing at a mile a minute. *What did Deandre want to see me about all of a sudden and why did I detect a lot of hostility in his tone? Is he mad because he hasn't talked to me in a while? But he has to understand my reasons for wanting to be alone. What happened to the warmth that I usually hear in his voice?*

I know he knows that Dearaye is dead. I saw the news the next day when they found the two bodies out in Hyattsville. The bodies were later identified as Dearaye M. James and Thomas J. Murphy, one shot to death, the other strangled. *Has Deandre connected their deaths to me? Deandre has to know Tommy and his crew. Has he seen the news where they reported that Thomas Murphy's brother Ricardo Murphy was murdered in DC a few days after he was murdered and dumped in Maryland? Has he put two and two together and come up with Angel? Even if he has made some connections, which ones could probably lead to me? Maybe I'm just overreacting. Maybe he's just distraught about his brother.*

I'm gonna have to calm myself down. If need be, I'll just send Deandre onto the next life, if he doesn't send me, first. I don't want to kill Deandre if I don't have to, but I might have to. I can't afford to start slipping now. I can't let myself be swayed by emotion. I called Deandre back and told him to come to Fatima's house. I don't think he'll try anything at Fatima's house I think I should get a reading on his mind-set.

Deandre's pearl white 600 SL pulled into Fatima's driveway a few minutes ago. I stood at the window and wondered why it took so long for Deandre to get out of the car. *What's he doing in there?* If he tries some stupid shit, I'm ready for him. I tucked the reloaded silenced Ruger in my pants and pulled my shirt over it. I had the .45 automatic tucked in the front waistband, also out-of-sight. I watched through the blinds as Deandre made his way up to the front door. I opened the door and hugged Deandre, but not real close. I could tell by the look on his face that something was on his mind. I tried to play it off like I wasn't hip to how messed up he was.

"Dre, what's up with you? What is so urgent?"

"We need to talk. I need you to break something down for me. And Angel, please don't lie to me." Dre said.

"Have I ever lied to you, Dre? You can ask me anything."

"Did you know that Dearaye is dead?"

"What? Dead? Stop playing, Dre."

"Does it look like I'm joking? Did you know?" he shouted.

"Did I know? How in the hell would I know that? I haven't watched TV, so naw, I didn't know that. What the fuck happened to Dearaye, Dre?"

The next thing I knew, Dre pulled out a gun. The barrel of the gun was pointed at me. I was suddenly afraid. My mind told me that I was about to die. *He must know. He must know I was involved in his brother's murder. But how does he know?*

"I was hoping that you could tell me what happened to him, Angel. He was shot in the face. He was beaten and stabbed. His body was thrown into a ditch. What do you know about that, Angel? Did you know that Ray was mad at you for messing with me?"

"Yeah I knew that. He called me and told me that back when we first started messing with each other. I told you that. Put the gun down, Dre."

"Did you ever find out who was robbing your workers? Did you find out who killed little Lil' Chucky?"

"No." I lied. "I tried to find out, but the streets weren't talking; nobody knows who those dudes were. Dre, you're scaring me. Why are you still pointing that gun at me?"

"What about your sister, huh? Did you find out who killed her?"

"What are you asking me, Dre? Why are you tripping on me, like this? Please put the gun down, Dre, before it goes off. What did I do, baby? Why are you treating me like this?" I wasn't lying about being scared. I really was. I was trying to stall for time. I needed a way to pull one of my guns.

"Answer my fucking questions! Better yet, shut the fuck up. I'ma tell you what you did. Somehow you found out that Dearaye was behind your sister getting killed. You beat him until he gave you Tommy Guns; then you killed him."

"Dre, baby, you're wrong. You've got it all wrong. I never knew that Dearaye did anything. I haven't seen Dearaye. Why do…"

"I know it was you, Angel. Just admit it."

"If you think some crazy shit like that, then you must be crazy. I just lost my sister and a friend of mine and you come up in here waving a gun around. You're accusing me of shit, when I'm the victim. Somebody killed your brother and you blame me? What the fuck is that all about? What are you gonna do, huh? Shoot me? You gonna kill me Deandre? Well, go ahead. Fuck it, I ain't scared to die. I ain't did shit to your brother. I didn't even know he was dead. Go ahead, Dre, shoot! What are you waiting for? I love you Dre, but if you think I crossed you in anyway, go ahead and kill me."

I turned around and walked to the table in the living room. I expected to be shot in the back. I was taking a chance by telling Deandre to shoot me, but I had to try something. When I turned back around, the gun was at Deandre's side. Tears flowed out of his eyes.

"Why didn't you tell me about Tony Bills?"

I walked over to Dre and wiped his face. He dropped the gun to the floor.

"I used to mess with Tony; I was there when he was killed. But what does that have to do with you, with us? I never told you that the coke was coming from me because I didn't want you to take advantage of me."

Deandre took his eyes off of me and that was all I needed to pull my gun. I pulled the silencer 9 millimeter from behind my back. As he raised his head to look at me. I shot him in the stomach. He grabbed his stomach with both hands. I almost felt sorry for him, almost. I knew that I had to kill him because I couldn't turn back. The look on his face was one of shock and anger. He tried to reach for his gun on the floor, but I shot him in the leg for his troubles.

"Deandre, don't you know that you never pull a gun when you don't intend to use it. You should've killed me when you had the chance. I really do love you, Dre. I was hoping that you left all the bullshit alone. I hoped that you mourned your brother, and left everything else at that. Let me tell you about your brother. He was fucked up, Dre. He was mad at both of us because we were together. He went down to Sursum Cordas and got the dude Tommy Guns and his brother and cousin to bring both of us a move. Who do think tried to snatch you? It was them and Dearaye was with it. You heard me right, Dre; they were paid to rob you, too. That's who robbed your workers as well. They kidnapped my sister, raped her, and killed her on the orders of Dearaye. They both admitted to it before they died. I paid some dudes to kill everybody they could until word got back to me that it was Dearaye. All the murders that have been taking place, that's my work. I stabbed your brother. I beat his punk ass. I shot him in the mouth and blew the back of his head off. I did that! I did that for my fourteen-year-old sister he killed. And I fucked Tommy in the ass and then I killed him. it was pathetic the way he cried and begged for his life. But I didn't spare him. They didn't spare my sister and she was innocent. Your bitch ass brother should have had the balls to take me. But, they didn't, so the same way my sister pleaded for her life, is the same way Tommy Guns pleaded for his life as I rammed a big twelve-inch rubber dick into him. He passed out several times. I thought about my sister the whole time I fucked him.

Angel

So, yeah, I killed your brother. Fuck your brother! I hope he's in hell right now. Ricardo Murphy, Tommy's brother, he's dead. Short-Short their cousin, he's dead too. That's the story Dre; a lot of people died. A lot of people lost their lives because your weak ass brother got strung out on some pussy! The funny part is, you're about to die for being stupid. I've killed a lot of people in my life, Dre; I'll pay for it one day, but not today. Say hi to your brother for me, Deandre."

I shot Deandre in the forehead and he fell back over the couch. He was dead before his body touched the leather.

******

I walked up the steps and knocked on Fatima's door.

"Fatima, wake up, girl. Fatima!"

After several minutes, Fatima opened the door, "What is it Angel?" she asked me annoyed.

"Deandre's downstairs."

"Damn, what does he want? Does he know about Dearaye? Where he at? You want me to talk to him?"

"Fatima! You can't talk to him." I told her as she turned around and faced me.

"Why not?"

"Because he's dead, that's why."

"What? Angel, please tell me that Deandre is not in my house dead. Please tell me that you didn't kill Deandre in my house. PLEASE FUCKING TELL ME THAT!"

My silence must've said it all because Fatima fell to the floor in tears, crying uncontrollably. I was helpless. It hurt me to see Fatima crying. I just wanted her to stop.

"Fatima, Deandre was going to kill me. He pulled a gun on me first. I swear! I didn't want to kill him. Somehow he found out about my connection to this brother's death. He came here to kill me. That's why his messages were so urgent. He pulled his gun on me. I

208

talked him out of pulling the trigger. When he let his guard down I pulled my gun and shot him. I had to kill him because he would've tried to kill me eventually."

Fatima looked up at me with tears running freely down her face. "But I didn't hear any gun. Oh, the silencer! That's why I didn't hear anything. So he's just downstairs in my living room now, dead?"

"Yeah, pretty much."

"Angel. I can't do this. I can't live like this. I can't take it anymore. Don't you see what you've done to me? I'm going insane. I hear voices. Why have you forced this life onto me? May Allah have mercy on my soul. I'm going to the hellfire for sure. I'm going to die or either go to jail for life. We're going down, Angel. Is that what you want? Well, you've done it. I hate you, Angel. I hate you. I hate you." Then she stared crying again.

"Fatima you can't fall apart on me now. I need you. I was always there for you. Whenever you were in trouble, who was there for you? Me! You're not going to jail because you didn't kill anybody. I did! I'm not going to jail because nobody's going to tell about us being at the Tourist Home, because no one knows. There's no witnesses to any crime. Nobody knows about Deandre being here. All we have to do is get rid of his body. I want you to come downstairs after you get dressed, to help me dig a hole so we can bury him.

Is this bitch crazy for real? I'm not fucking digging no hole to bury nobody. I fucking hate Angel, I wish she'd go somewhere. She should go to California and never come back.

"If you don't come downstairs. I'll know that I'm in this alone. Come on Tima, don't lose it on me now. After this one thing, you can do whatever you want or go wherever you want and I won't bother you again. If you don't want to be friends with me anymore; that's cool. You can have my apartment until I buy you another house anywhere you want it. Or I'll just give you the money and you can do whatever, but tonight I need you. There's blood all over your couch that we have to clean up. We have to bury his body. It's up to you. I'll be downstairs."

Even though I told Fatima it would be alright if she didn't want to be friends with me anymore; it really wasn't. *I'm going to have to kill her. Why won't she act right? I don't want to but she knows too much. Damn.*

I went out to the shed and got the shovel. I started digging a hole. About thirty minutes later Fatima came outside dressed in boots and sweatpants. She grabbed the other shovel and helped me dig a hole big enough for Deandre. It took both of us about five hours to dig his grave, but we did and then we dragged him through the house wrapped in a blanket and some plastic.

We rolled Deandre into a hole that had to be at least four feet deep. My back was sore and my feet felt like sand in my shoes, but overall we got the job done. All those nights at Run and Shoot Gym paid off. I dropped his gun into the hole with him. I already had his car keys and the money that he had on him in the house. We covered him up and sat down for a while. Then I had to get rid of his car. The 600 Benz was the new joint where you didn't need a key. All you needed was a black plastic card. You could carry the card in your pocket or wallet, like a credit card. As long as the card was on your person, the car would unlock, start and lock back. I drove the Benz while Fatima followed me. I drove down to Anacostia Park, jumped out of the car, and let it coast into the Anacostia River. And that was that!

I looked at Fatima on the way back to her house. I'm glad that she decided to come and help me out. I had already decided that Fatima could really be next to meet the Grim Reaper. When I went to dig the hole for Deandre, I marked a second spot in the dirt. I don't think she noticed it. That spot was to be another hole; a grave for Fatima Muhammad's body. I was afraid that she was going against me, but by digging the hole and burying Deandre, she showed me that I might be wrong. *Maybe I'll give her another chance.*

Back at the house; Fatima quietly packed a bag of clothes and told me that she had called Wop and told him that she was going to stay with him for a while. I made her promise not to say anything. *I'll crush him too if need be. I know she doesn't want to jeopardize him. She doesn't want that.*

Things have gone from bad to worse, and I just want to move on, get past all this. I've given my sister's death honor in what I've done. *They didn't get away with it, I showed them they wasn't fuckin' wit' an average bitch.* Now, I just want it all to be over with. I look in the mirror and sometimes I don't know who I see staring back at me.

Who am I? What have I become? Fatima called me a monster today. *Am I really a monster? I just wish I knew what my future held in front of me.*

CHAPTER TWENTY-SIX

FATIMA

I need a serious vacation. Angel got me playing Bonnie to her Clyde while she kills people. It's been a week since Angel made me bury Deandre in my back yard. Why mines? What is wrong with me? But, how could I say no? I just got to stay clear of her. I can't even sleep in my own house no more. I don't feel comfortable. Don't she know my backyard ain't no cemetery? I think I'll just stay right here with Wop at his house.

I have to figure out what I'm gonna do. Buy a new house maybe or move to a whole new state all together. Either way, I got to get away from Angel. Girlfriend is trippin' for real. It's like something evil done possessed her and she's gone mad, killing all them people like she's crazy. And she got me all in the middle of her shit. I feel so bad. I need to atone for my sins and try to save my soul. I'll have to offer all my salats and even a few optional prayers to Allah to have mercy on me.

I'm having the worst nightmares. I watched two people die and I was involved in four murders. I've been running around with a person who killed god knows how many people in the past two weeks. She's a lunatic, a lunchbox, the devil incarnate. But, she's also my best friend, my sister. I love that girl with all my heart, but she's out of control.

Every day I offer salat and I say a prayer for her. I say a prayer for me as well because I never did anything to stop her from killing over and over again. Even though we never talk about it, I thought that after she killed her father, she'd be okay. I knew that her father molesting her was like a thorn that grew from concrete. I've always known there was a deep, inner secret place within Angel. Somewhere, far inside her and it's dark, real dark. I always blamed it on her dad and the molesting.

I really think that's what set her off, you know. But, then she killed Andre in college and that's sort of when I knew she was crazy. But, I never imagined nothing like this. Angel used to be sweet and soft, that's what trips me out about her now. She can be the nicest, best person you'd ever want to meet who would do anything for you. But, if you violate her, she goes to a whole nother level. That's where she takes it, she takes it to death.

I don't know how she does it and lives with herself. I've taken maybe a hundred showers since I left that Tourist Home on Talbert Street, but I still feel dirty. My body and soul feels unclean. I can still smell death in my nostrils. Some days I wake up seeing blood on my hands. The nightmares all end up with me crying bloody tears.

I sit around and think about the innocent woman who got killed in the Tourist Home. I think about her family. Her name was Ernestine Wiseman. She had a big family too, five children and a husband. She was forty-six years old and her only crime was going to work. I can still see her face in my head. I can see her face hitting the floor as she died. The picture that the news ran of her continues to haunt my dreams. They showed a family portrait of her with all of her children. I cried when I saw it and my conscience feels so guilty, I hate the way I feel.

The police don't have a clue about the murders at the Tourist Home. Angel was right. They quickly blamed it on the escalating drug war that was taking place in the streets. *What drug war? The Angel War would be more accurate.* The two dudes who died with Ernestine Wiseman, Andre 'Stink' Reese and Mark 'Boochie' Murphy, were mentioned, but the press ran with the story about the lady, wife and mother of five.

I know Wop probably thinks I'm acting strange because in the week that I've been here, I barely said twenty words to him. I want to talk to him so bad; I want to tell him so much, but because the twins were his friends, I can't. Plus, he's crushed enough as it is about Dearaye. He doesn't even know about Deandre. If he knew that Angel killed both brothers and that I helped to bury Deandre in my backyard we'd definitely fall out.

Plus, I need him right now and if I talked, he'd either blame me or do something crazy and Angel would kill him, too. I can't win for losing. That's Angel's saying, but it's the story of my life.

Yesterday, Wop came home at around one o-clock real agitated and paranoid. Then thirty minutes later the Feds kicked the front door in. They had a warrant to search the premises and a warrant to arrest Wop for first degree felony murder, armed robbery, and kidnapping. Unbeknownst to me, Wop had a small cache of weapons in the bedroom where I was when the cops came in the house. One gun was under the mattress on the side of the bed where I slept. So they arrested me too. I was kicking and screaming for Wop to do something. But, he couldn't do shit. He was too busy fidgeting with his hands behind his back to save me.

Now it's about two in the morning and I've been processed, fingerprinted, picture taken, strip-searched, and questioned. It's freezing cold in this cell. It stinks in here, and I'm scared. The big policewoman looked like she enjoyed seeing me naked as she searched me. She was probably a big ol'bulldyke. I can't believe what's happening to me. *To have to sit in this cell like this is definitely my punishment. I never thought I would ever be in jail, not like this.* All I was trying to do was duck Angel. I'm really afraid of her. I go to Wop's house for comfort, safety, and peace and I end up in jail.

I was formally charged with ten counts of carrying a firearm without a license and possession with intent to distribute a controlled substance, cocaine, within a thousand feet of a school. They found three kilos of cocaine. One key was in powder form and the other two were cooked up and broken down into ounces, seventy-two ounces in all. I didn't even know all that stuff was in the house.

Wop tried to tell them that I had nothing to do with the guns and drugs, but I'm a young black woman so they locked my ass up too. *I swear I don't think I can take this cell much longer. The silence is deafening. I'm hungry and I'm tired, but my body won't let me rest in this foreign place.* I used my phone call to try and reach Angel, but she didn't answer. So, I called my mother and she promised to reach her for me.

I heard footsteps coming down the hall. *I hope it's someone coming for me, to let out and maybe apologize for the misunderstanding. But it wasn't.*

A policewoman handcuffed me and then led me to a small room with nothing but a table and chair. I sat in the chair and my left wrist was handcuffed to the desk. Two male officers came into the room. I immediately became conscious of how terrible I must have looked.

The had dragged me out of Wop's house as is, so all I had on was an oversize T-shirt, raggedy jeans, and flip-flops. My hair was a mess and my face was undone. The two plainclothes police dudes introduced themselves as Homicide Detectives Rick Jordan and Peter Gertz. I instantly wondered what they wanted with me. It wasn't long before I found out.

"Ms. Muhammad, can I call you Fatima?" said the black cop, Rick Jordan.

"Yes.:"

"Fatima, you've been booked on numerous firearm violations and serious drug offenses. Tomorrow morning you'll be arraigned in District Court and you'll see a magistrate who will most likely, due to the severity of your charges, hold you without bond. Fatima, we did a back ground search on you and you have no prior criminal history.

"We know that you're employed for Angel's Beauty and Barber Palace on Queens Chapel Road in Northeast; you live in a rented town house in Maryland, and you drive a 1997 Nissan Maxima-blue. You have good credit, you pay your bills on time, and you're Muslim. The way I see it, you're facing twenty-years on drug charges. You'll be in DC jail for years before you even go to trial. DC jail is the worst place on the planet.

"Trust me, I've been there undercover. Imagine living in a small cell with rats, roaches, and a butch broad named Joan locked up for murdering her kids. You wouldn't like DC jail, Fatima. Now that DC is run by the federal government after you're convicted of these charges and you will be convicted, you'll end up in Wala Wala Washington State on the West Coast somewhere. No family visits, no friends, no nothing. Is that what you want Fatima?"

"Those guns and drugs weren't mine. I don't even live there. I was only visiting. I don't know why y'all charged me with this stuff. I don't know anything about it."

"You're right, we know the guns and drugs weren't yours and you're totally innocent. We know that. But life is not fair, Fatima. You were in a room that had ten automatic weapons in it. So, unless you cut the bullcrap and talk to me, you'll be convicted on all of the above charges and three counts of felony murder."

"Three counts of felony murder! For what? You must be crazy?" I told Detective Jordan. "I don't know anything about no three murders."

"Oh! Is that right?" he said. "Check this out, Ms. Smartass Fatima. I'm a homicide detective. That means I investigate murders. While investigating a murder scene a week ago, I came up with several fingerprints. One set of prints belong to the deceased, the other set, well we didn't know who they belonged to. Then after we put your prints into the database to search for a match; you happened to have a match already in the system.

"Technology is a beautiful thing Fatima. Because every time someone gets arrested and fingerprinted, the computer automatically cross-references unknown prints with any print entered after the first one. When we fingerprinted you, the computer came up with a match. You were at the Tourist Home on Talbert Street when three people were killed and guess what? You're about to be charged with an additional three counts of murder. And guess what else, Ms. Smartass Fatima? The feds are going to give you the death penalty. No Hazelton for you; life in prison is too easy.

"You'll go to Terre Haute, Indiana. Have you been to Indiana, Fatima? It's a nice place with a whole lot of white folks who don't give a damn about Ms. Smartass black Fatima Muhammad. The whole nation is upset about what happened to Ernestine Wiseman. No one cares about the two thugs that were murdered. But, the public outcry for blood is over the mother of five who was killed while working to feed her family. And now we have you."

I couldn't believe my ears and I didn't even realize I was crying until the detective handed me some tissues. My whole world came tumbling down. I broke down into an outburst of screams. The officers left the room and let me cry myself out. I cried for myself, I cried for my mother, I cried for my boyfriend, Wop. I cried for Angel's sister Ahdeerah who was kidnapped, raped, and murdered. I cried for the twins, for Ernestine Wiseman, and Tony. Angel killed them. And then I cried for Angel. I always read in the Holy Qur'an that Allah doesn't place a burden on a person who they cannot beat. Well my burden is too great. *Oh Allah, please help me! What do I do now? I love Angel with all my heart, but I can't go to jail and then be put to death for things that I didn't do.*

Angel

And Angel she would never forgive me, never. If I betray her. She would definitely seek revenge against me. If I did. I could sense something was strange about her the night she killed Deandre. I saw her make a second spot in the dirt after we buried Deandre. She thought that I didn't notice. That spot was for me. I know it. *Why is this happening to me? I'll just lie and say that somebody else committed the crimes.*

The detective came back in the room and I lied like hell for an hour or so. But the cops were seasoned. They saw right through my lies. Before I knew it, I was knee-deep in lies. The detectives got mad.

"Fatima, you've been lying to protect someone. With or without you, we're going to find out what happened at the Tourist Home because guess what, Fatima, we found another set of prints, too. And eventually, we'll find out who your accomplice was and do you think that person will protect you? Trust me, it won't happen. We're trying to save you Fatima. I'm trying to help you; can't you see that? Help me too, Fatima. Tell me what you know. Help me solve this case and I'll personally see to it that all the drug charges and gun charges are dropped and you'll never do a day in jail. We won't charge with the murders. You'll help us and we'll relocate you in another place to live. So what's it going to be; death or life, jail and death row or a new life and a fresh start? I'm going to take my partner and step outside for a few minutes to let you think about what I've just said. Then I'll come back and hopefully we'll talk some more. Okay?"

I nodded. Then they left. *What do I do? I can't stop crying and I'm scared. What would Angel do in this situation? I need to stop kidding myself because I'm not Angel. Angel is not Angel. Angel is sick and she needs help. Maybe they'll find that she's legally insane. I saw that on TV once. They can't lock her up or kill her because she's crazy. That's it! I'll tell the truth about the murders, but I'll make it look like Angel's insane. That way, we can have her put in a mental hospital where she can get help. I'm scared myself, but I'm scared*

218

for Angel more. If she keeps acting like a professional hit woman, pretty soon it will catch with her and she'll be killed. I don't want her to die. So if I tell what I know, maybe just maybe, I'll help save her life. She definitely needs help and I'm not going to jail for nobody's bullshit...

I made up mind to do the best possible thing for Angel. The detectives came back into the room. I told them that I was ready to talk. The white guy produced a tape recorder.

"I went to the Tourist Home with a friend of mine Kareemah El-Amin. We call her Angel. She went meet two dudes who she knew, about some business, what, I don't know. She was under a lot of stress because her sister Adirah El-Amin was recently raped and killed a few weeks ago. She was acting all strange and she definitely hadn't been herself since the attack on her sister. When we arrived at the Tourist Home, she met two dudes in the lobby.

"Angel and one of the dudes rented a room while me and the other guy stayed in the lobby talking. About ten minutes later Angel came back downstairs with a gun in her hand. Boochie saw Angel with the gun. He reached into his waistband to get a gun, but Angel saw him. She shot him. Angel had this look on her face like she had snapped or something. She told me Stink tried to rape her and kill her but they wrestled for the gun and it went off, killing him. She got the gun and fired some more out of fear.

"She never looked so crazy before. When she came downstairs I guess the guy figured out what happened, and reached for his gun; so she shot him too. The clerk startled Angel when she suddenly came out of the office. Angel shot her thinking it was Stink coming to grab her. She didn't mean to kill the lady or two dues. She went crazy after her sister died. She's crazy. You can help her. Please help her. Please!"

"Fatima, I want to help you. But you're not helping me. I want to help Ms. El-Amin, but again, you're lying to me Fatima. Don't say anything; let me finish. The evidence at the scene doesn't fit your version of the story. Mr. Reese or 'Stink' was not involved in any struggle. The room would've been in disarray. The bed wasn't even messed up.

"If Stink had tried to rape Ms. El-Amin, wouldn't the bed have at least show that? Unless of course he had her pinned up against the wall, but the dresser or something would've been out of place. Nothing was. Nothing in the room showed a struggle. Mr. Reese was lying on the bed on his back. His penis was exposed and we did find were traces of saliva, saliva that didn't belong to Mr. Reese. So for lack of a better term, whoever killed Stink, gave him oral sex before they did it. She caught him off guard. After sucking him off, she shot him.

"That was the best time to shoot him because most close their eyes during oral sex, which leads us to believe that Ms. El-Amin went to that Tourist Home to kill Andre Reese. Why Fatima? It was her suggestion to get a room wasn't it? She could have talked to Stink anywhere. But she wanted to isolate him. After killing him she knew that Mr. Murphy or Boochie was downstairs with you. She had to kill him, too. Our investigation shows that the shell casings that were ejected from the gun bore a slight indentation.

"It was later learned that the murder weapon used in all three killings had a silencer attachment on it. That's why Boochie never heard the shots upstairs, isn't it? Isn't that right, Fatima? Ms. El-Amin then came downstairs and shot Boochie. How am I doing so far Fatima? She came down the steps and opened fire, didn't she? He never stood a chance, did he? Then Ms. El-Amin noticed that the clerk, Mrs. Wiseman; was a witness who could describe the two of you; isn't that right!

"Ms. El-Amin knew that she couldn't leave the clerk alive. Ms. El-Amin then shot Ernestine several times in the chest, killing her instantly. Ms. El-Amin was very sane that night, Fatima. The murders of Mr. Reese and Mr. Murphy were premeditated. She went to that home to kill them. Mrs. Wiseman was just unfortunate.

She used you to keep Boochie and Stink separated. She knew she was no match for the both of them; they both had records as long as your arm. She performed oral sex on Stink; then killed him, then came downstairs and killed Boochie and Ernestine Wiseman. That's what really happened; isn't it Fatima? You must think we're insane if you think we'd believe that crock of shit you told us. Tell me the truth Fatima, or I swear you'll go down for everything too."

I couldn't handle it, I broke down. I told them the whole story starting with Tony Bills her boyfriend who she killed. I told them about Angel and Carlos Trinidad and how we picked up drugs every week from his associates. Angel basically took over Tony's business. I told them that I stayed in the background while Angel made all the deals.

I told them about Tommy Guns killing Lil' Chucky and about the robberies. I told them about Tommy and his homies killing Adirah on the orders of Dearaye and how Angel found out and that's why she killed Dearaye. I told them about Angel paying Stink and Boochie to kill all those people in the streets. She wanted to kill all those kidnappers in hopes that he people holding her sister would release her. I told them about Angel raping and killing Tommy. I told them that Angel had to get rid of Stink and Boochie because they knew too much. And I told them about Stink finding Tommy's brother and cousin, and killing them. I then told them everything that happened at the Tourist Home. *I can't believe it, I'm a snitch.*

But after I finished the whole story, to my surprise I felt better. I had all that balled up inside of me and it was killing my conscience. I know that Angel will kill me for what I've done. I probably won't be able to ever forgive myself for ratting on my friend, but I know in my heart, I did the right thing.

The detectives made good on their promise to take care of me. They put me in an office with a comfortable couch and I went to sleep. When I woke up, they fed me and then made me tell my story over and over again to different people. That's how I became a witness for the state and a traitor.

CHAPTER TWENTY-SEVEN

ANGEL

Shit is really wild. Just when I thought everything was under control, some more shit happens. Fatima's mother just called me and said that Fatima's in jail. She was arrested with Wop on gun and drug charges. She said she talked to Fatima yesterday, but that's all she would tell me. I don't think Fatima's mother likes me very much. Actually, I don't think she ever did.

I went to the Superior Court and the District Court. No one has heard of a Fatima Muhammad. That's strange because if Fatima's mom talked to her yesterday at around 8:00 p.m.; Fatima should be in court this morning. I saw a list of people arrested the day before who had to appear in front if the judge in courtroom C-10 but no Fatima Muhammad.

I checked the docket in District Court and I saw a time for an appearance for David Lee Jones. That's Wop, but where's Fatima? I called my lawyer Rudolph Sabino and had him check into the matter. He called me back. There was no record of a Fatima Muhammad ever being arrested. Red flags went off in my head. *What the fuck is going on? This is some shit that I don't need.* In the last week since the Tourist Home incident, I had been trying to keep my business and drug empire together. Wack and J-Rock from Barry Farms started buying more bricks and so did Russell, Doodie, Nome, and Romeo. Face from Uptown is pressuring me for a better price on his 10-keys weekly. Dip from Congress Park got robbed and shot. They put some work in, and now Squirt is locked up and Dip is on the run. So, that's 6 keys a week and $150,000 dollars weekly that I lose. The dude

Angel

Vest from down the valley got killed over a broad, but Deemo and Moosy are still onboard picking up the slack. Pretty Lady is up to five keys a week, business as usual. Everybody else is pretty much the same.

Right before the situation with Adirah, I had pulled in some dudes from out in Baltimore and a few from Virginia. I still had all my youngings in Simple City, Eastgate, Benning Park, 54th and D, Central Avenue, 49th and Call Place, and several other strips, business was booming. Killing Deandre made me lose money, of course, but I'm still fulfilling my obligation to Carlos, so he's happy. He knows what's going on and I mean the man know everything.

He wasn't bullshitting, he's like God. The only problem is, Fatima. Now she's missing. I went to the 1st District Police Station and no one cooperated with me. I was very careful not to give them my real name. When Fatima didn't materialize the third day, I went to DC jail to see Wop. Again I gave a phony name. It took over two hours before he was finally escorted to the cage. There's a phone receiver on both ends of the glass in the visiting hall.

"Wop, what's up?"

"Angel, what's up with you, boo?"

"Did Fatima get locked with you?"

"Yeah, I didn't mean for her to get caught up in my shit, but they grabbed her when they came to get me. I tried to tell them that she wasn't involved in anything and that she was only visiting me but they weren't trying to hear that shit."

"So, where the hell is she?"

"I don't know. The last time I saw her was when they put her into the paddy wagon. I never saw her at the precinct and she wasn't in court with me. I don't have a clue. Fatima doesn't know about my business so they can't trick her out of any info about me, so I'm not worried. I asked my lawyer if I had co-defendant and he told me no.

They must've let her go. I don't know what's up. I've been calling her house and her cell phone. But, she ain't answering. I can't figure it out. Shit is fucking, crazy."

"I'm hip, I'm hip. I done tried to find her because her mother said that she was locked up and needed a lawyer. I've been all over the judicial system looking for her with no luck. I'm starting to get nervous. She's not at home; she's not at her mom's crib, she doesn't have any other friends. I'm lost. Look, remember this number, it's my cell phone. Call me if you hear anything from her or about her. Call me if you need something. The number is 202-438-7073. You got that?"

"Angel, have you see Deandre? I've been trying to get in touch with him. I missed Dearaye's funeral and everything. But I need Dre to come over here and see me. So if you holler at him, give him my message."

"I'll do that, Wop; you take care of yourself. Don't forget, call me if you hear or need anything." I didn't want to tell Wop that Dre was dead. That's the last thing he'd want to hear. I left DC jail in a daze. I was trying to face reality, but it was hard. Wop hasn't seen or heard from Fatima; but they did get locked up together, that's weird. Something is definitely up.

Outside of taking care of street business, I've been running the Palace because Fatima had been lunching and shit. So I'm either there or at the communication outlet. Then another week passed and still no word from Fatima. I had all kinds of thoughts, but I tried to think positive. She could've just ran away due to the stress. Then on July 15; 2003, my world came tumbling down. I opened the Palace for business and the day started off as usual. At around 1:00 in the afternoon, the whole Queens Chapel Road was blocked off and surrounded by cops. *Some serious fugitive must be on the loose or something*, I thought. Then the police swarmed the Palace. Men and women dressed like SWAT members put all my customers against the wall. I walked out of my office and stood patiently waiting for them. I knew that the fugitive was me, and the pieces began to fit. Fatima caved in and gave me up. The police placed me under arrest and then closed up my shop. They placed me in the back of one of the police cars. In my mind all I could think about was Fatima.

What did she tell them? Did she tell them everything? What was she thinking? Why? The police were too cocky, and sure of themselves the way they sent forty patrol cars, had a warrant for my arrest, the whole nine. As the police car raced through the city, I wondered if I'd ever see the streets again.

I was taken to a building and told it was the Homicide Headquarters. For about forty-five hours straight I was interrogated. I was questioned in shifts by several different detectives. Although I asked for my lawyer on several occasions, I was never afforded the opportunity to call him. I was held in a little room and caught maybe thirty minutes of sleep whenever I could. I was given cold bologna sandwiches and sodas. But I didn't answer any questions and that made them mad. For two whole days I played the fool and acted like I had no clue as to what was going on.

I was wise enough to know how to keep quiet because the detectives had a strange way of tricking people into saying what they didn't mean. I saw an article in the Washington Post before that talked DC police detectives forcing and coercing confessions out of people and that a case can be made from what he person says while being interrogated. Fatima was the only person who could've gave them the information that they had. All they needed was her testimony to convict me of murder.

They threatened me, lied to me, wheedled, cajoled, shouted, laughed, and then tried to rough me up a little. They pretty much tried everything in the book to get me to confess to those crimes.

But, I pretended that I didn't know what the hell they were talking about.

"Make it easy on yourself." They said. "You're facing the death penalty." They told me. I wasn't even paying them any mind. When they mentioned Carlos, I got scared for a minute. If these folks get to Carlos, he'll think that I gave him up and he'll hurt my family. I'll have to get word to him ASAP.

These folks can't hold me forever and violate my constitutional rights. I took criminal law in college, so I knew that for sure. When they finally realized that I wasn't going to give them any information, they took me to the 5th District Police Station and processed me. This was my first time being locked up, but I had a general idea of what was going down. I was stripped, searched; and fingerprinted. Then I was finally given permission to make a phone call. I called Rudy. I told my lawyer everything that happened to me since I was arrested two days ago. He was livid. He screamed cold-blooded murder, threatening the whole city establishment. *And he better do something for all the money I pay him.*

The next morning I was taken to court. I was learning firsthand how the wheels of justice turn. I asked the other females locked in the cage with me a rack of questions. The females in the bullpen where I was ran the gamut. All sizes, shapes, colors, and crimes. Most were crack heads, prostitutes, boosters, and dope fiends. There were a few young girls in jail for hustling drugs, assault, bad checks, credit card fraud, and then me. I was by far, the worst off since I was charged with three counts of felony murder. I played the innocent role to the fullest and kept my 'I don't know what they're talking about' face on. I went in front of the judge that afternoon and the proceeding only took a few minutes. I noticed that the courtroom was filled with spectators and reporters. The government stressed to the judge the severity of my charges and the judge agreed. I was ordered held without bond.

My lawyer told me that I was remanded into the custody of the Central Detention Facility. In other words, the DC jail. I was handcuffed and shackled. Then I was transported with about four other females to the jail. I can't say for sure that I was scared because I think that I was too upset to be scared. Then I figured, *what the hell should I fear? Why be scared of what officers and big bulldyke broads can do to me when Allah is going to fry my soul?*

Now that's scary. I was going through all that bullshit because of my best friend, my sister, my heart, Fatima. She has betrayed me and that hurt me like hell. I've been with Fatima since we were kids and I love her to death, but she has to go. Her life is not worth the paper that her birth date is typed on.

I was hauled off to the female block in DC jail, South Two. DC Jail had about two thousand men housed there. Our block was the only female block there. The block has eighty cells in it with two females to a cell. I knew that I was in for a long haul, so I decided to make the best of it. I was assigned to cell # 73. The cell was empty when I first moved in, but the next day they put a young girl into my cell with me. She caught her boyfriend cheating and stabbed the girl he was with. She was charged with assault with intent to kill and is facing ten years if found guilty. Her name is Latesha.

I was in the Washington Post for a few weeks. The media frenzy that surrounded my case was crazy. I was dubbed 'The Female John Gotti'. I was linked to several homicides in the city. According to the Post, I was behind all the recent execution style murders that took place that last several weeks.

The paper ran the story about the mother of five who I was charged with killing, and the story about Adirah being rape and killed. My alleged motive was revenge. I personally felt like a celebrity. The local news stations and papers were all vying for an interview with me. The story even went national. A lot of my old friends came out of the woodwork for their fifteen minutes of fame. My name was even linked to the infamous Carlos Trinidad and that brought national and international coverage. Carlos was infamous in other countries as well. I closed both of my businesses indefinitely. The least on my apartment was paid so I gave the keys to one of my uncles and let him stay there in my absence. I gave my Benz truck to my lawyer as a down payment on my legal bills. Money wasn't a concern for me, as I had invested wisely over the years.

I had $700,000 dollars hidden in my bedroom at my mother's house. There is a little over $500,000 dollars in the safe at the apartment. The wall safe in Angel's Beauty and Barber Palace contains about $250,000 dollars. The safe at the communication outlet contains about $170,000 dollars. The business banking accounts for both stores have roughly $400,000 dollars apiece. I invested heavily into the stock market and I have mutual funds and CDs. There's an unspecified amount of cash at Fatima's house that I hadn't even counted. My net worth is definitely in the low eight figures.

Speaking of Fatima, she still has yet to surface. My guess is that the feds are hiding her somewhere until she testifies against me. Nobody has talked to her or heard from her since the night of her arrest. I hired two more lawyers. My defense team resembled the OJ's dream team. I already had the savviest lawyer in DC; Rudolph Sabino. Now I have Rubin Rabinawits and Jennifer Roberts. I went to a couple of bond hearings but the result was always the same. The political climate that surrounded my case made it virtually impossible for me to get a bond or any type of release.

My visiting days at the jail were Mondays and Thursdays. I get visits from my lawyers whenever; there's no limit. I've gotten several visits since I been at the DC jail; mostly my family. But, a few of my homies from the street have visited and other associates have been writing me letters, that's love. I'm even offering my Salats and going to Jumah in here. I read my Qur'an for daily nourishment and I'm really back on my deen.

Jail is hard and never ever let anybody tell you it isn't. Every day was the same, tedious, and monotonous. I prayed dominoes, cards, and scrabble every day. The days turned into nights and weeks passed by turning into months. By the time I turned around, five months had passed by. The government still had not returned the indictment. My lawyers say that their evidence is shaky. They need more than Fatima to indict me.

The discovery packet shows what the government has is actually nothing. They have no fingerprints that belong to me, no guns discovered, no nothing. All they have is Fatima Muhammad, her testimony, and her prints at a crime scene. I can't figure out for the life of me why Fatima hadn't told them about Deandre being buried in the backyard because that would do me in. They say that they have DNA from the saliva that was found on the penis of the deceased Andre Richardson. My lawyers have been fighting a court order of me to submit a sample of saliva for a DNA test. But eventually we'll lose and the government will have my DNA.

But even if they prove I sucked the nigga off, so what? That alone doesn't prove that I killed him. My mother's still torn apart by Adirah's death and my arrest has made her condition worse. She's on some kind of anti-depressant. When I walk through the hallways going on visits or to the infirmary, all the dudes in the jail be trying to holler at me but I be shooting them down. *What do I want with a dude that's locked up?* Then one day out of the blue, I got a visit.

I wasn't expecting a social visit and most people stopped coming to see me long ago. I guess the novelty wore off when the cameras turned off and the fame died down. I heard the cops calling my cell number.

"Cell 73 El-Amin! Cell 73 El-Amin!"

"That's me, CO what's up?"

"Kareemah El-Amin?"

"That's me." I told her again.

"You have a social visit." She said throwing my hall pass in my face. *See bitch if I fucked you up in this motherfucker then I'll really be in trouble. She just don't know.*

I walked to my cell wondering who could be out there. But my gut feelings told me it was somebody close. I brushed my teeth and tightened myself up before leaving the block and heading to the visiting hall. At first glance, I didn't recognize anyone in the waiting area. As I turned to leave, a man motioned for me to come to the phone. The female visiting hall was made just like the one for the men. There were twenty booths with telephone receivers attached to both ends of a three-inch fiberglass separator. When the dude sat down in front of me and picked up the phone, I recognized his eyes. He was wearing a disguise, but the man in front of me was none other than Carlos Trinidad. I smiled.

"What are you doing here? You know these folks are probably watching to see who visits me. They've already publicized our involvement with one another, or what they believe it to be. You shouldn't have come here."

He smiled at me and I swear his smile warmed me. He had one of those devious 'cat ate my canary' smiles.

"Whoa! Slow down for a minute. I covered my tracks. I have several identities. Right now I'm Bill Tate. So call me Bill. These phones are not tapped or monitored, so we can speak freely with each other. Just kinda cover your mouth a little when you talk. I had to come to see you at least once, Angel. But after today, I'll keep in touch through my lawyer. Who happens to be your lawyer."

"I appreciate that. But I already have three lawyers."

"Rudy Sabino is great, I like him. Rueben Rabinawits is a piece of shit. He's good, but he's known to work with the prosecutor's office a lot. Jennifer Roberts is new in town, but from what I hear, she's the one to watch in the future. I know about your lawyers. I want you to have the best. Have you heard of J. Alexander Williams?"

"Of course. I saw him on Oprah Winfrey once."

"He's the best criminal defense attorney in the country. With him on your side, you can go to trial at 8:00 a.m. and beat your case, then beat the jury home so that you can beat eggs for an omelet for breakfast. That's how serious J. Alexander Williams is. Consider his services a gift from me. I like you Angel. I respect the way you do business and take care of business. You should've never gotten your hands dirty, but I admire the fact that your principles are strong. You showed more heart than a lot of men. I noticed that about you when we first met, remember? Did I ever tell you about my sister?"

"No, you didn't."

"When I was twenty-years old, my sister was raped too. She was sixteen, going on seventeen at the time. A close friend of mine turned out to be the rapist. I tracked my friend down and killed him. With that one act, I lost two people close to me, my sister and my best friend. My sister was never the same after that. That's why I'm here to help you, Angel. I understand why you made the moves you made. I did the same thing once. One day we'll have the chance to really talk and we'll talk then. J. Williams services are just advisory, because you won't really need him. I have good news for you."

"What could possibly be good news?"

Carlos smiled the Kodak smile again.

"This case will not even make it to trial."

"What? How do you figure that?"

"I have friends in high places. I'm like God, remember? I do what I can to take care of my friends and they take care of me. I have a judge in my pocket and several people inside the DA's office. Those DNA samples that they have will disappear and the government witness will never show up for court."

I couldn't believe my ears.

"How do you know that Fatima won't show up? No one even knows where she is."

"I know exactly where she is. She'll never make it into a courtroom. I know she's your closest friend, Angel, but Fatima's a rat and rats are rodents. What do you do when rodents get out of hand? You call the exterminator. In this case, that would be me. Give me the word and Fatima will cease to exit. I have people on the inside. She's being held at Embassy Suites Hotel in Crystal City, Virginia. She's in a suite on the top floor with six armed guards around her all day and all night. Killing her is the easy part. I just want to make sure that's what you want. Without Fatima, they had no case. Her video-taped statement won't hold up in court with her gone. What do you want to do?"

"Damn, you don't be bullshitting? Okay. You have my okay. Take care of that and I am forever in your debt."

Fatima is my heart, but that bitch gotta to go. Like Carlos said, she's a fucking rodent.

"The next time I sit in front of you, I wanna be a free woman."

"Consider it done. I'll send word when everything's finished. Except a visit from J. Williams. Take care of yourself in here and be strong. Get some rest." Carlos hung up the phone and walked out of the visiting area.

When I got back to my unit I was ecstatic. I felt like a big boulder had been lifted off my shoulders. I'm going to beat the case. It's me against the world. I felt like Tupac; all eyes on me. When I walk out of the courtroom, I'm going to buy me a convertible Bentley and put a $10,000 stereo system in it. I'ma ride around all day pumping Jay-Z and R. Kelly's joint, 'Not Guilty'. *I hummed the words to myself. Jigga Kelly, not guilty. Angel El-Amin, not guilty, Not Guilty!*

CHAPTER TWENTY-EIGHT

FATIMA

I'm tired of running. I've been to twenty different hotels in the last six months. Ever since I agreed to testify against Angel, my life has been a non-stop scene straight out of the movie Godfather. I feel like I'm on the Sopranos. But, I have to absolve myself of these criminal sins. I still have nightmares about all the things I was part of. I dreamed about Angel killing me. There's nothing stopping her from eventually deciding that I was in the way, too. I can't even call my mother out of fear that somebody may be listening in.

The Feds believe that there are people out there trying to find me. They say that if it was just Angel all of this wouldn't be necessary. But ever since I linked Angel to Carlos Trinidad, they say that I have very dangerous enemies. So, they've placed me in the Witness Protection Program. I'm tired of all this with the police around me twenty-four hours, seven days a week. I don't know what to do. I'm tired of fast food. It's okay but I miss my own cooking. I want to run away from all this but I know that they'll eventually find me, either Carlos Trinidad's people or the feds.

They say after I testify against Angel, I can get on with my life. This whole process may take me a few years though. *What life will have then? No job, no friends, and probably a contract out on my head.* I hated this closed in feeling. I feel like a caged gerbil. I don't go outside unless I'm moved. I don't go anywhere by myself. I have six armed guards around me twenty-four hours a day. I've grown to know them personally.

Angel

There are two women and four men. The two women are cool as hell. One is black. Her name's Valerie Ward. She's from Georgia. She transferred to DC to be closer to her boyfriend, who's a lawyer at the department of labor. The other woman's white. Her name is Dorothy Benigan. She's single, childless, and loving it. They keep my company all day so we talk a great deal.

The four male marshals are cool too, but they rarely talk to me. The Hispanic marshal's name is Miguel Vasquez. He's fine as hell. He looks like the dude from NYPD Blue. What's his name? Oh! Jimmy Smits. The black cop's name is Maurice Tolliver. He's twenty-eight; an Aries and was raised in DC. I know a lot about him, he's real nice to me. He's smart and sweet. The other two marshals are white cops who come off racist. So I don't mess with them.

The feds told me that Wop, copped out and took 120 months. That's ten years behind bars, but it's better than life. I'm happy for him, he got off the light. I wanted to see him and talk to him so bad, but the feds wouldn't let me. If it's meant to be, I'll see him again one day. I often think about Angel, too. I know she's in DC jail. I know that she's probably miserable as hell, too. I know that she hates me. I hate myself some days. But, then some days I feel that I made the right decision. *Why should I let Angel take me down with her? I didn't ask to be caught up in all of this. I didn't create this mess. This is all Angel's fault.* The first law of nature is self-preservation. That's what Angel always says. Or does that only apply to her? I cry myself to sleep some nights. I know that everybody is gonna be mad at me because I'm helping the cops. But, I have to do what's right. On the day of Judgement when I stand before Allah, I'll be questioned about my sins. Hopefully, Allah will forgive me because I tried to atone for my sins.

When all this over, I want to relocate to Atlanta. People say that Atlanta is the new mecca for black people. I can go down there and get lost in a sea of black faces and that's just what I plan to do. I dozed off and woke up hungry as hell. I walked into the living room of the hotel suite and asked Valerie to call room service for me.

"Can you order me the fried fish dinner with a raspberry iced tea?"

Twenty minutes later, Officer Benigan went down to get my food. I was watching Friday on my portable DVD player when the food came. The fish is the best thing on the menu. I gobbled up my food, like a starving Somalian. Then out of nowhere I got this sharp pain in my side. I rushed into the bathroom to throw up, but nothing came up.

I couldn't breathe as the pain in my side spread toward my chest. I was getting light headed. I stuck a toothbrush down my throat to try and force the off back up. I tried to defecate, but the pain was too intense. My chest felt like it was on fire. My heart started racing and I knew then that what I was experiencing was more than just cramps.

I started throwing up yellow bile. I couldn't even stand up erect. I got dizzy as the room spun around. The next thing I know, I was staring at the ceiling. I heard voices calling my name. At first it sounded like the officers in the next room. Someone was banging on the door. I saw a great big light being flashed in my eyes.

Then I recognized the voices calling me. It was Ernestine Wiseman, the lady from the Tourist Home. *How did she get into my room?* I looked into the light and saw Deandre, Dearaye, Stink, Boochie, Tony, and countless others. They all beckoned for me to follow them into the light. I heard the banging on the door and my name being shouted through the door. The last thing I remember seeing is the light. I followed everybody into the light.

CHAPTER TWENTY-NINE

Detective Sean Jones

"What do you mean she's dead? How the fuck can she be dead with six armed guards watching her twenty-four hours a day? I can't believe this shit. When did it happen? Nobody knows how or why? This is crazy, Rick. What the fuck! Okay, Rick, call me back when you hear something more."

I hung up the phone and popped two Aleves. I tried to walk my headache off. I can't believe what I just heard. Fatima Muhammad's dead and the federal marshals who were guarding her don't have a clue as to how she died. It's being investigated. Yeah right! I had no idea that Kareemah El-Amin's reach was so strong. But she's been linked to Carlos Trinidad, so it was probably his reach.

To kill a government witness under the eye of six armed guards is big. Really big! Now what the am I going to do? I already marked the murders of Dearaye James, Thomas Murphy, Ronald Fletcher, and Anthony Phillips, closed with the arrest of Kareemah El-Amin. I was anxiously awaiting to extradite her to Maryland to face felony murder charges which would guarantee her the death penalty. DC is bullshitting about capital punishment, but the good law abiding citizens in the state of Maryland will gas chamber and lethally inject her ass. That's why I like Maryland.

Now everything is back to square one. Without Fatima Muhammad, I don't have shit. I still remember about six and a half months ago when Rick Jordan from DC homicide division called me with the good news. I was going over some evidence from another cold murder case that was quickly going nowhere. Then the phone rang.

"Hello?"

"Sean, are you sitting down?" Rick asked.

"Yeah, why? What's up Rick?" I asked.

"I have somebody who you definitely need to talk to."

"Who?" I asked him, tired of playing games.

"Fatima Muhammad."

"Fatima who?"

"Fatima Muhammad. The only living breathing witness to the Tourist Home murders and she can connect the dots in four of your homicides out there. For, example remember Tony Bills murder case? "Yeah."

"Well, you were right. Fatima Muhammad is a close personal friend of Kareemah El-Amin and she swears that Ms. El-Amin killed Tony Bills, Tommy Guns Murphy, and Dearaye James."

"You said four murders; that's only three."

"Remember the other guy who was killed at the deli when Dearaye James was kidnapped? Well according to Ms. Muhammad, he was killed by the guys who were found dead in the Tourist Home Motel. She says that Kareemah El-Amin pulled the trigger in all the killings. She's been talking for forty-eight hours and still going. She says Tommy Guns killed Kareemah's sister and that Dearaye James gave the order. How's that for starters?"

"Rick, I swear, I could kiss you!"

"No kisses, fruitcake, the next vacation we take is on you. We'll do lunch and discuss how we can all benefit from our star witness.

That was six and a half months ago and I thought that everything was wrapped up. Fatima confirmed Kareemah's link to Carlos Trinidad. She said that Kareemah killed Tony Bills for the money. She came off with over a million dollars. What she didn't know was where Dearaye James and Tommy Guns were killed. That info would've helped a lot. Now what do I say to the families of the deceased? Hello, this is Detective Jones calling back to say that our witness is dead and there will be no closure for you.

I talked to several of the victims' relatives myself and I kept in close contact with Tina Brown, Tony Bills, girlfriend and mother of his daughter. I found myself starting to like Ms. Brown. She was overjoyed to find out what happened to her daughter's father. And her daughter, who was thirteen at the time, had to hear the brutal truth about what happened to her dad. I respect the fact that Tina was so open with the child. I believe Honesty had a right to know what happened to the most important person in her world. Tina told me that she had to put Honesty in a school for troubled youths because she started acting out after the death of her father. They prescribed some medication for the young girl, but Tina said it didn't seem to be working.

I visit them periodically and believe that Honesty is starting to come to grips with her father's death. She doesn't fully understand it, but she accepts it. I remember one day when I was at their home and we talked for a few moments.

"Why did that lady kill my daddy?"

"Because the lady was a bad lady who wanted money from your father."

That's all I could think to say. The closure part was in the fact that Kareemah El-Amin was in jail in DC facing life and then she'd be sent to Maryland to stand trial where the penalty for murder was death. But now I have to be the bearer of bad news. Tina and her daughter won't have any closure because the reality of the matter is without Fatima Muhammad the case against Kareemah El-Amin is weak. She's going to walk. She's going to go free, scott free. Life is never fair. I have to look this woman in the eyes and tell her that the woman who killed her boyfriend is going to walk the same streets as she. Our criminal justice system is not just at all. We have no witness and her signed confession can't talk and her story can be refuted. You can't cross-examine a dead witness. So like I said, we have nothing.

I decided to talk to Tina personally before she heard about all this on the news or worse through the grapevine. I called to make sure that she was home and then went to Kettering, Maryland. I pulled my car into the driveway and got out. Tina and Honesty both came to the front door. I hugged them and stepped inside. I told Tina that I needed to talk to her alone.

"Whatever you say to me, you can say in front of my daughter. She's almost fourteen-years-old and she's mature enough to understand what's going on. I keep no secrets from her."

I would have preferred if her daughter wasn't there; but Tina said it was okay. She wanted her daughter to know the truth about her father's murder.

"Fatima Muhammad is the only person who could bring Kareemah El-Amin to justice for Tony's murder. But I'm sorry to say that she won't be doing that, because she's dead. She was in police protective custody, however, someone got to her. They penetrated her security and it's believed she was poisoned. At the moment no one knows who killed her, but all bets are it came from Kareemah El-Amin. Who, without the testimony of Fatima Muhammad, will end up walking scott free."

"What do you mean, she walks?" Tina asked me. Honesty stared me dead in the eyes.

"I mean she beats the case. She walks away free. She'll be free on a technicality. The tech being that there's no one left to testify against her. With no witness, you have no case. She literally gets away with murder."

"But they have her testimony. Doesn't that count for something?"

"They have her recorded statement but it's not worth jack without her. In order to convict Angel, you need a live witness. So with the demise of Fatima Muhammad, convicting Angel is virtually impossible."

"I can't believe this." Tina said.

"That's exactly what I said earlier. Listen, Tina, I know how you must feel. I wanted Angel as bad as you, but we never counted on the fact that something would happen to Fatima. They blindsided us and it hurts. When I say they, I mean Carlos Trinidad. He's the only person with the power to pull of killing a federal witness. It had to be him. Angel is a big fish these days but her power is limited. When you start reaching your arms in the tree of law enforcement, it's all branches, that takes money, influence, and power.

"Hold on for one minute. Did you say Angel was hooked up with Carlos Trinidad?"

"Yeah."

"I never knew that, Sean. I know him from when he dealt with Tony. I wonder if he knows that she killed Tony? He was like a father to Tony."

"I don't know the answer to that, but I do know one thing for sure, and that is that Carlos Trinidad is helping Angel."

"Maybe Tony did something and Carlos told Angel to kill Tony."

"I don't know. What I do know is that unless a magical witness appears, Kareemah El-Amin is coming home soon." I looked at Honesty and noticed that she was crying. My heart was hurting for her. She turned and ran into her bedroom. I looked at Tina and she was crying too.

"Detective Jones, tell me one more time what happened to Tony."

"Okay; what we know about that night is that Kareemah El-Amin cooked dinner for Tony and then she had sex with him and he let her tie him up, then she shot him in the back of his head. She concocted the story about the intruders. She went to Fatima Muhammad's house and counted out over a million dollars that she took from the safe Tony kept in their apartment. That's what happened."

"Sean, do you think he suffered a whole lot? From the gunshot, I mean?"

"From what I know about these situations, Tony died instantly. He didn't even know what hit him."

"That's good." Tina said and wiped her eyes. I can see him in my dreams, you know. I talk to him every day. You just don't know how hard it's been."

"I can imagine, that's why I came all the way out here to tell you the news of Fatima."

"Thank you for coming out here and telling me this face-to-face. God bless you, Sean."

She turned and walked into her house. I stood there for a minute and wiped a tear that threatened to fall from my eye. After twenty-two years in the game, I still get misty when tragedy strikes good people. At least it shows that I'm still human and death has not desensitized me. I went to Ernestine Wiseman's house and spoke to her family, and for the second time in hours, I had to wipe away another tear from my eye.

CHAPTER THIRTY

ANGEL...

"Cell 73. Cell 73. Who's in cell 73?" the CO asked.

"Which one do you want out of cell 73, CO?"

"Cell 73 El-Amin has a legal visit."

"Sheila, go tell Angel that she has a legal visit. Tell her to hurry up because the CO has been calling her cell number for a while now."

I just met with my defense team yesterday. If they come back today it must be to bring some good news. When I walked into the visiting hall I saw a black, well-dressed man motioning to me. I went into the back room reserved for lawyer conferences and I knew who it was. He stood up as I entered the room.

"Kareemah El-Amin I presume?"

"Yeah, that's me. Who are you?" I asked.

"Please excuse me. I'm J. Alexander Williams. The J stands for Jasper. You can call me Jay. How's that?"

"That's cool with me. Tell me something good."

"Our mutual friend, sends his love and respect. I'm here to tell you that you will soon be a free woman. The government's case died with Fatima Muhammad. They have no witnesses and their DNA samples are missing. Without those two components their case against you is in the toilet. So, pretty soon they'll have to flush it before the back draft stinks too bad. Right now, as we speak, they're scrambling to find something to hold you on. They have to present something to the judge that will justify holding you longer than nine months. They don't have it and from what I gather, they won't find

244

anything. So just relax as much as you can and think about what you're going to do when you get out."

"That's is the best news I could possibly get, Jay. Tell our mutual friend that I'm forever in his debt. Mr. Williams, I mean Jay, how much does it cost to retain a lawyer like you?"

"Too much Kareemah, too much."

He smiled as he gathered his things, and got up to leave. He was halfway out the door when he turned around and faced me. "By the way, you look much prettier in person." Then he was gone.

Back on the block, I went to my cell and thought about what I had just heard. Fatima was dead, she was my closest friend in the whole world and now she was dead and I had her killed. All my life she was like my sister, my Muslim sister, and my best friend. The last time I cried was when my sister was found dead. I never knew that pain could be so great. I glanced at the picture of Fatima on my wall. We were at a club; I think it was the Black Hole. We were fly as hell against me, she was dead to me. She's been dead for six and a half months. When I walked into the TV room, the whole room got quiet. A breaking news bulletin was on live and the topic of the newscast was me.

CHAPTER THIRTY-ONE
THE NEWS

"This is Maria Wilson from City Under Siege Fox News reporting to you live from the Municipal Center, which is the headquarters of DC Police Chief Arthur Ramsey. Fox News has just heard that the key witness in the Kareemah El-Amin multiple murder case is dead. Fatima Muhammad was the only person at the scene of the Tourist Home where three people were shot to death, including Ernestine Wiseman, a forty-six-year old mother of five.

Fatima Muhammad also implicated Kareemah El-Amin in three other murders. The state of Maryland is waiting to try Ms. El-Amin for the murders of Anthony Phillips, Thomas Murphy, and Dearaye James. Ms. El-Amin was also linked to over thirty-three murders that took place several months ago. Fatima Muhammad turned state evidence over seven months ago and agreed to testify against Kareemah El-Amin.

"Ms. Muhammad was in the Witness Protection Program under armed guards. However, she was poisoned to death. Investigators are working around-the-clock to determine how security was breached. I have with me here, Deputy District Attorney Susan Rosenthal, DC Mayor Mervin Berry III, and DC Police Chief Arthur Ramsey.

First I'm going to talk to DC Mayor Mervin Berry. Mayor Berry there was a public outcry for some type of closure in the Kareemah El-Amin murder case. There was political pressure to bring someone to justice. Ms. El-Amin was brought to justice and it appears that she won't even stand trial in light of the recent of Fatima Muhammad. There are over thirty families grieving over the deaths of their loved ones. All these deaths have been attributed to Kareemah El-Amin. How do you feel about the recent turn of events?"

"Good afternoon Maria, like the 600,000 constituents in the District of Columbia; I am appalled at the new development in this case. When I campaigned to become Mayor of Washington, DC I made a promise to the people of this great city to lower the crime rate. I personally feel that our justice system has to help me bring criminals to justice and to keep them there. I'm truly dismayed about this situation. And my administration will do everything humanly possible to assure the people of DC that they can be a witness to a crime and feel safe. We really do depend on the public's help in solving a lot of crimes and it's very important that there is an element of safety provided when our public helps. Now, if you don't mind, I'm going to defer any more questions to my chief of police, Arthur Ramsey."

"Good afternoon, Chief Ramsey." Maria Wilson said. "Can you please tell us what's being done to keep Kareemah El-Amin behind bars and are there any new developments we should know about?"

"Good afternoon. The department it truly disturbed about what has happened. We're trying to turn over every leaf in this case to secure evidence that will lead to a conviction. We believe that Kareemah El-Amin is a very dangerous young lady. We believe that she belongs behind bars. We would like to implore anyone with any information about these cases to please come forward. And most importantly on the behalf of the whole police department, we would like to express our condolences to the family of Fatima Muhammad, a woman who had the nerve and heart to turn against a monster. She died because of her courage. Again, anyone with information regarding this case please call our crime solver hot line at 202-232-6767."

"Thank you, Chief Ramsey. Now I have Deputy District Attorney Susan Rosenthal here. DA Rosenthal, what can you tell us about the status of the government's case against Kareemah El-Amin?"

"Hello, Maria, we at the District attorney's office have been diligently trying to bring this case to trial for months. Our case wasn't very strong from the beginning. But Fatima Muhammad strengthened it. Without Ms. Muhammad, it's going to be very hard to put this case in front of a jury. We're working in conjunction with several police agencies in an effort to find out who poisoned Fatima Muhammad so that they can be brought to justice. At this time, I decline to comment on the status of the case because investigations are ongoing. As we receive information, we'll make that information known to the public.

"DA Rosenthal, if no witness is produced and if the DNA samples are not found, what happens to Kareemah El-Amin, who's being held without bond at DC jail?"

"Well, Maria if we're unable to secure another witness in this case, I regrettably have to say that Kareemah El-Amin will be released and the charges will be dropped."

"Thank you so much, DA Rosenthal. This is Maria Wilson from City Under Siege Fox News with a live broadcast from the Municipal Center in Northeast Washington. Please tune in at 5:00 for more coverage on this story."

I watched the news every day for the next two months and I read all the newspapers I could find and the info was always the same. I already knew that no witnesses would be found because I didn't leave any. On the morning of my court date, I knew that I had taken my last shower as a resident of DC Jail. I knew that by the time school kids got out of school at 3:00 o'clock, I would be a free woman.

CHAPTER THIRTY-TWO

COURT

"**G**ood morning your honor, Rudolph Sabino, on behalf of Kareemah El-Amin. Ms. El-Amin is present. Your Honor, the government doesn't have the DNA Samples that it promised the court in December in 2003. Your Honor, the government has no witness what-so-ever. My client has been held without bond and has been held in jail for nine months.

Your Honor, the government has had nine months, which is more than enough time to secure an indictment, procure witnesses; and match DNA samples. Your Honor, DC law requires that if the government has not indicted a person in confinement for nine months, then that person is released. On behalf of Kareemah El-Amin, I have presented the court with a motion to dismiss all charges against my client. Thank you, Your Honor."

"Good morning, Your Honor, Christine Weinstein, standing in for DA Susan Rosenthal who could not be here today. The government is unable to produce any evidence that would aid in the prosecution of Kareemah El-Amin. We do not foresee any evidence coming along in the future. As the court knows, our only witness was killed under federal protective watch. So, I regrettably say to the court that the government doesn't oppose defense counsel's motion to dismiss all charges."

The judge sat in his chair up on high, looked at me with sincere contempt, and then said. "I'm going to grant Mr. Sabino's motion to dismiss all charges, but I must say for the record that I'm truly disturbed by the unfortunate events of this case. I'm going to dismiss all charges with prejudice, so that at any time that the government

Angel

can secure evidence against Kareemah El-Amin, this case can go to trial. So ordered. The court is adjourned."

I hugged all of my attorney's and hand in hand we walked out of courtroom 113 into a waiting throng of cameras, reporters, and spectators. People on cell phones were relaying the outcome of my case to their friends. I walked out of Superior Court a free woman and was rushed through the crowd into a waiting Jaguar. I looked around at the world and couldn't believe I was free. The first thing I did was go to the bank and withdraw five thousand dollars. My second stop was a Post Office where I got a money order for the five and mailed it to Latesha Garrison; DC Jail #292-730, my cell partner and new best friend. I wrote on a piece of paper, 'Keep your head up'.

In all the commotion going on, Angel never saw the blond-haired woman watching her come out of the courthouse.

"Hello, Carlos? It's me Dorothy. Yeah she's free. She just walked out of the courthouse. Okay, will do. Bye."

She got into a silver Mercury Sable and pulled away from the curb.

CHAPTER THIRTY-THREE
TINA & HONESTY

"This is Maria Wilson from City Under Siege Fox News reporting live from the DC Superior Courthouse where Kareemah El-Amin is in court today to find out if she'll still be prosecuted for numerous murders. Our sources inside the court predict that Ms. El-Amin will be indicted and therefore released. Wait a minute, I'm receiving information now. We have just received word that District Attorney's Office has dismissed all charges against Kareemah El-Amin. Yes, it is confirmed, Kareemah El-Amin is a free woman. She's on her way out of the courthouse as we speak. She should be coming out this door right behind me here. Hold on here she comes now. Ms. El-Amin, can we ask you a few questions? Ms. El-Amin do you have anything to say to the people of DC? Ms. El-Amin, is it true that you had Fatima Muhammad killed so that you could be free? Ms. El-Amin, Ms. El-Amin? We tried to get a few words from Kareemah El-Amin, but as you saw, she wouldn't give a statement."

I turned off the news and tried to swallow what I just witnessed. Angel is out of jail. She got away with all those murders. I wiped away tears from my eyes and from the eyes of my daughter.

"Mommy was my daddy a drug dealer?"

I was taken back by her question, but I have never lied to my daughter.

"Yeah baby, your father sold drugs."

Angel

I realized at that moment how little I knew about Honesty. With me working every day, I rarely see Honesty now that she spends most of her time at my mother's house. Tony left us well-off, but I still work to set an example for Honesty. I had no idea that she even knew what drug dealer was. I'm eternally grateful to Tony for making it possible for us to get out of DC and out of the ghetto. I always wanted a better life for Honesty.

"Honey, your father was a good man; he was a great father. He loved you more than anything in the world. Your father grew up poor, so he did whatever he could to make life better for us."

"But Mommy, isn't dealing drugs wrong?"

"Yes. Dealing drugs is definitely wrong and there's no way to sugarcoat it."

"So, why did Daddy sell drugs; why didn't he just get a job?"

"Honesty, where did all this come from?"

"I don't know mom; I've thought about this a lot of since Daddy died. Why didn't he work?"

"Your father once had a job. But he was always stigmatized because he was an ex-con. He had been to jail and had a criminal record so people treated him different. So selling drugs, although it was morally wrong, was your father's job. It's what he did and now I wish to God that he had just kept working, because he would be here with us now."

"Mom, I don't know who to blame. Who should I be mad at?"

"What do you mean, baby?"

"I mean, my father's gone. I can't be with him again until I die, right? That's what is so upsetting. I don't know if I should be mad at Daddy for messing with that woman. Should I be mad at you? Or should I blame the lady Angel for killing my father? I'm so confused."

"Honesty, listen to me baby. Don't blame anyone. Don't consume yourself with hate wondering who's to blame. There's nothing that anyone could've done to prevent this from happening. Your father was stubborn. He was going to do what he wanted to do and nothing I said or did could change that. He wasn't perfect. He made mistakes. But he should not be dead because of those mistakes. I don't care with Tony did in the street; he never killed anyone. He was killed for his money. Over money, sweetheart! I blame Kareemah El-Amin. She should be in jail for the rest of her life, but no, she's as free as a bird. And she's prospering off of the money that she stole from Tony. She owns a beauty salon and a communications store. God will deal with her. God always repays evil deeds with punishment."

"Mommy does God love us?"

"Of course he does, baby."

"Then why did he let that lady kill my father?"

I never got a chance to answer Honesty's question because she ran upstairs to her room and slammed the door. I could hear her cries as I sat on the couch and tried to answer her question. I had no answer. I continued to ponder the question as I rewound the tape in the VCR. I pressed play. I taped the newscast that Honesty and I had just watched. I was hoping to record the moment when the government announced that they had found new evidence that would convict Kareemah El-Amin. But all I got was sixty inches of television screen that showed Kareemah 'Angel' El-Amin being released from the courthouse. I pressed the slow motion button and watched the killer of my dreams as she defiantly walked through the crowd. Her smile stabbed me in the heart. As she got into a waiting car at the curb, I hated her more and more as every minute passed by.

CHAPTER THIRTY-FOUR

ANGEL

It doesn't seem like it's been a whole year since I walked out of the courtroom a free woman, but it has been. I can still remember those days locked up behind bars. I really thought my life was over. I remember riding handcuffed and shaken through the streets in the backseat of the police squad car. I remember seeing the world so differently on that long trip to the Homicide Building. I honestly never thought that I'd see these streets again.

But here I am, back on the bricks and better than ever. The first thing I did was retrieve my money that was in my hiding spots in Fatima's old Town house. Her mother moved into the house after Fatima's death. I was positive that the locks would've been changed, but they weren't. I waited until Fatima's mother wasn't home, and I went in and got my money. Alice Muhammad believed all the stories that cops and the newspaper fed her about me having Fatima killed. There was no reconciliation between us, there would never be. Before leaving the house, I checked on the shallow grave in the backyard. It was unbelievable, but the grass had grown over Deandre's grave and one would never know he was four feet deep. Word on the streets was that Deandre left town after the death of his brother. I'm the only living person who knows where Deandre James 'body will forever rest.

When I got released, my uncle went on back to his house and I moved back into my apartment in Oakcrest Towers. It didn't feel right. It didn't feel like home and I couldn't seem to get comfortable in my space. So, I quickly reconnected with my old friends James, who sold the real estate. Thirty days later I moved into a three-bedroom house in Clinton, Maryland.

And you know me, I couldn't help but to get caught up in the happenings in the streets. I rode through Barry Farms and hollered at J-Rock who happened to be running the drug business in Barry Farms because Wack decided to square up and live right, which was cool with J-Rock because everything was now his.

I rode up Park Chester and kicked it with Scrubber. He told me that this brother Skeet got locked up on a probation violation. He got sentenced to two years. He also told me about his man, Boobie. Boobie was hot. Scrubber said paper work had been floatin' around proving Boobie testified against the dude named Airron Davis. Boobie had disappeared, but Scrubber let me know he was now the chief and it was business as usual.

I talked to Pretty Lady over the phone; she was onboard with Robbie and Duck from the Gangsta Gear Shop. Mike and Sam on Minnesota were down with Duck and 'nem too. I never talked to Romeo. I couldn't catch him, but I heard he was still the man on 48th Street. Jay-Jay on Evans Road took a fall. He lost all his money in the Vegas casinos. The dudes from Wellington Park ran Juvenile out and was now controlling. Where they got their drugs from was anybody's guess.

I hollered at Face and found out that he's the numero uno uptown. Everybody cops their bricks from him. The Gangsta Gear dudes, too. He surprised me by not going to jail. I heard that Gambino and Ron is only selling weed now and word on the streets is that they're caked up.

I visited the SAHNA shop; The Smash All Hot Niggas Association; and talked to Antwan and Poo. It was all love. The whole time I was in jail, Nome and Doodie always kept in touch with me. I spent a lot of time talking with them. Everything's still the same on MLK and on Condon Terrace. I found out that Russell from Trinidad is in jail in Maryland on conspiracy and murder charges.

The word up Congress Park is that everybody was in jail. Squirt, Dip, Marcus, and Jo-Jo. 'The Park' was beefing with another hood and the shit hit the fan. I told myself that I might go see Squirt, since my old boyfriend Buck is his brother. Last I heard, Buck was in some federal pen in Terre Haute, Indiana. *These police really got everybody locked up, damn. I'm just glad they didn't get me.*

My homies on 54th, Hillside, Central Avenue, Simple City, East Gate, and Benning Park were all pretty much doing their thing. They easily rebounded after I went to jail. I ain't mad at them. They say that one monkey don't stop no show.

I keep in touch with my Maryland and Virginia contacts because if I decided to come back, I'll need them. The feds think that they're so slick, but I see their unmarked cars following me every day. They watch my house and my businesses. I literally can't make no type of moves right now.

They wanna catch me doing something wrong. Or they think that I'll give them Carlos. I know that's what they want. But, it'll never happen. The cops are geeking to lock me back up. They're mad as hell at me. They thought they had me on serious charges and I beat them in court on a technicality. That has to hurt and you and I both know they'll be on my ass for the rest of my life.

I came out of my house one day and saw the detectives who were on Tony's case. He stopped me and tried to rattle my cage.

"Hello Ms. Angel."

"Do I know you?" I asked him.

"I'm the detective who investigated the murders of Anthony Phillips, Dearaye James, Ronald Fletcher, and Thomas Murphy. You know the people you killed. I just wanted you to know that even though you walked away free on those charges, you'll slip and I'll be there to catch you and I'm going to personally see to it that you get the needle for it. I don't care how long it takes me; I'm devoting the rest of my career to bringing you down. So please enjoy the clean fresh oxygen that you're breathing, because one day, you'll be breathing recycled air that bounces off the walls of a jail cell; on your way to the chamber where a lethal injection will be waiting for you."

"Ewww, I'm so scared."

"You probably think you did something real slick by having Fatima killed, but you didn't. Who am I? I'm the person who's going to put your ass back in jail."

"I don't appreciate or respect threats, Mr. Detective. So you can save the bullshit for somebody who feels intimidated. Do your investigation and watch me all you want. But here's a little advice for you. Do it away from me, my residence, and my places of businesses or believe me, I will have so many high-priced lawyers eating lunch with the Maryland Chief of Police that you'll be checking parking meters until you retire. Don't call me, and don't come around looking for me." I said smiling like I was in a Colgate commercial. Then I jumped into my truck and left. By the way, I forgot to mention that as soon as I got out of jail, I copped the Hummer H2 in candy apple 'fuck all you' red.

Roy came back to the Communications Outlet to run it for me, thank God. The place is booming. He had to hire an additional three people as sales associates. Tamara came back to Angel's Beauty and Barber Palace and is in charge of all the day to day operations. I wooed most of my old barbers and stylists back, but some had other commitments. I hired new people in their places and then updated both floors of the Palace.

I opened a new store, too. A clothes store called Top of the Line Fashions. I went to New York's garment district and purchased all designer clothes at below retail prices. I dealt with the same people that Solbiato and Lifestyle clothing stores dealt with. I lowered the markup and made designer clothes more affordable. I banked on the quick flips like the drug game. I sell Versace, Dolce and Gabanna, Moschino, Prada, and Ferragamo, to dudes in the hood. Then I put shoes in the store, boy or boy was that the right thing to do to make some money. My next investment will be a shoe boutique and a jewelry store. I want to eventually spin off with my own clothing line. I got big plans, as usual.

One of the other things I did when I first got out of jail was that I went home to my mother. I sat her down and I told her everything. Well pretty much everything. I didn't tell her about Tony. You know some things are better left unsaid, but I told her everything else. I wanted her to have sense of closure for Adirah. And you know what, my mother understood. I came away from our conversation with the feeling that she understood that the end justified the mean. Those dudes hurt my sister for no reason. Nothing can bring my sister back, but it feels good to know that everybody involved in her death is now dead, eternally sleep. Personal justice is good for the soul sometimes, along with a little chicken soup, so me and my mother made a pot of chicken soup together.

I've done almost two years now in the streets without starting no shit or getting into trouble. I'm doing so good, I just wish that things had been a little different. I wish Fatima was here and I miss my sister terribly. I've been thinking about starting a non-profit organization. My mother will handle all the paper work of it, but we could call it the Adirah El-Amin Foundation and we could help underprivileged kids go to college, assist pregnant young girls in health care, offer drug abuse classes, HIV screening and treatment and a host of other things.

I've often thought of the past and now I look at where I am and I just think how funny life is, you know. All that stuff I did, all the lives I took. It's weird because Allah has guided me to this place where I am now and I can tell you that I love life, I really value it these days. I'm so thankful because the very life structure that I value now, I didn't and 'life' meant nothing to me.

I started seeing a psychiatrist, too. You know so I could work things out in my head. It's hard, sometimes to go back. Honestly, I don't want to think about the past, but my psychiatrist, Dr. Heringer says I really need to get it out of my system. He says that it will help with the nightmares. I've had them all my life, especially the dreams of my father molesting me. For me, sleep had been my worst enemy, that's sort of why I liked staying at Fatima's house. For some reason I slept more peaceful there. Nowadays, I see everybody in my sleep; my father, Andre, Tony, Stink, Boochie, Ernestine Wiseman, Fatima, Adirah, everybody. I see them all the time in my sleep. And they aren't happy, to say the least.

Sometimes, I really wish I could change things, go back. See what I see now and erase the past and fix things, make things right. I heard from Carlos, too. I was wondering where he was at. On the anniversary of my one year of being released. I received a phone call from a female who said that a mutual friend wanted to see me. I was to come to the Bally Fitness Center off of East/West highway. I laughed to myself because there are signs in everything that Carlos does.

The Bally's is where we met for the very first time to put our deal together. I remember wanting to sex his caramel ass up. Carlos is one fine Spanish dude. I went to my mother's house and parked the Hummer in front. I went to the front door and left out the back door in my mother's 94 Toyota Camry station wagon. I did that to duck whatever car was trailing me. I drove around for a while to make sure that I wasn't being followed. Satisfied that I wasn't, I drove to PG Plaza and the Bally Fitness Center. I looked around the center and didn't see anyone but a few people running track. It dawned me me that our meeting was to take place in the sauna.

I got undressed and put on a towel. I expected to see Carlos alone, but to my surprise he was seated next to a white woman. She was pretty with long blond hair and green eyes. Carlos introduced us. Her name was Dorothy Benigan.

"It's so nice to meet you, Angel, finally."

I didn't really catch the finally part but she seemed nice. Carlos must've trusted her because he talked as if she wasn't there.

"Angel, how's the free world treating you?"

"I'm okay, it's treating me good. How about you?"

"I'm just fine, even more so now that everything's over with your situation. You had me worried for a minute. But I had people around you at all times. At first I was concerned that you mention to bargain yourself out of jail. I underestimated you and I apologize. But, I had to take precautions. I had women locked up who were on the block with you all day. The young lady that you shared a cell with for eight months is my niece."

"Latesha Garrison?"

"She's my niece. She was your protection and your watcher. She's home, now that all her troubles have disappeared and she'll be here before you leave. There was a girl across the tier from you in cell 74 named Shelia Tucker, do you remember her?"

"Yeah, I remember Shelia."

"She also works for me. And so does Sergeant Wanda Jackson who worked the 4 to 12 shift. If you would've so much as breathed my name once, you would've never made it out of DC jail. But like I said, I underestimated you. I appreciate your strength and I respect that to the fullest that's why I sent Jay to help your lawyers. I took care of your problem because you were loyal, trustworthy, and strong; it's hard to find those qualities these days. I respect the fact that you are low-key now; that's good. But as soon as you're ready to go the dance again, call me and I'll play your favorite song. But I must ask you something."

"I don't mean to cut you off, but did you call me down here to insult me and threaten me in front of your friends?" I glanced at the blond woman.

"Angel don't be so impetuous. I wanted to see you. I wanted to verbally express my gratitude and respect. As I was saying, I need to ask you a question. Did you kill Tony and if so, why?"

Carlos caught me off guard with that question and that's when I noticed Dorothy Benigan staring at me. She was fiddling with a towel in her lap. I looked into Carlos's jet black eyes and worded my response.

"Carlos, I can't lie. Yes, I did kill Tony. I didn't think about the act; I just acted. I knew that Tony had a large amount of money in our apartment. I wanted his spot. I wanted the money and the position. I killed Tony to advance my career. I've been killing people since I was sixteen-years-old. I wanted to get in touch with you and build an empire. And that's what I did. So that we could both prosper. That's the truth."

"I appreciate your honesty. You have the balls of a four-hundred-pound man. Tony was like a son to me. I'm deeply dismayed that you killed him. What you did is not unlike the American Mafia. You killed to get ahead. I forgive you. What you did in the past, we must go on. I had an idea that you killed Tony but I was never sure. You're ambitious, smart, and treacherous, but also loyal to a degree and that's a lethal combination. I often thought about having you killed, even as I made your DNA disappear. But I can't do it. What can I say? I'm getting soft. Dorothy here has a small caliber handgun that has been pointed at you since you sat down. Had our conversation not gone right you would be dead now. But, as I said earlier, I'm getting soft. Never con me again, Angel. Do I make myself clear?"

I nodded.

"Dorothy, you can leave us now. Stand outside the door and make sure that Angel and I talk without any interruptions. Go on!"

That's when I recognized her. She was the same white woman who was on the treadmill next to me at the Run and Shoot one night. She was at Applebee's restaurant the night I brought Carlos the big bag of money. And she was outside the courtroom the day I was released. She was always with me, and I never knew it.

I was alone with Carlos wondering what else he had to say. I was still upset because I hate listening to Carlos threatened my life and tell me how he's sparing me and whatnot. I might have to kill Carlos one day. *Stop it, stop thinking like that, remember what Dr. Heringer said.* To my surprise Carlos got up from his bench and came across the sauna where I sat. He pulled me up until I stood inches in front of him. Then he kissed me and you know me, I kissed him back. It was instantaneous, his tongue traveled all over my face and neck. It was already hot and steamy in the sauna, but he ran my temperature up and made me wet. I was soaking wet in every way possible. I felt his finger enter me and probe my warm center. I snatched his towel off. My hands found his manhood and I massaged it until he was hard as cement. My towel fell off. Carlos licked and gently nibbled on nipples. Then he sat me down on the bench, dropped to his knees, and put his face in the place. He licked and sucked me to about three orgasms. He kissed me and I was turned out by the taste of my own juices. The fact that we were making love in a public sauna made it more exciting. I was turned on to the tenth power. I sat Carlos down on the bench and returned the favor. I sucked his dick until he came deep down my throat. As I swallowed his load he went crazy on the bench. When I released him from my mouth, he was still hard. I sucked on him some more to keep him stiff.

Then I climbed on top of him and rode him until we both came. After he came in me, I became conscious of the safe sex thing, but I was definitely caught up in the moment. Without saying a word, I covered myself with a towel on the floor and left the sauna. I walked past the guard dog Dorothy Benigan. I looked into my would-be executioner's eyes and saw the same thing in her eyes that lived in mine.

I got into the shower and stayed under the hot water for a long time. Then I dressed and headed for the door. I heard a familiar voice call my name. I turned around and looked into the face of Latesha, my old cell mate.

"Angel thank you for the money, I appreciate the fact that you trusted me and always looked out for me. You're good people and I respect you. Here, take this."

I took the envelope form her hand.

"My uncle is really thorough. I'm glad everything worked out for you. I never wanted to hurt you. Take care of yourself; Angel; you're a good friend."

She left quickly. I opened the envelope and saw a wad of cash and a letter. It was from Carlos; it said:

Dearest Angel,

Thank you for the memorable moment in the sauna. Call me whenever you need anything. My number will never change. I hope to hear from you soon.

*PS The money is from niece.

Carlos!!!

I counted the money and it was $5,000 in cash. On the way home I pulled up to the intersection. A lady held a sign that said. 'Please Help Me Feed My Children'. I dropped the envelope into her pail and pulled off.

Angel

I remember that day like it was hours ago. I haven't spoken to Carlos since that day. He doesn't know that his child is growing inside of me. I'm six months pregnant and my sonogram shows the sex of a little girl. I may never tell Carlos. I figure, why should I? It ain't like we're going to be together anyway. So my daughter by Carlos is my secret and for the first time in my life, I'm scared.

Everything has changed now. I no longer want to move to California to be in movies, so Halle ain't got to worry. Honestly, I've been living a movie. I think I'll stay right here in DC so my mother can help me when the baby gets here. I was thinking of relocating, but not too far away, maybe Virginia or North Carolina. I don't want my enemies to hurt my daughter. I had been telling myself that one day I'll probably pick up where I left off in the fast life, but I doubt that very seriously now. I have another life to look after. If it was just me, then maybe I would take my spot back. I'll probably just open more stores and focus on my clothing line, my baby clothing line. I might end up in Forbes or Rich & Famous Magazine one day. Picture that.

I looked around my office, the same room upstairs in the Palace where I killed Dearaye and Tommy. It's painted, carpeted and decorated now. But the memories of what I did before the decorations would stay with me forever.

I walked down to the second floor, I figured I'd talk to Tamara about ordering some products we need and I couldn't help but notice a young girl seated in the waiting area. She caught my attention and I knew her from somewhere, but I'd never seen her before. It was the strangest thing.

Friday was on the big screen so I watched it, while Tamara was on a call. Every now and then I would catch the young girl staring at me, but I thought nothing of it. People always stare at me. About twenty minutes later the young girl went to the back of the salon to where the bowls were and ended at Felicia's station.

As the afternoon turned into evening, I waited for everyone to finish up so that I could close up the shop. I went to the first floor and hollered at my barbers. They were all like night and day, but all the fellas loved me. They heard about the things I was accused of and figured that I was a thorough broad. Besides, I only charge them $150 a week to rent their chairs, so they should like me. After everything was cleaned up on the first floor, I went back upstairs. The salon was empty except for a few of the stylists. We talked for a while, then they all went home. I cut off all the light in the salon and was headed to my office, when I heard a knock on the front door.

At the door I peeked through the curtains and saw the young girl who had been in the salon earlier, I opened the door and let her in.

"Hey, baby, did you forget something?"

She just stared at me.

"Is something wrong with you, boo? Did you forget something?"

"Can I talk to you for a minute? I need to some help."

I closed the front door and led her into the barbershop.

"Sit down, what's the matter, did someone hurt you?"

"No, but I'm thirsty; can I have a glass of water?"

"Sure, I have some Aquafina in the fridge. I'll be right back."

I left, grabbed two bottles of water out of the fridge and walked back in the room to see the young girl standing with a gun pointed at me. *This is it, this will be the end.* I knew that someone had sent her, I couldn't believe I wasn't more careful. *Who sent this young girl to kill me?*

Then I saw the tears streaming down the young girl's face and fire erupted from the gun. The girl bucked from the force of the gun. I never even felt the first bullet, but I felt the second, the third, and the fourth. I felt a burning sensation all over my body. The room had changed positions. Either I was up against the wall or I had fallen to the floor. I felt the weight of something holding me down. I stared into the eyes of the young girl standing over me and wondered why she was shooting me. I could literally feel the life slipping out of me. All I could think about was my unborn baby, my child. I couldn't even protect my child. The last word I heard besides my own cries were...

"That's for my father."

As I drifted off to a quiet place, everything was getting dark. *Who turned out the lights?* I thought to myself. I tried not to panic as I felt my heart race and my blood ooze out of me. Then it hit me. I remembered the little girl's face. How could I have forgotten it? She looks exactly like her father, but I couldn't remember her name. Then it came to me like the bright light I saw.

Honesty, her name is Honesty, Tony's daughter, Honesty!

THE END...

A Novel by Anthony Fields

COMING SOON

ANGEL 2

BODYMORE MURDERLAND

IN THE BLINK OF AN EYE

ANGEL 3: THE FINALE

HERE'S A SNEAK PEEK INSIDE OF ANGEL 2...

CHAPTER ONE
ANGEL

2013

A small bell chimed as I pulled the door open to enter 3 Salsas, a Mexican bistro on 14th street. The bells caught the attention of my long time business partner, James. He stood as I approached and we embraced.

"Ang, as always, you look stunning."

"So do you, James. So do you." I replied and meant it.

"Sit, Angel, please and order some food. This place is under the radar but they have the best Mexican food in the DMV. Try either the enchilada verdes, a tightly rolled tortilla filled with fresh salad and grilled chicken sautéed with roasted corn. Or you can try the quesadillas, filled with kabob meat, bell peppers, cilantro, onions, ropy lengths of fresh Oaxaca cheese, your choice of chicken, beef or fish."

"I'm good on the food, James. I'll just have something to drink, then you can stop wasting my time and just give it to me straight. How much money are we losing?"

James smiled. "Still haven't changed, I see. Ten years of doing business with you and you still haven't changed."

"Is that a bad thing?"

"Depends on how you wanna approach the question. What are you drinking?"

I picked up the beverage menu and read it. "I'll take a sangria. Virgin."

"Coming right up." James signaled the waiter and ordered the drink and his food. Once the waiter had left, he said, "Your beauty parlors are cash cows that need to be jettisoned. Fast. The hair that you're purchasing in bulk from overseas along with all other haircare products are getting more expensive every quarter. You don't charge enough booth rent in any of the salons to recoup the money that you're putting into them. I know that the B and B Palaces are your babies, Angel but they have to go. If they don't make dollars, they don't make sense and you know that better than I do."

I thought about what James said and knew that every word of it was true. Money was always good to make, but sometimes loyalty superseded money. "The salon on Queens Chapel road is operated by the woman that saved my life. Without her quick response and action, I wouldn't be here. The salon on QC road feeds her and her children and I could never take that away from her. I don't care if that location never makes money. I owe her. Closing the salon on Queens Chapel is out of the question. We can close the other two shops. No problem. What's next?"

"The communication outlets. Apple, Google, Amazon and Samsung have become behemoth entities that care nothing for the little guys. They swallow small businesses up whole. Circuit City has gone outta business and Radio Shack is next. Best Buy is soon to follow. Your outlets are not gonna survive another year. Cut your losses and sell them. Take all the money made from those businesses and invest that in real estate. The resurgence of job growth in the US is powering a rebound in the housing market. Home sales in the DMV are at their highest levels since 2006. Prices have increased since bottoming out 3 years ago. Government data shows that the economy added twenty thousand jobs last month alone. I have a friend at the National Association of Realtors and she advises me to get in the game now. A healthy job market means that those who buy a house now are less likely to fall behind on their mortgages. More people are able to save for a down payment. Working families-----"

The waiter returned with a tray of steaming hot quesadillas and the drinks. I sipped my drink as I watched James bite into his food, chew and swallow.

He sipped his drink. "Mexican food is great lunch. Sure you don't want any?"

Angel

"I'm positive. Listen, I'm feeling you on the real estate ventures. Put something together and run it by me in a week or two. I'm in. What about the space that I wanna lease at the newly opened Center City DC Mall. Are they fucking with me?"

James devoured another quesadilla before answering. "Of course they are. As long as we can pay all the expenses and leasing fees, which we can. I'm waiting on them to give us a date to move in. But there is one thing though, Ang."

"What's that?"

"You can't do business at Center City as Top of the Line fashions. This mall is upscale. Rodeo Drive upscale. Versace, Alexander Wang, Diane Von Furstenburg and Hermes all have stores there. You gotta change the name of this one and I have an idea of what the name should be. Wanna hear it?"

"Come on with it." I replied as I continued to sip my sangria.

"Modus Vivendi. It's new, it's chic, it's fresh. It's Latin and it sounds expensive."

"What does it mean?"

"It means, 'A way of life'. Clothes should not only be fashionable but represent your way of life. And that's the marketing scheme that I've been thinking about. It sounds urban, yet foreign. We bring in student designers trying to break into the game to make our clothes, but we still will feature all the other big name designer lines. That is if we can get them to agree to distribute to us. What do you think?"

As always, James impressed me with his business acumen. The ton of money that he made me legally over the years was undeniable. I walked into the bistro knowing that I would acquiesce to anything that James offered. Anything but closing the palace on Queens Chapel road. "I like it. As a matter of fact, I love it. Get the paperwork done and then fax it to me for my signature. Take care of all the sales of the salons and get back at me when it's done. I hate to drink and run but I gotta prior engagement that I can't miss."

James wiped food off his face with a napkin and then wiped his hands. He stood and we embraced again. "I'm glad that you trust me, Ang. I appreciate it."

"Don't mention it, James. In ten years, you have never steered me wrong. Keep it that way and I won't have to kill you."

The color visibly drained from James' face. He opened his mouth to speak but no words came out.

"I laughed to break the tension. "Just kidding, James. Damn, you didn't think I was serious, did you?"

"I, uh----"

"Stop taking me so seriously. I was joking. I'm out. Call me in a few days. "I reached into my purse, pulled out a fifty-dollar bill and tossed it onto the table. "Enjoy the rest of your lunch. It's on me."

****

I wheeled my Porsche truck through the streets of DC, taking notice of all the construction taking place in the city. What James had said about the real estate boom was accurate. I made a mental note to myself to invest in a construction company and purchase some construction equipment to rent out to contractors. I rode through the streets and remembered when they were mine. I remembered when I controlled over eighty percent of the drug flow into the city. The quintessential queenpen, coronated by none other than the man who controlled everything, Carlos Trinidad. Pulling into a parking space in front of the Whitman Walker Clinic, I killed the engine, hopped out the truck and went inside the building. Ten minutes later, I was walking into my mother's office area.

Her receptionist, Valerie looked up from a call and waved, then she moved the phone and said, "Go ahead on back, Angel. Your mom is in her office."

I did as I was told and walked into my mother's office.

My mother walked around her desk and embraced me. "Assalaamu Alaikum, baby."

Angel

"Wa laikum assalaam. What's up, Ma? How is the nonprofit life treating you?"

"Everything is good, marsha'allah. What brings you to Northwest today?"

"You forgot about our lunch date, didn't you?'

My mother smacked her forehead. "You're right, baby. I forgot all about our mother-daughter luncheon for today. Where are you trying to go? And what are you trying to eat?"

"Anything but Mexican." I told her with a grin.

"I'm not even dressed for a power lunch."

"Cut it out, Ma. You look great and you know it. Stop fishing for compliments."

Naimah El-Amin gave herself the once over look. "I do look okay, don't I? Especially for a fifty year old widower Muslimah."

My mother was right. For a woman who'd witnessed as much death as she had, her skin remained flawless and her youth seemed forever young. Her figure was better than mine and only her naturally curly hair betrayed her by showing hints of grey. That grey now covered by a multicolored hijab that matched her Red Bottom heels that I'd gotten her a few months ago.

"Ma, you're a widower because you choose to be and not because you have to be."

"Child, I have no time for anything else. You, my grandbaby and this foundation takes up enough of my time. I'm good. I'm married to this life I'm living right now. Keeping Adirah's memory alive is my life's work. Speaking of which, sit down and let me finish watching this graduation on TV. Michelle Obama is about to speak."

I watched my mother return to her chair and sit down. Her face on the TV screen mounted to the wall by her desk. I found a chair opposite her and sat down to watch the first lady do her thing. "Whose graduation is this, Ma?"

"Howard University. We have seven young ladies from the worst neighborhoods in DC that we gave scholarships to graduating today. A

100 percent graduation rate and I am so proud, baby. I was gonna attend the ceremony but changed my mind at the last minute. It's not about me or us as a foundation, it's about them. Wait---here's Michelle Obama."

Michelle Obama spoke for about twenty-five minutes and I hung onto her every word. In all her radiant splendor, the most powerful black woman in the free world gave Howard's commencement speech like a seasoned vet. She encouraged, admonished, advised and captivated her audience. She was the epitome of the baddest bitch in the world and I respected her. I stared into the faces of all the young women sitting in the audience and remembered when I was them. Young, hungry and wanting to rule the world. Back then, the only person that believed in me was Fatima Muhammad, my best friend. My best friend that later betrayed me and snitched on me to the cops. The best friend that I ordered to be killed.

Thunderous applause broke my reverie. Michelle Obama was now replaced by Howard's female president. The matronly woman spoke for a few minutes and then announced the graduating class of 2014, starting with the valedictorian. I reached into my purse to grab my phone and check my messages. The name that I heard next stopped me in my tracks. Slowly, I raised my head to look at the TV screen. I couldn't believe my eyes. My cell phone dropped from my hand. The name. Her face. I couldn't believe it was her. Anger rose in my chest and constricted my breathing. "He lied to me! He lied to me!"

My mother's head spent around as if on a swivel. Her eyes bore into me. "Who lied to you?"

"Your brother lied to me. He looked me right in my face and lied."

"My brother? Which one?"

"Uncle Samir. He lied to me about her." I emphatically stated and pointed at the TV.

Confusion etched itself in my mother's face. "Angel, what the heck are you talking about? Who are you talking about that Samir lied about?"

Angel

I stood up and walked closer to the TV. "I'm talking about her, Ma." She had grown a lot and her hair was a different color under her graduation cap, but her features were unmistakable. Riveted to my spot in front of the TV, suddenly I was in another place, in another time, 8 years ago............

The Beauty and Barber Palace was empty except for a few stylists who were preparing to leave. All the barbers had left already. After everyone had left, I was about to turn off all the lights and head for my office when I heard the knock at the door. I peered out the door to see who was knocking. I assumed that it was somebody who had left something, so I saw the l girl and opened the door. She had been in the salon earlier. "What's up, baby? Did you forget something?"

"Can I come in and talk to you? I need some help."
I opened the door wide enough for the girl to walk in to the shop. "Sit down. What help do you need?"

"I am a little thirsty, can I have something to drink?"

"Sure. I have some Aquafina waters in the fridge. I'll be right back." I left and got two bottles of water. When I came back into the room, the girl was holding and gun and it was pointed straight at me.

To be continued.......

Made in the USA
Las Vegas, NV
16 July 2022

51716599R00154